BLACK LIGHT: PROTOCOL

BLACK LIGHT SERIES

SHANE STARRETT

Black Light: Protocol
by Shane Starrett

Published by Black Collar Press
Don't miss a release! Sign-up for our newsletter here!

EBook ISBN: **978-1-947559-87-5**
Print ISBN: **978-1-947559-88-2**

Cover Art by Eris Adderly, http://erisadderly.com/
Thank you to Eris Adderly & Jennifer Bene for edits!

BLURB

"Yes, sir."

Galen Harmon lives to hear those two words. And for fifteen years he lived the dream with a submissive who'd knelt at his feet and offered that simple phrase over and over again.

But then she was gone. Ripped away in a heartbeat of savage betrayal and anguish that still haunts him.

Until he met Alex.

She's everything that was taken from him. Obedience and submission, willing to follow his every rule, his every protocol...

Perfection.

But Galen Harmon is a man with secrets. A past and present that could put *her* life at risk.

If he tells her.

And when she *demands* the truth, he has a decision to make.

Give her the very thing she insists to keep their relationship alive...

Or let her go.

Before it's too late.

CHAPTER 1

GALEN

"*O*hmygod! Yes, yes, YES!"

My temple throbs.

But not my cock.

I shouldn't be feeling this way right now. In fact, I should be thrilling to the flush of raw energy and power that comes from having a submissive spread out on a spanking bench, back arching as I weave the Hitachi in a sinuous pattern over her pussy, focusing on her clit. I should be captivated by the sight of a beautiful woman who's clearly on the edge of falling into an intense orgasm.

Except I'm not. Instead, I'm clenching my jaw.

Because she shouldn't be.

That's the problem.

There was a time when everything happening to the woman below me would've had me deep in my Dom headspace. Because there was a time I'd known exactly how the woman whose sex I was teasing was going to react. How fierce she was going to fight to maintain obedience to my dominance.

"Oh fuck, oh fuck, oh fuck, I'm gonna come!"

But that was a different sub than the one in front of me now, a

1

different time when I thought nothing could ever change the keen, razor-sharp joy I felt when listening to the same sounds I'm hearing right now. Especially when they were threaded through with the powerful undercurrent of struggle to maintain discipline to what I demanded. Goddamn me for feeling frustration rather than desire because she's a gorgeous little sub, and she *is* trying to comply in her own way. There's just one problem.

It's not good enough for an asshole like me.

"FUCK!"

Ms. Love—at least I think that's what she told me her name is — wrenches against the restraints, twisting on the bench. I don't need to ask what's just happened: it's clear as fucking day. I pull the wand back, watching as she holds herself rigid. Even if I'm not in a *good* Dom headspace it doesn't change where I am and what I should be doing. It only increases my anger I can't force myself to fake what experience tells me I should. Instead, I just want to be out of Black Light, away from the club and the music and the scent and the sounds of a woman coming down slowly from the sexual high I've put her in.

The gasp that escapes her trails into a breathy moan. The massager *brrs* in my hand and I switch it off, my only thought telling me to walk away from all this…

Forever.

"Holy fuck," she whispers as she slowly lowers back to the padded leather.

"Reach between your legs," I growl.

She does so immediately, without hesitation. She knows exactly where I want her fingers to go and she does, two digits disappearing inside without another word. Her eyes close ever so briefly as she hooks them within, opening to stare up at me as she waits for my next command.

"Show me." My voice is harder than it should be. I'm being severe, and while that's served its purpose in past scenes, it isn't how this one started. I sense her confusion, see it in the tight press of lips, the searching scan of her eyes.

I reach out and grab her by the wrist. "Did you come?"

She trembles in my grasp. "I…"

"*Did. You. Come.*" I clench her hard enough she winces, the tension from her body tracing up through my fingers as she tries to pull back.

"I…"

"Yes, or no?"

She falters. Her mouth opens then closes before she finally whispers, "Yes."

I grit my teeth. I have no right to be this upset. This is our first time sceneing together, and she admitted she was only 'experimenting' with the idea of higher levels of submission. And even though I was clear what my expectations were, I shouldn't be angry by the slickness coating her fingers.

As a Dom, what I should be doing is using this situation to my advantage. At the bare minimum this is the perfect opportunity for a 'funishment,' and I'm imagining that's exactly what she's expecting. Now, though, I'm treating her coldly, my grip on her less an '*ooo you've been a naughty girl*' signal and more a '*God what a disappointment you are.*'

A good Dom would be taking care of the sub staring up at him. Except I'm not being that Dom right now. I hate myself for it but —*fuck*—I just don't have it in me. This was a mistake, and I have to own it, even if she did exactly what I'd told her not to.

I turn away and unplug the Hitachi before dropping it in my bag. Once I've zipped the duffel closed, I go back and wordlessly undo the cuffs at her ankles.

"What…?" Her voice wavers.

"We're done here," I say tonelessly.

"We're… what? Aren't we… aren't you going to—"

"Was any portion of the instruction I gave you earlier not clear?"

"I…" She's blinking, unsure, but her confusion is also building toward something else. Something I knew would happen and yet hoped wouldn't.

Resentment. Anger.

I'm not going to let her off the hook and I'm also not going to let her use the excuse she expects will make up for her disobedience.

"I asked you a question."

"I… you said…" She snaps her mouth shut, sitting up, and I see the tautness in her body heralding what's about to begin. "I know what you said but… you… you…" She pins me with a piercing gaze. "You *made* me come." The accusation in those final words is unmistakable.

"No, I didn't. You *let* yourself orgasm."

"Are you kidding me?" She gapes at me. "How was I *not* supposed to after everything you did?"

Just walk away. Just walk away…

I should listen to myself, but I don't. Everything that's about to happen is going to be fruitless, but I stand there anyway. "So, you're saying you *did* understand me. Did I give you permission to come?"

She stares at me, the wheels in her head racing. "You didn't stop me!"

"Then you clearly *didn't* understand what you were told."

Should have known, Galen. You should have known.

"Look, I don't know what your fucking problem is, but you do understand the whole point of us being here, don't you?" Her hand cuts an arc as she indicates the room we're in.

"I understand what it means for you," I say quietly, "but it's not the same for me. At least not with the topping-from-the-bottom attitude you seem to be coming from."

Her eyes blaze. "What! Are you accusing me of…?" She leans toward me, seething. "That's bullshit, you fucking asshole!"

I nod because she's right, even if she's missed the point

entirely. I knew—I could tell from the moment she worked so hard to convince me—she didn't have a clue what *'high protocol'* really meant. But against my better judgment...

Again, Galen.

...I went through with her request. Because I thought maybe this time, maybe with this sub, it might be like it was with...

Go on. Say it. Say her name.

No. "This was a mistake. For that, I take full responsibility. I should have known better. I'm sorry."

"And that's it? You're just going to get me off and then fucking... leave?"

"Do you need aftercare?" I'm barely able to muster a trace of sincerity in my words, and her eyes narrow in recognition.

"Go to hell."

"Don't worry," I say with quiet conviction. "I am."

I move to the chair next to us to retrieve my jacket and put it on. She watches in silence as I reach down and pick up the neat pile of her clothing.

"Leave it," she snaps. "I'll get it myself when I'm ready."

Nodding, I put it back down. "Again, I'm sorry for all this."

"Wow." She shakes her head in disbelief. "I don't know if you're just stupid, or a colossal prick, but leave me the fuck alone."

"Both," I murmur in response to the first part of her statement, and I grab my bag as I move off to comply with the second.

It's as I'm walking away I first notice him staring at me from across the room. I don't know how long he's been standing there, but the look on his face is one of concern, so it's clearly been long enough. There's no pity in his gaze, but it's still irritating.

Terry 'Muscles' Robertson is a Dungeon Monitor at Black Light and he's a good man, but right now I don't want good. I want someone to match my mood and I've never seen Terry act like an asshole to anyone, ever. He's always smiling, always cheerful, always ready with a helpful hand or a terrible joke. All things I'm not sure I'm ready to deal with considering my current frame of mind.

I draw close, and the look on his face turns into a crooked smile.

"So, looks like you had a nice scene going on ther—"

"Don't, Terry. Just… don't."

He falls into step beside me. "Whoa, whoa, whoa, now. I'm just making sure you're okay."

"I'll be okay after I get about ten drinks in me."

"I really don't think you should—"

"Are you my mother? Because unless you're my mother, I don't give a damn what you think I should or shouldn't do."

He goes silent as we walk through the club, and a part of me says I should apologize even though I know I won't. I'm in a foul mood, and though there's no reason for me to take it out on him, he says nothing to remind me I'm behaving like a dick nor what he could do about it if he really wanted.

We weave through the crowd until we make it to the large, curved bar. Fortunately, there are only a smattering of people at it, and most of those already have drinks in hand. Klara's working tonight, and she moves to Terry and me as we come up.

"What can I get you, Master Harmon?" she asks with a bright smile.

"Three fingers of Weller on ice. Two cubes, no more, no less."

"Of course, sir." She turns and moves down the bar to get the drink.

I turn and stare at Terry.

"So. It looked like she had a good time—"

"I'm quitting," I say with quiet determination.

"You're quitting… what?"

"Black Light. The lifestyle. All of it."

He rolls his head. "Aw, man, don't say shit like that…"

"I fucked up."

"No, you made a *mistake*. You ain't the first Dom in Black Light to do that and you won't be the last."

I tense. I realize Terry means well, but I'm not someone who takes making a 'mistake' lightly. It's not in my nature. Besides, this isn't the first time something like this has happened lately. In fact, it's becoming a recurring theme. Perhaps not always as bad as what just took place, but sufficient enough my flippant remark carries some weight.

"I understand what you're doing, Terry." I pause long enough to take my drink from Klara, letting the first sip burn a cool path down my throat. "But... seriously, I think it's time to reconsider. I'm not doing Chase and Jaxson any favors by pissing off the clientele, and there's honestly no point in me continuing with this if all I'm doing is making myself into The Bad Dom of Black Light. That's not who I am, and it's not who I want to be remembered as."

"You quit, and that's *exactly* what they're gonna remember, though. I ain't the only one who's seen you struggling since..." He catches my look and doesn't say her name. "Since it happened. When it's just the staff it doesn't matter because we all know you're a good Dom. But if word gets out among the customers about why a longtime member suddenly disappeared..."

I take another sip of my drink. "Terry, why would you care what people in the community say about me if I leave? What vested interest could you possibly have in my reputation?"

"Because you're a good man," he says, smiling sincerely. "You're just going through a rough patch, that's all. What's been happening to you"—he motions to the room I fled a short time ago—"ain't because you're a bad Dom. It's because you're not finding the right sub for yourself. You're trying to play with people who aren't the right fit for what you need, or who think they know what you're offering when they really don't." He reaches out and pokes me in the chest. "When you were with her, you were one of the best I've ever seen, and that ain't me blowing smoke up your ass. It was a joy to see you in the club, and I ain't the only one who's said it."

I start to argue, but he cuts me off.

"Listen, I know you ain't on top of your game right now, but that's a shitty fucking reason to just throw everything away. And I'm not gonna lie; I've never taken you to be the kind of man who just gives up and walks away when things get tough."

Ouch.

"So, yeah, maybe you haven't been at your best lately. But that doesn't mean it's *always* gonna be that way." He leans back, crossing his massive arms over his chest. "We just need to find you the right submissive."

I turn my head toward the playroom before slowly looking back at him. "You *did* see what just happened in there, didn't you?"

He purses his lips. "I did. And like I said, it wasn't exactly your finest moment but that doesn't mean—"

"Terry, it was a fucking shitshow."

He takes a step toward me. "She didn't listen to a thing you said before you started playing. She told you one thing and then went off and did what *she* wanted. She set you up to fail."

"Wait," I say slowly, narrowing my eyes. "How do you know all that?"

A startled look scrambles across his face before disappearing. "I'm a Dungeon Monitor. It's my job to..." He makes a nervous flicking motion. "Chase and Jaxson pay me good money to make sure the customers are taken care of."

"You stalked me."

"Listen," he says, bringing both hands up, "it ain't like that."

"It isn't? You seem to know an awful lot about what we negotiated before we went in there to play," I tell him pointedly.

"Okay, so maybe I might have overheard a few things, but that don't mean I was stalking you."

"It's a textbook definition of it."

He crosses his arms back across his chest. "I was just doing my job," he huffs.

"Just doing your job?"

Terry has the nickname 'Muscles' for good reason. He's *big* and intimidating as hell until you get to know him. That's served him well at Black Light on more than one occasion, and it's part of why him standing in front of me right now looking like a petulant child who got caught with his hand in the cookie jar takes some of the edge off the anger that's built up in me. He's trying to sound gruff, but instead it comes out half pleading.

"Yeah, I was looking out for you. And her. But mostly you."

"Why?"

"Because I told you! We care!" His voice is loud enough a few heads turn, and because it's Terry more than a couple of the looks are 'oh shit that guy's about to get his ass kicked.'

"Listen," he continues, lowering his voice, "I know this is an exclusive club and all, and Chase and Jaxson are real big on confidentiality and shit, but you've been here for a long time. And, sure, you were never one to get involved in events like Roulette and the rest, and—yeah—you and her kept a low profile while you were playing, but... don't think for a moment people still didn't notice you, man. You thought you were flying under the radar, but we saw you. And maybe you think all that 'community' stuff people in the lifestyle talk about is just bullshit, but I'm gonna tell you this: where it concerns me and some other folks here, it ain't. So, yeah, we care. And when we see one of our own hurting— especially someone like you—we're gonna sit up, take notice, and do the right thing."

"Like stalking me."

"Whatever it fucking takes." His voice is so sincere, so full of conviction, and... I can't stay mad. If his only purpose was to calm me down and talk me off a ledge then he's succeeded, and it's worth taking note he's done it better than people I've actually paid to help me.

"You are something else, my friend," I say with a wry chuckle.

"I mean, I've been told that. I don't see it personally, but... you know..." He gives me a wide grin.

I smile back. There's a moment's pause, and then I say, "So... you and the other DMs think I just need to find the right submissive, huh?"

He nods emphatically. "Exactly! The way we see it, your biggest issue is you come here to play the way you used to play instead of coming here just to fuck."

I choke. "What?"

"Well, it's the truth. You're too close to the situation to recognize it, but we do."

Terry's acting almost paternal and it's hilarious, but I keep the smile off my face.

"See, your kink is high protocol, and that's a bit more intense than what a lot of the subs coming to Black Light are looking for. Not only that, but it's more of a slow-burn kinda thing, and a lot of folks are looking for something with a little more... instant gratification. They ain't got the patience to wait for the build-up." He makes a dismissive motion with his hand. "If you came here just wanting to dominate some sub and then nut, you'd be golden."

"Jesus, Terry! Does Chase know you talk about the members like this?"

"He knows we don't talk about *every* member like this."

Hmm.

"Thing is, there's nothing wrong with a sub just wanting to get spanked and then fucked hard. Hell, for a lot of people it's all they need, and God bless'em. But we both know that's not what you're looking for. And what's that saying? The definition of insanity is—"

"Doing the same thing over and over expecting different results." I tilt my head. "Damn, Terry, I'm impressed."

"Yeah, well, unlike what some people might think, I'm not just a big, dumb, slab of meat. I know a few things too." He taps his finger to the side of his head.

"I've never made that assumption, I assure you."

"Thank you. I appreciate that," he replies quietly.

I finish the last of my drink, then set the glass down. Klara looks my way, motioning to wordlessly ask if I want another. I shake my head.

"So, I just need to find the right sub for myself, huh?" I look around the club slowly before bringing my gaze to rest on Terry. "Clearly my track record lately hasn't been stellar in that regard. Don't suppose you and your friends have any suggestions?"

I watch as a broad grin creases his face. "Funny you should mention that…"

CHAPTER 2

ALEX

"Kneel, slave."

I falter.

Slave? Did he seriously just call me slave?

"I'm not a slave," I say quietly, and I do not kneel. Instead, I close my eyes tightly. *How? How can this be happening again?*

His hand comes up, gripping me at the back of my neck. "What did you just say?"

"I said 'I'm not a slave,'" I repeat a little louder this time.

His fingers tighten, and in a different situation I'd thrill to the tendrils of pain snaking along my muscles but... dear God, why does this keep happening to me?

"Tonight, you are whatever I tell you that you are," he rumbles in a low tone, and where his voice had initially been an attraction, right now it grates across my nerves like sandpaper. I know all too well where this is headed.

I so wanted it to be different this time. Why couldn't he be the one to understand?

Why, why, why?

"Did you hear me, slave?"

I sigh. Even within the tension of his grasp I manage to lower my head, and my voice sounds so weary when I say, "Red."

His hand tightens for a millisecond before it comes away completely. "Did you just safe word?" he asks incredulously.

"Yes."

"What the fuck!"

He pulls back a step, and I turn to face him.

"I didn't do a fucking thing!" His voice is a mixture of wounded pride and displeasure that matches the look on his face.

"I'm not your slave."

"You said you wanted Gorean when we were negotiating!"

"I did not. I said high protocol."

"Same fucking difference!" He jerks his hand upward in a gesture of disgust.

"No," I say quietly, meeting his eyes. "No, it isn't."

Redness creeps up his neck as his muscles tense. The tendons flare outward like an angered cobra, and he takes a step toward me. "Don't you fucking lecture me, slut."

Oh, Jesus. Seriously?

I stand my ground even as he towers above me. He's a big man, strong, and while there's no doubt he's attractive... right now I'd rather grind on a cactus than play with him.

"I'm not lecturing you. I'm simply saying there *is* a difference."

He brings his hand up, finger pointing in my face. "You listen to me. I've obviously been in the lifestyle for a lot longer than you and I think I know what high protocol is. *You* clearly don't, so you might want to read a couple of fucking books before you come waltzing in here announcing how you want to play to an experienced Dom and then safe-wording the fuck out at the first indication of it!"

I keep my eyes locked to his, my voice calm and cool. "Duly noted. I'll remember to do that when I find an *experienced* Dom."

It's an unnecessary comment, and a bit foolish of me to make because now his eyes bulge outward as the red deepens. I should have just turned and walked away but I'm a bit angry myself, and he plainly doesn't have a clue what he's talking about beyond whatever he's picked up in some BDSM subreddit or forum.

He leans down into my face. "You fucking bit—"

There's a sudden grip on my arm, and for a split second I think he's grabbed me. It's not him, though. Someone has stepped up to us and this person is the one pulling me back now.

"Hey, folks. Is there a problem here?"

My supposed Dom for the evening jerks back. I turn my head to find one of Black Light's Dungeon Monitors at my side, interposing himself between us.

"We all doing okay?" the DM says, a warm smile creasing his face.

Many of the members of Black Light call him 'Muscles,' but to me he's always been Terry. It'd be forward of me to call him friend, but we've always gotten along well. He's looked out for me in the past and—honestly—he's part of the reason I'm here right now, trying yet again to find someone who'll understand exactly what it is I'm looking for. If it wasn't for Terry, I'd have given up long ago because Black Light isn't cheap, and even though I do truly want to fulfill this part of my life that's been missing, I'm equally certain it'll never happen.

What's going on right now simply reinforces that opinion.

"She"—the Dom stabs a finger toward me—"needs a course in Sub 101."

Terry cocks an eyebrow upward. "Is that so? Man, that doesn't sound like Alex at all. She's always had a really good idea what she's looking for, and I ain't had any Dom tell me she hasn't been straight up front with them during negotiations." Terry glances at me with a grin. "Well, any *good* Dom, that is."

The other man grunts. "Yeah. Sure. Whatever."

"I think we've decided not to play tonight," I say in a quiet, polite tone the man does not deserve.

"Oh." Terry slaps a faux pout across his face. "Well, that's a damn shame."

"It's fucking bullshit," the man mutters, looking away from us.

"Sorry?"

"Nothing," he mutters again, glowering.

"So," I say after a moment of awkward silence, "thank you for at least trying. I appreciate it." I reach my hand toward him.

His mouth drops open. For a second he appears to be trying to speak but nothing comes out. Finally, he sputters, "I should—"

"What *I* think you should do," Terry says, cutting him off, "is shake the lady's hand and wish her a good evening."

The Dom is big, but Terry's bigger, and even though Terry's voice is polite, there's an undercurrent of 'try me, pal, and I will mess you up' that doesn't go unnoticed.

"Fine," he snaps, and the touch of his hand to mine is so brief it doesn't even constitute a shake. "Have a fantastic fucking evening."

Before I'm able to respond he's spun away from us both, stalking off with his hands clenched at his sides.

I let out a deep breath. "I think I need a drink."

"That sounds like a great idea," Terry says softly, his palm coming to rest between my shoulder blades. "Come on. Let's go get you one."

◆

"I'M JUST NOT SURE."

I take another sip of my wine, looking over the rim of the glass at Terry. I hate even saying the words because I'm not someone who waffles over a decision. However, right now…

I'm really just not sure.

"Listen, Alex, I'm not trying to pressure you in any way, shape, or form, okay? But…" Terry raises a hand to cut me off as I start to respond. "I've been a DM a decent amount of time and I know meeting someone can be stressful, especially if you're a sub. I mean look what happened tonight. It's enough of a pain in the ass just putting yourself out there, and then the guy bullshits you and turns out to be a jerk and..." He gestures with his hand back toward the main floor of the club. "It all goes to shit and you're right back where you started."

"Yeah..." I mumble.

Terry tilts his head, giving me a sympathetic look. "I get it, okay? All I'm saying is—in this case—I personally vouch for the guy, alright? And even if you only spend a minute with him and then tap out, it's no harm, no foul. No matter what, I guarantee you he ain't gonna feed you a line of crap." He gives me a reassuring smile. "If he does, I swear I'll mess him up bad."

It's sweet Terry thinks he needs to protect me from being set up on a bad blind date, especially since *he* is the one arranging it. We both know my success rate with Doms in the club is atrocious; tonight being a perfect example. It's sort of what brought us together, and why we're sitting at this table having this conversation.

"It's not that I'm worried about him being a bad Dom. I seriously doubt you'd put me in that position." He gives me a warm smile at the praise, which makes what I'm about to say a little harder. "It's just... since we last talked—and especially after tonight—I've been considering whether what I've been looking for is truly worth pursuing. Like you said—and God knows I've experienced—the kind of Dom I'm trying to find is easily mimicked by fakes and pretenders. And I know you wouldn't set me up with someone like that, but what would be even worse than him being *that* kind of Dom would be finding out he's one who understands everything I want, but we're just not compatible otherwise."

Terry shakes his head emphatically. "No way. Ain't gonna happen."

"Terry." I look down at the tabletop for a second. "How can you possibly be so sure of that?"

He looks at me with a sincerity that's palpable. "I just am."

I sigh. "I don't know."

He covers my hand with his. It's huge, and he's strong, but the gesture itself is one of the gentlest and most tender I've experienced in a long time. It's comforting and kind and thoughtful and a sudden sense of warmth pushes away some of the lingering taint of what took place this evening out there on the floor.

"Please," he says quietly. "I ain't above begging, especially when I know in my heart of hearts this is gonna be the best thing that's happened to two people in a long time."

I blush. I shouldn't, but I do. "Terry..."

"You really wanna make me beg?"

"No!" I roll my eyes before letting my gaze come back to rest on him. "Are you *really* sure about this?"

"One hundred fucking percent."

I take a deep breath before letting it out slowly. I'll probably regret this. Not just for the disappointment of being let down yet again by a Dom who says they know what high protocol is but clearly don't, but because I'd be letting Terry down, too. He's so convinced, so sure, and I've been there so many times myself. *This one has to be the right Dom. He has to be.*

And I want to believe... right up until they aren't.

"What's his name?" I ask softly.

"Galen."

I tilt my head. "Master Galen?"

"Nooo," Terry says slowly, shaking his head. "At least not at first."

He pats my hand gently.

"But maybe someday."

17

CHAPTER 3

GALEN

*S*he's going to be late. I can feel it.

I'm sitting at the bar in Black Light, sipping a San Pellegrino because this is where we agreed to meet for the first time. Terry ultimately whittled away at my reluctance until I finally said yes to meeting with this 'Alex,' and I've no real reason to be so sure she won't show on time. However, he set the invitation for nine PM, and it's eight fifty-five, she's nowhere in sight, and I've got this gut feeling.

"You stay here. I'm going to go… check around."

Terry pats me on the shoulder and moves off through the crowd.

Jesus, he's more nervous than I am.

He doesn't need to be. I've already made it clear that while I respect him and his efforts, I don't have high expectations. If this Alex was someone well-versed in all things high protocol, I'm certain we would have crossed paths by now, and that's not been the case. I said as much to Terry, and he brushed it off by saying 'she's pretty new to Black Light.'

Sure. And pretty new to the entire concept of high protocol, I'm betting. In the last eight months I've had a lifetime's worth of

18

experience seeing how well meeting up with someone like this has ended, and so I have a right to be wary.

I glance across the club floor one more time before turning back to the bar. Taking another sip, I watch the people reflected in the mirror, and there's no one who remotely looks as if she's who I expect her to be.

It's a typical Friday night at Black Light, with the typical lifestyle crowd mixed with the D.C. elite who want to play at BDSM for the weekend in a safe space. I don't begrudge them their thirty-five-hundred-dollar Brunello Cucinelli suits, or forty-five-hundred-dollar Balenciaga mock leather dresses, nor the ones who've come decked out in their best fetish gear.

While neither is my style—to each their own—I'm also half-expecting her to show up in some homebrewed version of bondage gear because... well, for some people that's exactly what they expect a high protocol submissive to be dressed in. And if I'm right, and she shows up late wearing some version of that, then...

Home by midnight, crack open a bottle of Woodford Reserve, and contemplate my final exit strategy from here.

"Pardon me."

I turn to my right at the sound of a quiet yet firm voice. *Oh.* It's an attractive woman, but clearly not Alex. She's elegant and sophisticated, and while everything about her is slightly understated in a way that doesn't scream wealth, it's equally obvious she's just here window shopping. Probably with her lobbyist husband who finally convinced her to 'check out' the lifestyle scene in a high-end safe space where they can both dip their toes in without having to worry about mixing with the—

"Galen?" she continues, extending her hand.

Well... shit.

Part of my job is being able to think fast on my feet and I kick it into high gear right now. She's caught me off guard, and shame on me for falling into the trap of being snared by my own biases. I take a moment to slowly set my glass down before turning to focus solely on her.

"Alex, I presume?"

"Yes."

We shake hands, and her grip is warm and firm. I slip from my stool and motion her toward it, and she dips her head politely as she takes my place, smiling.

"A glass of white wine?" I ask, gazing at her.

"Water, please."

"Of course," I murmur. I motion to the nearest bartender, and she crosses over a moment later.

"A San Pellegrino for the lady." I cock an eyebrow up questioningly, and Alex gives a slight nod.

The bartender moves off, and I take a second glance at the woman I almost dismissed a moment ago.

Still elegant, still sophisticated looking. I place her height at about five-foot-four or five-foot-five, and her dark hair is styled short, cut off at her jawline. I guess she's in her mid-thirties, working either in government or the corporate world. As I'm appraising her, she's doing the same to me, and neither of us are hiding it.

"So," I begin, "I'm curious to learn how you knew it was me."

"An educated guess. You're probably one of only a few Doms here tonight unescorted and you weren't roaming, and, admittedly, Terry did give me a brief description."

"Something he failed to do for me," I say wryly.

"I hope you're not disappointed," she says with a wry smile of her own.

"Not yet."

"Hmm." She narrows her eyes. "Not exactly a ringing endorsement for your expectations of the evening."

I say nothing for a moment, tilting my head slightly. "Terry told me you were fairly new to Black Light."

"That's true," she says, nodding. "I've only been a member for five months."

"Ah. That would explain why we haven't crossed paths before."

"Probably. My understanding is you've been a member here for some time."

"That's correct."

The bartender returns with her water and for a moment we both sip our drinks. She doesn't break our eye contact to scan the crowd, nor do I.

Interesting.

"So, why *are* you here?" I pick up the conversation again.

"I'm pretty sure you already know that," she counters.

"Fair enough. Still, if you'd indulge me."

"Alright." This time she does break eye contact, staring off into the distance. "I came here in the hopes of finding someone who I'd be able to connect with over my particular kink."

"And which of the multitude would that be?"

She pauses for a moment before answering. "High protocol."

I take another sip from my glass. "Do you consider that a kink?"

"I think that's the general umbrella term most people use for the things they come here to experience." She purses her lips. "I take it you don't?"

"I think, even within these walls"—I motion to the club around us—"there's still a bit of a negative stigma attached to the word."

"So, you don't subscribe to the notion of taking ownership of it and giving it agency beyond the outsiders' *Fifty Shades of Grey* point of view?"

"I think you'll find I'm someone who doesn't put great store in what other people think, at least in general."

"I see," she says politely. "That suggests you feel I'll have the opportunity to see that philosophy put into action."

"Is that something you'd like?"

She gives me a smile to match the one I gave her earlier when I said 'not yet.' "I suppose we'll have to find that out, won't we?"

Touché.

I'm beginning to warm to her. Still, nothing she's said has given any indication she has experience with our mutual 'kink,' nor what version of it she's looking for, *nor* if she has any real idea of what it is at all. She's able to hold her own in conversation, but if she truly wants to be involved in high protocol in the same fashion as I, it's going to take more than just being able to verbally spar.

"Have you ever been in a high protocol relationship before?"

"Relationship? Or do you just mean playing in a club?"

"Both."

She folds her hands in her lap. "Relationship? Yes, one. It was... it was before I came to Black Light. It..." For the first time this evening I see a brief flash of nervousness cross her face. But it disappears almost as quickly as it came, and she continues, "It started as an online relationship, progressed from there until we agreed to meet in real life, and..."

I glance down, and her fingertips are pressed tight together.

"It... it didn't work out." Again, she looks away and out into the club.

It's a story I've heard before.

"Was he abusive?"

Her gaze snaps back. "In so many words, yes."

"And when it all began, he claimed he wanted a high protocol relationship too, knew all about it, could provide you everything you were looking for."

"Yes."

"But that was a lie, wasn't it?"

Her eyes grow cold. "From his perspective, no. From mine..." She goes silent.

"And playing in the club?"

"Suffice it to say my experiences so far have been... lacking."

"And yet here you are."

"And yet here *you* are too."

This time I voice the word. "Touché."

"Terry said you have experience. In fact, he was quite confident our desires would align." She gives me a pointed stare. "If you don't mind my asking, have *you* been in a high protocol relationship before, or is your experience solely playing in the club?"

"Terry was right. I have experience."

She waits for a moment. "Okay. That wasn't really an answer to my question."

"What do you know about high protocol? I mean, *truly* know. You've admitted your one relationship was a failure, and that your experiences in the club have been 'lacking.' I mean you no disrespect, Alex, but is there a chance you *don't* know what high protocol really is, or that maybe your understanding of it is incorrect?"

Fire lights her eyes. "That's a bit presumptuous, don't you think? You've been quizzing me for all of ten minutes and from *that* you form the opinion I don't have a clue what I'm talking about?"

"I simply asked a question."

"No, you didn't. A question would've been 'I'd like to hear your thoughts on what you're looking for in a high protocol dynamic,' or 'could you please tell me what was missing from your previous attempts at high protocol?' Instead, you presumed to tell me I might not even know what it is I'm looking for." She leans forward. "Now, I mean *you* no disrespect, but as delightful as this little tête-à-tête we're having is, you've given me no reason to believe *you* have a clue what high protocol is and—if I may be perfectly frank—I'm beginning to get the feeling we're just wasting our time here."

Ooo. I'm starting to like this woman.

"Alex, trust me when I say with one hundred percent conviction, we're not wasting our time."

She leans back slowly, her eyes narrowing as she stares at me. "Well, I have to say, Galen, you certainly aren't giving me that impression."

"You've been burned before, haven't you?"

"Yesss," she says.

"So have I."

For a moment we simply stare at each other.

"Okay," she says eventually, her voice quiet. "I'll take the first step here. I want to explore high protocol with someone who doesn't mistake it for a free pass to be abusive or believe the only way for me to experience it is to become their slave. Someone who understands the structure inherent in the dynamic, who understands my *desire* for the rules and formality but who doesn't want to twist them into me giving up all my rights and doing everything they say at all times without question. Someone who'll give me the opportunity to show I can be submissive for them without shoving me to my knees right out of the gate and demanding I submit with blind obedience."

She takes a slow, deep breath, and I give a small nod to encourage her to continue, already deeply intrigued.

"You're right: I don't have a lot of real-life experience in what my *expectations* of high protocol are because I've never been given the opportunity. No one has ever bothered to listen to my wants and needs nor bothered trying to understand them. Instead, it's been *'kneel, slave'* or *'I'm the Dominant and you're the submissive and you'll do what I tell you to because that's how this works.'* God knows I've heard that spiel far too many times, and I'm not naïve, nor a fool, Galen. I've done my research. All I've ever looked for is someone who is like-minded and will give me the chance to show what I'm into and what I'm willing to do."

I open my mouth to respond, but she raises a finger and points it toward me with emphasis. "What I will tell you is this: you may be different than all the others who've come before you, Galen—only time will tell whether that's true or not. But let me make one thing perfectly clear: you will *never* make the decision for me on what high protocol is, and if you underestimate me one more time this evening, you'll *never* know just what I'm truly capable of."

Damn.

Before either of us can speak, a voice cuts us off.

"Hey, there you are!"

It's Terry.

"I'm really sorry, guys. I got caught up taking care of some shit but—look at you! Looks like you found each other without me, and things are going well!" Terry's grinning as Alex and I share a glance with each other.

"We've made introductions," she says with a polite smile that doesn't quite reach the corners of her mouth.

"In fact," I add, "we were just discussing how the rest of our evening might go. That's assuming one of us doesn't take the other for granted."

Alex flicks another look toward me. "Yes. Exactly."

Terry looks a bit confused, but since no one's tossed a drink on the other, we're still here at the bar talking, and both of us are smiling in some fashion, he seems pleased well enough. "Alright, alright, that's good. So, umm, is there anything I can get for you? You, uh, need a private place to… talk or anything?"

Alex dips her head to hide a smile. "I think we're fine right here for now."

"We'll let you know if we need anything, Terry."

He takes the hint. "Sounds good. Well, I better get back to work. Things are crazy tonight." He takes a step back. "It's good to see you two together. You make sure to let me know if you need anything." He shoots me a pointed look, his grin even wider, then he's gone.

"He's a good man," I say quietly as he disappears into the crowd.

Alex pins me with a gaze. "He is. If it wasn't for him, I wouldn't even be here tonight, I can tell you that."

"Then I definitely have something to thank him for."

She narrows her eyes before laughing. "Wow. Has anyone ever told you that you have a way of making hard right turns in conversation?"

"It might have come up a few times."

She picks up her glass and finishes the last of her water. "So."

"So." I've got an idea, and I make a quick, searching glance of the room to see if I can find what I'll need to make it happen. A second later I find it, and if I make my pitch quickly I'll be able to put my plan in motion and see just how far Alex is willing to take this.

Or I'll prove to myself I was right all along.

"I have a proposal, Alex, if you're willing to entertain it."

"A proposal?" She gives me a guarded look.

"Yes." I put on my most charming smile. "Do you enjoy a challenge?"

"A challenge?"

"Yes."

"Okay… an odd question, but… yes, I enjoy a challenge."

I turn and look back at the empty table I spotted a moment ago. "You see that table right there?" I point, and her gaze follows my finger. "I'm going to go over to that table and sit down. What I'd like for you to do is go to that bartender right there"—I point to Klara, who's working at the opposite end from where we sit—"and ask her to pour you two fingers of Weller Twelve-Year over two cubes of ice. When you're done, I'd like you to bring it to the table and serve it to me the way you think I'd want it served."

The expression in her eyes slowly shifts as I describe the challenge, and by the time I've finished she's wearing a look of intrigue.

"And that's it?"

"For now."

There's a moment's pause. "Challenge accepted," she says with quiet determination.

I'll be damned. Without a word I turn from her and move across the bar area to the table.

Once there, I sit with my back to the bar. For this little challenge it's important she understand I'm not going to watch her nor give her any visual cues as to what she should do. I'll give her credit: she didn't balk when I offered the challenge, nor did she act confused or question what I told her to do. I'd expected her, at a bare minimum, to ask me to repeat some portion of my instructions, but she didn't even do that. She talked about rules and structure and formality regarding her vision of high protocol, and I'm curious to see how she puts those into application in a situation like this.

She thinks she knows high protocol; let's see just how much she really does.

The minutes slip by, and I keep my vigil—back to the bar, eyes scanning the crowd as it ebbs and flows around me. Five minutes pass, and there's no sign of her. By seven I'm guessing she's given up all pretense and has fled the club rather than admit she really doesn't have a clue. I'm a fair man, however, and I'll give her until ten before I turn to confirm my suspicions. When I glance at my watch again almost nine minutes have passed, and as I bring my eyes up, I feel a quiet presence at my back.

I start to turn, then stop as she moves beside me. She kneels slowly, gracefully, a glass with a deep, rich, amber liquid held in her hand. When her knees hit the ground, she spreads them slightly, bringing the drink up with both hands and offering it to me, head bowed, eyes down.

Son of a bitch.

I say nothing, raking her with my gaze, and I almost do a double-take.

Fuck. She's taken off her dress.

She's kneeling beside me, offering up the glass, a goddamn

picture-perfect pose of submission and obedience, and aside from a black lace bra and matching panties, she's removed every other stitch of clothing she came in here wearing.

Fuck, fuck, fuck.

Okay, okay, first score in the game to her. She accepted my challenge, and where I anticipated her running away in abject failure, instead she's gone all-fucking-in.

Alright, Galen, keep your shit together. Don't get too *excited just yet.*

Too late. My dick's gone hard because... damn. This... this I did not expect, and yet here she is beside me in a position I haven't seen from a sub since...

No.

No, I won't spoil this by thinking about... her.

This woman... she's done what no other submissive has recently: she surprised me. Earlier I felt certain Terry was naïve about what she really knew, and I was equally as sure she was going to be yet another failure. But for the first time since... since everything I've been trying to forget... she actually seems to be someone who gets it.

She understands.

She sees the inherent beauty and subtlety in this poised form of submission which doesn't have her spread lewdly over a spanking bench, or bound splayed to a St. Andrew's cross, and yet is just as fucking sexy—if not more so. I let her stay in position presenting my drink and savor this moment I've missed. I watch to see if she'll waver; turn her head up to glance at me, or shift her hips to relieve the strain from kneeling in the position, or a hundred other little signs to say she's uncomfortable or isn't enjoying this one tenth as much as I am.

She does none of those things. Instead, she simply remains in position, silent, unmoving.

Perfection.

I let another minute pass before I reach for the glass and take it from her hands.

"What is this?" I ask quietly.

"Two fingers of Weller Twelve-Year Bourbon over two cubes of ice," she answers just as softly. "Sir."

Sir.

I take a sip of the drink. It's exactly what I asked for. But she didn't just stop at the drink. No, now I understand what took her so long. I want to ask how she did it, where she hid her dress and shoes, but… honestly, the game's still on, and that's a question for later.

"Okay, Alex, I'll admit it. I'm impressed. Very impressed." I take another sip of the bourbon. "Good girl. Well done."

I expect her to look up.

She doesn't.

Damn. Is she… could she…?

There's no time for that kind of thinking. *One step at a time here, Galen.* I challenged her, asked her to play my little game, and she's done it far better than I have any right to expect. Now I need to decide just how far I'm willing to take this, and what my next move is going to be.

Just… if you think there's even the remotest chance she might be the 'right sub,' don't fuck this up.

"I do, however, have one further question for you."

She remains still, eyes down, waiting.

"Why are you wearing *any* clothes at all?"

CHAPTER 4

ALEX

hat did he just say?
Did he just... did he seriously just ask me why I'm still wearing clothes?

I begin turning my face up toward his, then stop.

No. No, you will not give him the satisfaction. You've beaten him at his little game so far, and he knows it. Now he's trying to get a rise out of you. Don't fall for it.

I hold my position because I'm positive I'm right. I'll admit there's a part of me that's thrilled this little contest we're engaged in because for the first time since I've come to Black Light—hell, for the first time in my life—it feels like he might be someone who gets it. Who understands the style of high protocol I'm looking for.

Maybe. Hopefully.

He's just sitting there, and I either make my next move quickly or cede the initiative to him.

You want to play, Galen? Let's play.

I stand smoothly, keeping my gaze glued to the floor in front of me. Wordlessly, I remove my panties, then drop back into a kneel. Without glancing his direction for a millisecond, I reach back and unhook my bra then carefully fold both and set them beside me.

Queen to E5. Your move.

He's thinking, probably contemplating what I've just done. He asked me if I liked a challenge, and now he's finding out just how much I do. And right now, he's either fuming that I'm not failing at his tasks, or he's coming up with new ones. I grin inside, because I'm picturing myself making the Morpheus *'come at me'* hand gesture from *The Matrix.*

He stands. I almost flinch but keep myself in check. He pauses for a moment then turns and walks away.

Okay. Either he's retreating or he's moving on to another challenge. Either way, I need to make a decision quickly on how I'm going to react. He's clearly intelligent, and aside from the 'why are you wearing any clothes at all' comment he's said nothing which could be construed as crass or sexual. And while I think he might be irritated by my matching him tit for tat, he also said he was impressed with me... and called me a 'good girl.'

Which I liked. Very much.

Okay, Alex, time to move. Do something.

I peek and he's moving across the room, not looking back, and if I don't make a choice quick, I'll lose him in the crowd.

Go.

I get up and follow him. I'm not sure whether he expects me to crawl, walk, or just stay where I'm at. Everything I've done so far has been based upon what I think a Dom who truly understands high protocol would want. I hurry to catch up and then walk a respectable distance behind him because I'm betting that's what *he* would like. For some reason crawling just doesn't seem his style and staying where I was doesn't seem right.

It doesn't matter, though. I've already made my choice. Leaving my panties and bra behind, same as he did with his drink, I keep my head down, hands behind my back, and thread my way through the club. He doesn't pause as he makes his way through the crowd, and

I suspect he hasn't even looked back to see what I'm doing. He either trusts me to follow—which sends a little tingle up my spine—or he set up this part of the challenge so no matter what I do, I'll fail.

And if that's his game it means he's a prick like all the rest were and I'll bail out of this so fast he won't have time to watch my ass disappear.

As I weave through the clubgoers there's an occasional murmur in my wake until he finally comes to a stop. I continue until I stop close behind him, then drop back to my knees, hands palm-down on my thighs. I'm pretty sure we're in front of one of the private booths, but I don't dare look up to confirm it.

I catch the soft rustle of fabric and then his voice.

"In."

It's all he says. A single word, but there's something in the way he says it, his tone…

Yes! Scoooore!

Okay, next move. I drop from my kneeling position onto all fours, and crawl through the opening he provided. Once I'm inside, I see the edge of a chaise lounge and head toward it. When I reach it, I come to rest in the same kneeling position I was in before. There's a soft swish as the curtain drops behind me, the noise of the club reduced to a low background hum.

He approaches. I wait, eyes still down, a tingle running up my spine before it becomes a frisson of electricity. This might be just a game but—*ho boy*—it's definitely having an effect on me, and one I'm not at all upset with.

For a moment neither of us moves, then he speaks again.

"Up."

Another single word, and the tenor of it shoots right to my pussy. This started as a challenge, but it's quickly turning into something else entirely. Not that I'm complaining; at this point I'm all in.

I stand and, for the first time since I knelt beside the table, I catch a quick glance of his face. There's not a trace of anger on it; if anything, he looks pleased, which only compounds the sensation between my legs. I don't let my gaze linger, however. I lower my eyes back to the floor as I'm supposed to and wait for whatever he's planning next.

"Present."

My pussy clenches at the command, and my hands shoot to my sides, fingers together and resting against my upper thighs like every image in every submissive position chart I've ever pored over, imaging this very situation. And it's happening. It's actually happening.

Oh, God. How far is this going to go?

The thought sends me into a tug of war of opposing emotions. Thrill of where this may end up tonight and fear it's happening too fast. I mean, I *wanted* this, but I really don't know anything about Galen. And the thing is, unlike the others, he's intense. He's not predictable, hasn't fallen into the same patterns the rest of them did, and he's not shown any trace of the latent or overt aggression I've felt around the other so-called Doms I've run up against.

What was it Terry said? 'I guarantee you he ain't gonna feed you a line of crap.' Well, that much has definitely been true. Still… what if he's just more patient than the others were? What if all he's been waiting for is to get me in here alone so he can pull some of the same nonsense they had?

I shove those thoughts aside because he's moving. If that's what's about to happen, I'll deal with it the same as I did before. Still, credit where credit's due; he's the first Dom to get me naked in the club, and as far as our game goes, for that alone he's scored at least one point tonight.

He circles slowly around me, and I hold my position, silent, unmoving. He starts a second pass but comes to a stop when he's directly behind me. It's hard not to tremble as he stands there because I have no idea what he's going to do. I wait for a sound, anything that'll let me know what his next move will be.

He touches me.

I almost jerk at the sensation of his fingers coming to rest on my biceps but, with every ounce of control I can muster, I hold myself rigid. He rests his hands there for a moment then slowly lets them drift down the length of my arms. The caress is featherlight, and goosebumps rise in the wake. He reaches my wrists, then takes my hands into his. Not a clench, but a light embrace, spreading the digits apart gently as he strokes each one. When he's finished, he drags his fingertips back up my arms until he reaches my shoulders. He stops briefly, his thumbs making small circles as he massages my shoulder blades soothingly. Damn, he's making it hard not to move, to shiver against the sensations dancing across my skin, but if he thinks I'll give up and melt into a puddle now, he's misjudged me.

Still, it's a good attempt.

He doesn't linger long before he moves his hands again, sliding down the center of my back on either side of my spine, and I'm certain where he's headed. If this is going to veer off the rails in the way I've worried it might, it'll happen in about two seconds when he—

His fingertips graze over the curve of my ass, but instead of stopping to dig his fingers in and clench a handful, he skates past without pause, moving to the underside of my cheeks before lightly cupping me as he comes to a stop.

Oh, this is getting interesting.

He's close. I hear his breathing and feel the proximity of his body to mine. He's not purposefully pushing against me, shoving his crotch into my backside. He's in my space, but not *in* it. I've zero doubt he's watching and waiting to see if I'll balk, judging my reactions, and I'm not about to give him anything to find fault with. I hold firm, and several seconds pass before he moves again.

He lowers himself, his chest brushing against me as his fingers continue downward in their exploration of my body. He's tracing a path down the back of my legs, and I stiffen, unable to avoid it because if he keeps going the direction he is, once he reaches the back of my knees there's no way I'm not going to—

I twitch, hissing as I suck in air.

In an instant his hands are no longer on me, the ever-so-slight press of his chest against my back gone as he stands.

"What was that?" he asks quietly.

"Sorry, sir. I'm ticklish there," I whisper in return.

The room goes quiet. There's no reason I should feel disappointed, and yet I do. I beat him at his own game, but right now it's the fear this might be over that threatens me most.

I wait for him to do something, anything, but the only noises are the muted sounds from the club beyond the curtain, and rather than being comforting the silence only makes the seconds drag by. Finally, after what seems like forever, I hear him move.

He drapes something over my shoulders, and the fabric of his suit jacket comes into view as he tugs it around me. It's such a simple act and yet it's one of the sexiest things a man has ever done for me.

He stands there for a moment, gently massaging my shoulders, and though I can't be one hundred percent certain, I swear the tempo of his breathing has increased. Finally, he pulls his hands away, moving in front of me. I keep my face down, but he brings a finger under my chin, lifting until our eyes meet.

Approval.

It's a look I've seen from men in my professional career, and I see it now in Galen's gaze. It's a first for me in a club situation however, and my body flushes in response. I had no idea how powerful this feeling would be, how much I'd crave it.

How much I'd want more.

His face is neutral, but the look in his eyes is as intense as everything else he's done tonight.

"I'm going to go back and finish my drink," he says quietly.

"Please get dressed and, if you'd like to continue this, come join me." He pulls the finger from under my chin then turns and strides from the room.

'...if you'd like to continue this...'

I exhale. *If* I'd like to?

Oh, yes. Most definitely yes.

Because for the first time, maybe, just maybe... I've *finally* found someone who understands.

CHAPTER 5

GALEN

G *od. Damn.*
    I push through the curtain and head directly for the
    table. Why I think it'll be empty or my drink still there I
don't know, but I move that direction anyway because...

Because—*Christ*—it's been a while since I've been in this
headspace, and I told myself before not to fuck this up and I'm
pretty sure I haven't, but this woman, *Alex*... she got inside my
head fast, and no sub has been able to do that since—

Okay, still not going to let those memories screw this up
because I'm not letting this opportunity get away from me now.
Fuck knows if it'll go anywhere substantial beyond tonight, but
like the old Wayne Gretzky saying, 'you miss one hundred percent
of the shots you never take,' and I'm not about to let that happen
here.

To my great satisfaction, our table's still empty, my glass sitting
there untouched exactly where I set it down. I move back to my
seat and, as I do, I see the neat pile of her underwear where she
left it on the floor. Bending over, I pick it up and set it on the
table. She's got two options here: either come by and snatch them
up or head straight for wherever it was she took off her dress and

then bolt from this place, leaving her underwear as my glass slipper. She needn't worry; if this wasn't what she was looking for, I won't pursue her. Merely on the basis of what she gave me tonight, I've far too much respect for her to do that. If this is done, it's done.

I take a quick sip of the Weller bourbon to soothe the edge of my nerves and, as the liquid warms me, I catch her approaching out the corner of my eye. She moves to the edge of the table and stands in silence, hands at her sides.

"I believe these are yours?" I say, standing up and handing the items to her.

"Thank you," she says, dipping her head. "And this is yours." She shrugs out of my jacket, handing it to me. Gone is the 'sir,' and she's making direct eye contact as she holds it out.

"You can wear it until you're dressed, if you like."

"That's very kind. I'll be okay."

There's something about the idea of her walking through the club naked now that makes me want to command her to keep it, but the moment for that has passed. The scene is over, so I say nothing as I take it from her.

"Is there anything I can bring you from the bar?" she asks, glancing in that direction.

"No, I'm good," I answer, motioning to my glass.

"Okay." She gives me a polite smile and another dip of her head then turns and moves off. I watch as she goes, admiring the sway of her hips, the grace with which she moves as she weaves through the clubgoers. I don't miss the turning of heads as she passes, and pride and possessiveness shoot through me in equal measure.

Don't jump the gun, Galen. Exciting as everything that just happened was, you don't have a clue what she's going to tell you once she comes back.

But she *is* coming back. The offer to bring me back a drink assures it, and I sit back down with anticipation pricking my nerves.

When she reaches the bar, Klara hands across the dress she clearly left there. As Alex dresses, the two of them talk, and there are smiles, which makes me pleased in a way I shouldn't make assumptions about. Watching her slip back into her panties and bra is not without its own appeal, and that only increases my satisfaction. Klara tilts her head back in laughter before reaching to pat Alex's arm as she moves off. She comes back a moment later with a glass of white wine in hand as Alex is slipping on her shoes. Alex takes the wine and—with a final parting comment—turns and walks back toward me.

She's wearing a Mona Lisa smile, and it doesn't drop even though she can see my entire focus is on her. As she approaches, I rise and pull out a chair.

"Thank you," she says, sitting gracefully.

I move the seat in and remain standing until she's comfortably in place. Once she's settled, I take my own seat again, and it's just the two of us staring across the table at each other.

"I won't mince words," I start, keeping my gaze locked to hers. "That was very impressive for someone who claims they've never truly been in a high protocol relationship."

She chuckles. "I believe I said I'd done my research." She takes a sip of her wine.

"Yes, you did." I swirl the bourbon in my glass, never taking my eyes off her. "So... was that what you wanted?"

She bites her lower lip, and my cock strains against the inside of my pants. "Yes, Galen. Yes, it was."

"Good," I reply, shifting slightly in my seat. "Just so you know, my name *is* actually Galen. If I could ask, is Alex your real name or your scene name?"

"It's Alexandria, though most people just call me Alex."

"That's a beautiful name," I say, shaking her hand. "A strong name. Very appropriate for you."

She grins. "Now you're flattering me."

"I prefer to think of it as simply telling the truth."

"We've known each other for less than an hour."

"What you just did… I don't need to have known you longer to recognize the strength it took to do that. You accepted my challenge and then you didn't just complete it; you took it a step beyond."

She shakes her head. "Okay, now you *are* flattering me."

"Fine. Even if I am, it changes nothing." I take a sip of my drink. "You clearly understand the basic precepts of high protocol, at least in the way I believe you and I wish to practice it. You're clearly an intelligent person, able to think quickly on your feet, and moreover you observed the situation presented to you and adapted to it, which I will tell you is not a common trait. You took what I'd initially asked—how do you think you should serve my drink to me— and you didn't just follow the letter of the law. No, you followed the *spirit* of it and in a way that completely surprised me." I raise my glass toward her. "Do I think you're a strong person? Yes. In fact, I know you are."

"You're very confident, aren't you?"

"I am. Does that bother you?"

"No." She toys with the stem of her wineglass. "As long as that confidence is warranted, I find it… attractive."

I give her a nod of acknowledgement.

"So, let me ask you this, Galen." She tilts her head, eyes narrowing slightly. "When we were in the private room together, before you put your jacket around me… why didn't you try to fuck me?"

My eyes widen, and not just because of the question she's asked. It's the first time this evening I've heard her use a curse word, and the sound of it coming from her lips throws me a bit.

Exactly as she no doubt planned.

"And there you go again, proving my point."

"About?"

"How strong you are."

She smiles. "Some would say that question only proves I'm more Domme than submissive."

"I've no time for fools who'd believe *that*."

She dips her head in appreciation. "Thank you." She looks up at me, her gaze assessing. "But you haven't answered my question."

"Because fucking you wasn't part of the game. That's not what either of us was looking for tonight."

She cocks an eyebrow. "That's a little presumptuous, don't you think?"

"Then tell me I'm wrong, Alex." I put just enough Dom-voice into it to make it clear I'm being serious.

"No," she replies softly. "No, you're not wrong."

"We'll have plenty of opportunity to explore a sexual relationship another time if we so choose. Tonight was to determine if there should even *be* another time. We've both already admitted we haven't had much success finding like-minded people who share our desires. I'm fairly confident neither of us came here tonight wanting bad sex after yet another failed encounter."

"So, you're saying sex with you would've been bad, or you're just bad at sex?"

I narrow my eyes. "I didn't take you for a brat. Clearly, I was wrong."

She laughs, and I can't help but grin.

"I'm sorry, I thought we were still playing the game," she says with a coy look.

"I think tonight's game has ended."

"Did I win?"

"I think we both did."

"I think you're right."

Each of us picks up our drink, staring across the table.

"I mentioned you impressed me before," I say, staring at her intently. "And you did. I'm not going to lie; when you were gone for as long as you were, I was pretty sure you'd bailed. Then you showed up in your underwear and that surprised me because it's the first true act of what I consider high protocol submission I've seen from a submissive since…" I continue after a slight pause. "In a while. And maybe I'm wrong, maybe I've misread you, maybe it's just wishful fucking thinking on my part, but my impression is it was much the same for you."

"You're not wrong," she confirms, eyes staring back with the same intensity I'm feeling.

"So, we have a choice to make here. We can either consider this a one-time thing, go off and tell Terry it was fun but nothing more, or we can choose to take this the next step."

"'We' language."

I scrunch my brow. "Beg pardon?"

"You're using 'we' language. Not 'I want' or 'you'll do,' but 'we' language." She gives me a warm smile. "Now *I'm* impressed."

I raise an eyebrow. "Oh, so I didn't impress you before?"

She laughs again. "Okay, sorry. Now I'm impressed even *more*."

"Better," I reply, shooting her a sly grin.

"So," she says after a moment, "I'd really hate to disappoint Terry."

"As would I." I reach into the inside pocket of my jacket and pull out one of my business cards and a pen. "I propose this. If you're as serious as I am, then I'd like for you to come to my home. If you agree, I suggest you set up a safety buddy check before you come, and then once you're there we can identify what high protocol might look like for us outside of a club setting."

"A safety buddy check?" She gives me a questioning look.

"Yes. Because it's the right thing to do."

"Oookay." She draws the word out, but the smile on her face is approving.

I hold the pen poised above the card, waiting.

"I accept."

"Awesome." I write out my address on the back. "I'll make dinner, we can discuss what we're both looking for in detail, what your limits are, and what you like."

"And what *you* like," she counters. "Aside from Weller Twelve-Year bourbon and cupping my ass in your hands. Because turnabout's fair play, right?" She gives me a mischievous smirk.

"I'm sure we can find mutual interests."

"I'm sure we can. I'm looking forward to it."

I finish and slide the card across the table toward her. "I assume you work during the week?"

She nods. "Yes. Monday through Friday, seven to whenever, which usually means after six."

"This coming Friday, then? Say seven-thirty?"

"I can do that." She picks up her glass and takes a drink, looking at me over the edge as she does.

I stare back. There's a dark, eager part deep inside me that wants to take her back to the room, tell her to take her clothes off again, and fuck her like she thought I might. But I shove it down as fast as it squirms up. Patience has always been a virtue I've admired, and one I've tried to emulate. I'm not backing away from that now, because everything I've seen from Alex tonight is a solid indication this is potentially the beginning of something I'd almost given up on.

"Testing the waters, Alex. Let's think of it as that. A pleasant evening, some discussions, perhaps even negotiations, and then back safe in your own home by bedtime."

"We'll see," she says with an enigmatic smile.

The answer is cryptic and yet filled with an undertone that has my cock twitching.

"Can I ask you a question?" She sets her glass back down.

"Of course."

"At the beginning of the evening, when I first approached you... you had reservations, didn't you?"

"I did." I finish my drink quickly, placing the empty glass on the tabletop. "But I don't now."

She nods once. "Same." She reaches for my card and picks it up. Reading it carefully front and back, she returns her gaze to me when she's finished, a wicked glint in her eyes. "Do you give your address to every girl you meet at Black Light?"

I say nothing for a second, then slowly lean across the table and pinch her chin between my thumb and forefinger. "What do you think?"

To her credit, she doesn't flinch. "I don't think you do, sir," she says softly.

"Good answer," I reply, my voice a rumble. Letting her go, I stand up from my chair. She starts to rise, but before she can, I move to her back and press down on her shoulder. She submits, slipping back into her seat.

I bend. I hadn't noticed it earlier but—*fuck*—she smells incredible. The conflict between my dick and my brain roars back to life.

"Thank you for a wonderful evening," I murmur, letting my lips brush her ear.

She shivers. "Thank you, sir."

Sir.

Damn. I love that word. I want to hear her say it again, give her a reason to. Instead, I turn away and stride across the club floor toward the exit.

A part of me says to turn back.

No, Galen. Patience. Patience.

Ugh. I hate my own conscience sometimes, I really do. Because this…

This is going to make for a really, *really* long fucking week.

CHAPTER 6

ALEX

"*S*o? So?"

Klara literally walked away from a customer to meet me as I approached the bar. I have no idea why she's so invested in this because until I came to her with Galen's drink order, I don't think we've spoken a dozen words to each other in the time I've been a member here. But her eyes are bright, and she's leaning across the counter, eager to hear my answer.

I hold up his business card.

"Yes!" She pumps her fist, a wide grin creasing her face.

"It's just to have dinner," I add dismissively as I slip the card into my clutch.

"Oh, sure, sure." Klara nods in agreement, but her tone and the look in her eyes tell a different story. "Pretty much every woman I know gets naked and walks through a crowded BDSM club before they go to 'just have dinner' at a Dom's house."

I roll my eyes. "That was just part of a game we were playing."

Her skepticism doesn't fade. "Uh huh. Well, I like to play games with Spencer too, and I know exactly how those end up going, especially *after* dinner."

"Oh my God." I sigh, shaking my head.

Klara glances back down the bar. "Shit. Okay, listen, I have to get back to work for a minute. Don't you dare fucking leave"—she stabs a finger at me—"until I come back and we can get your head screwed on straight about what's going to happen at this *dinner* he's invited you to." Before I'm able to respond she turns away and heads back to her customers, leaving me to my thoughts.

And I *am* thinking. Because... yeah, she's right. This is likely to be more than just a dinner. Galen only spoke about us 'testing the waters,' as he called it, and while that thought's exciting enough, there's another part of me that hopes it turns out to be more.

You're horny. Go home and take care of yourself, girl, before you start blowing this up into something it may not be.

Yeah, I *am* horny, but that's his fault. I've never felt as excited, challenged—or *understood*—by a man as I do right now. I asked him why he didn't fuck me not simply as another shot across the bow in the game we were playing but because... honestly, after what we'd done? I wouldn't have minded if he had. Admittedly, the choice he made only solidified for me I wanted to see him again just to see where this might go. Still, considering everything that happened up to that point, if he chose to push the boundary in the private room and tried...

I'd have let him.

"Hey."

I jump. I was so lost in my own thoughts I didn't notice Terry approach.

"So... good?" He leans against the bar beside me, a goofy grin on his face.

"Terry! Jeez, don't sneak up on me like that!"

He laughs. "Thinking about him, weren't you?"

"No!" I run my hand through my hair, brushing it back. "Yes. Maybe."

"Soooo... good?" he asks the question again, staring at me pointedly.

I groan. "Okay, yes, Terry. Yes, it went good."

"Told you," he says with no small amount of pride before he narrows his eyes. "So, when are you seeing him again?"

Just like Galen earlier, it's a presumptuous question. Not only that, but it's also a little irritating Klara and Terry *both* assumed I'm going to see Galen again. Klara to the point of intimating I'll be getting laid when I do, without giving me the benefit of the doubt I can make the decision on my own.

"Who says I'm meeting him again?"

Terry's face falls for a second, but then he squints, his mouth forming a frown. "You ain't trying to bullshit me, are you, Alex?"

I drop my gaze to the bar top. "Okay, so maybe we *might* be having dinner together on Friday."

"I fucking knew it," he says with glee, clapping me on the shoulder.

Oof.

"Well, we might have had dinner, if you hadn't just dislocated my shoulder."

Terry snorts. "Right, I know you're strong, so I figure you'll recover by then." He shoots me a roguish grin.

"Yeah," I say, grimacing. "Thanks."

Klara comes back at that moment, moving in front of Terry. "Did she tell you?"

"Not everything, but she's got a date."

"Yep," Klara nods emphatically. "She thinks it's just to talk, so I've got to work that notion out of her head."

"Well, wait now," Terry says, stroking his chin. "Galen is a patient man. Could be that's all he intends to do until he's certain Alex is comfortable."

"Terry, it's been how long? Master Harmon may be patient, but every person has their limits…"

'Master Harmon.' He didn't ask me to address him by that title, nor did he mention it tonight, but Klara used it almost casually. *Hmm.* He mentioned he's been a member here for a while, but what did she mean by 'it's been how long?'

"I'm just saying…" Terry turns away from Klara toward me. "I told you Galen wouldn't bullshit you. You feel like he is?"

"No," I answer quietly. "Not in the slightest."

"Then all I'll say is, be patient and take your time." He gives me a warm smile. "It'll be worth it. Trust me."

My eyes dart between the two of them. It was a leap of faith trusting Terry in the lead up to tonight, and he wasn't wrong. I probably should still be a little wary, but what few remaining doubts I have are quickly fading because…

This was better than I could have expected—or hoped for.

I blow out a sigh. "Klara, I think I need another glass of wine."

She chuckles and starts to turn.

"Oh," I add, holding up a finger. "And bring me a small glass of the Weller bourbon." I look at her with a calculating gaze. "You and I need to discuss a little pre-planning for this coming Friday."

"ALEX, it's Ms. Kuhlman from Cogent on line two for you."

"Alex, we really need to pin him down on whether he's going to move forward with these folks or not."

"Alex, sorry to interrupt, but are we still on for three-thirty with the folks from Oracle?"

It's chaos. In other words, just another typical Wednesday.

"Tell Edda to hold just a minute longer; I'll be right there."

I turn to the two team members sitting at the conference table. "David, put out an email to James Hawkins reiterating these people won't wait forever for him to commit, and while we value his experience and expertise, this is a business matter, and we must advise him to move quickly. And that means by next week, or we'll find another client eager to take on talent of this caliber."

I switch my gaze to Bri. "Bri, apologize to them for the delay but let them know we've put a shot across Dr. Hawkins' bow, and if he doesn't move, we have other opportunities waiting for them.

Emphasize that because we can't afford to lose these people to SourceAmerica or George and his folks over at St. Onge." The two of them nod and rise from the table.

"Alex, Oracle?"

I look to where Seth is still leaning through the conference room door. "Yes, we're still on. I'll come grab you at two forty-five and we can head over."

"Wait," he says, looking confused. "The meeting's there?"

"Yes, Seth, the meeting's there. Did you forget?"

He gives me a grim look. "Thank fucking God you remembered, or I'd be sitting on my ass in an empty conference room wondering why the client hadn't shown."

"All good," I reply with a smile. "That's what I'm here for."

Managing chaos. That's me.

The title on my door says Director of Human Resources and Acquisitions, but it really should read 'Cat Herder.'

Years ago, there was a viral video that made its way through HR circles about cowboys herding cats, and I still have the link saved where I can grab it at a moment's notice. It described what I've been doing for the past ten years at GSR better than any written description could.

The atmosphere in the financial industry as a whole is frenetic; add the controlled yet manic energy of the US government and attendant lobbyists blanketing the D.C. metro area, and on any given day it's the equivalent of being in a daycare filled with children hyped up on Cap'n Crunch and Coke.

I love my job, though. I thrive on the energy of it, controlling the chaos, bringing the disparate parties together and creating unity, making sure all the balls are in the air and the plates still spinning. I don't think of myself as vain, but I'm good at what I do, and my position at GSR—and the compensation they give me—is evidence of that. From the moment I step through the doors until the moment I leave back through them, I'm the archetypical poster child for the Type A working woman professional. But when I put my work cell on 'do not disturb' at home?

I cringe sometimes to imagine what my contemporaries might think of the person I am in private. They'd accuse me of perpetuating a stereotype, a trope some women would just as soon see disappear entirely. Tiger in the boardroom, submissive in the bedroom. But the problem is outside my job that's what I am.

I'm a submissive. I always have been. I can't alter that part of me any more than I can change how I am when I'm in charge of a project. Call it the Janus Effect or whatever, but both sides are equal parts of me, and I *like* the person I am. My problem is while the career half of me has found complete fulfillment, the other part?

Yeah… not so much.

I've tried it all. 'Swipe right' dating apps, Fetlife, even 'drop into my DMs' on Reddit. The sum total of my experiences could be described as 'much effort was expended for little return.'

In every case it always ended the same: they claimed to know and understand what I wanted, and yet unless I was willing to roleplay Princess Leia in a slave girl costume they had no clue. I had a brief relationship with a Dom I met online who talked the talk while we were strictly in DMs and phone sex, but the minute he came down from upstate New York and we met in person —*nope*.

In desperation I looked for real-life venues where I might find someone and, at a munch I attended in Annapolis, I learned about a couple of clubs where I might have better luck than the online cesspool I'd been flailing in. One was The Crucible, the other a club called Black Light. A couple invited me to an introduction event held at the latter, and when I got there, I was convinced this would be it. The place was both intimidating and affirming at the same time, and there were so many people so obviously well-versed in the lifestyle and the myriad kinks therein, I just knew there'd be someone there who understood mine.

Famous last words.

I joined—which wasn't cheap—and it was one failure after another. True, the clientele was definitely more high-end than my previous encounters but... money doesn't buy everything, and in this case that was definitely true.

The Doms I found myself partnered with either just wanted to fuck me or expected immediate and total submission. Master/slave right from the start. The thing is... Master/slave isn't even a component in my version of high protocol. I knew it was for some, clearly many, but for me? No.

And before the night we met, I'd convinced myself the odds my evening with Galen would end in yet another failure were pretty good. I like Terry and respect him, but... experience has taught me not to get my hopes up, no matter how much something seems like a sure thing.

Then it went well. Better than anything else.

But meeting him at his home? What were you thinking agreeing to that?

I could have—should have—just negotiated for a second club date at Black Light. Scened with him there and had the chance to see if any quirks bubbled to the surface, but no. I let him get inside my head as much as I got inside his, and now on Friday I'm heading out to his house in Laurel.

Jeez.

Only one of the most expensive suburbs in the D.C. metro area. No pressure there. Whoever Galen Harmon is, he doesn't roll cheap. His home is on a five-acre plot right off I-95 along the Patuxent River, and from Sotheby's, to Zillow, to Redfin, none of them had a listing or pictures showing what the house looks like. It's completely off the grid, and the only information I could find was what showed on a satellite view from Google Maps—which was stalkerish, I'll admit that, but I was curious. I could see it was large, but beyond that there weren't any additional details I could glean.

I'm not someone who typically second guesses themselves, but I've gotten so used to guys not having a clue what I want it feels almost unnatural that someone might be on the same wavelength as I am.

But Galen Harmon might be.

God, he was so intense, so commanding, so in control, and... I want that. I *need* that. I've waited forever to find someone like him, and now?

He owes me.

Okay, that's not *entirely* true, but still. He set the bar pretty high, and while I may be nervous, I'm also excited. For once hope doesn't seem foolish and all I can say is the bastard better not screw this up. Because if he does, I swear to God he'll find out just how un-submissive I can be.

Two more days. Thursday and Friday, and then I'll know for sure. And if this does turn into a flaming dumpster fire...

I'm giving up on high protocol. For good.

CHAPTER 7

GALEN

*Y*es. I'll be there at 7:30. See you then.

I stare at the text one more time before slipping the cell back into my pocket. Glancing first at the chicken piccata simmering in the skillet, my gaze travels to the pasta laid out on the drying rack, ready to drop into boiling water fifteen minutes before serving, and there's a salad chilling in the fridge. Dinner seems to be under control, but maybe I should double-check whether I need to run the vacuum through the playroom a second time just in case.

Jesus, Galen, what the hell? Calm the fuck down.

Yeah. As if. I knew this would be a long week, and it was, but her text on Wednesday confirming the date—and the one last night reconfirming it—should have eased my nerves. And they did... until they didn't because it's coming up on six forty-five and she isn't here and now I'm second guessing everything I did to prepare for tonight.

You've dropped weapons into war-torn countries and had less anxiety than this.

Which might be true, but this... this is different. This is personal. This relates directly to a part of me I was ready to give up on and walk away from a week ago. Now, instead of abandoning it completely, I'm striding headlong toward it.

One night at Black Light, no matter how well it went, didn't mean shit if she showed up tonight and dropped the bomb. Which was still a possibility, but I didn't think it was likely. Alex commented on my confidence, and her observation was typically true where it concerned me judging people. Still, everyone can make mistakes.

So what? By the end of tonight you're gonna know, one way or the other.

The phone in my pocket buzzes, cutting off the circular train of thought I'm riding. I tug it out, and it's an alert from the security camera. A car has stopped at the front gate, and I watch as a slender arm reaches through a window and taps the code into the access pad.

I push every negative thought, every self-doubt, every concern aside. The time for that shit is over. Game face on because no matter what might happen, Alex deserves my best.

Putting the phone away, I check on dinner, waiting as she makes her way from the gate to the front drive. A few minutes slip by before I hear the chime of the doorbell, then I head across the kitchen to the foyer and open the door.

Alex's appearance is understated in a way that doesn't make her stand out at first glance and yet it doesn't diminish her beauty a single iota. I first noticed it that night at Black Light when she walked up to me at the bar, but it strikes me again now because the dress she's wearing under her wrap is another black one, simple yet sophisticated. As she steps through the door, the subtle fragrance she has on—the same she wore when I bent close and told her goodnight at Black Light—is a featherlight caress as she moves past me.

"I forgot to ask what you were cooking for dinner, so I brought both." She holds up two bottles of wine: one white, one red.

I chuckle. "That wasn't necessary but… thank you." I usher her in, taking the two bottles, then turn toward the kitchen. "Come with me. It's chicken, so the white works best. I already have a bottle chilling, if you won't be offended."

"Not at all."

"I don't want to spoil the surprise, but I think you'll enjoy what I'm making." Setting her white wine in the refrigerator, I place the red on the back counter out of the way. Taking out the wine I chilled earlier, I pour us both a glass.

"To meeting expectations," she says, raising her glass.

"Have you ever *just* met expectations?"

"Depends on who you ask."

"Well, you exceeded mine the other night. So, here's to *exceeding* expectations," I retort, raising my glass. It earns me a cheeky smile before we both drink.

I move behind the island, checking on the dish and starting the pasta water to boil, and toss a pinch of salt in. Alex taps something into her phone, and I've got a pretty good idea what it is. "Safety buddy check?"

She looks up at me. "Yep. Just like you suggested."

"Excellent."

She finishes with her phone, then glances around to take in the kitchen and what she can see of the living room and the dining room beyond. "You have a lovely home."

"Thank you."

"Have you lived here long?"

"I built it about fifteen years ago. A present to myself and—"

Goddammit.

"Someone I knew."

"I see." Alex narrows her eyes but doesn't push me further. "Well, you have good taste. It's beautiful."

"I like structured things. Clear delineation, clean, simple lines, no clutter, no muss. I built this with those concepts in mind. I mean, I had help, make no mistake. I'm not a designer nor an architect by any stretch of the imagination but…" I look up from the stove at her. "I think you understand what I mean."

She nods. "It makes sense." She gazes into the living room again, and her brows scrunch as she focuses on something. "Is that… is that a real Mondrian?"

I chuckle. "I should be so lucky. I do well for myself, but not *that* well. It's a limited-edition triptych lithograph. The closest I'll ever come to owning an original unless I somehow hit the Powerball." I shoot her an assessing look. "I'm impressed you recognized it." I shoot her an assessing glance. "I'll have to note this on your performance evaluation, Miss…"

She smiles, chuckling a little as she realizes she's never shared her last name with me. "Carre."

"Ah, Carre. That means… square, *en français,* if I remember correctly. How apropos, given the conversation."

Her eyes widen slightly. *"Tu parles français?"*

"Juste un peu. Assez pour me mettre dans le pétrin." I grin at her.

She laughs. "And has your French got you into trouble in the past, Mr. Harmon?"

"Galen. And… maybe." The water is steaming, and I have a sudden thought based on our first encounter.

"Dinner's almost ready, I just need to cook the pasta. Go and set the table for us, please."

Her mouth starts to open, but she stops herself before saying a word, instead giving me a measured look. "Of course, sir."

And there it is. The word I wanted to hear her say again the other night, which has the same effect on me now as it did then. She turns away and disappears into the dining room without another word.

After a moment of silence, I hear her opening and closing the doors and drawers of the buffet. I drop the pasta into the now boiling water and as it begins to bubble away, I hear the sound of plates being moved. I cringe at the *skkerek* of china grinding against china but I stay where I am, not interfering. I gave her a task and I need to let her handle it as she sees fit. She managed herself without my input at Black Light; I've no doubt she can do just as well here setting a table.

Once the pasta's cooking nicely, I step away from the stove and move into the dining room. Alex stops what she's doing, looking over at me. She's almost finished setting the table, placing the last of the silverware beside one of the plates.

"Napkins?"

She cringes ever so slightly. "Sorry. I... I'm not sure where you keep them, sir?"

I love how she's fallen into using the word and, like the other night, I want to hear her say it again and again and again. Three simple letters, and yet they have a powerful effect on me.

"Lower door of the cabinet, right hand side. They're in a small box, folded."

"Thank you, sir." She nods, straightens the silverware she just put down, then turns back to the buffet.

I don't stay and watch. Instead, I return to the kitchen without a word. I want her to understand I trust her, that I won't hover over her while she completes a task. We played a game the other night, but there were no winners or losers. That was never the intention. The challenge was to see if we understood each other, if our needs aligned, if the form of dominance and submission we each desired was compatible. More and more we're proving it is.

Or so I want to believe.

By the time I've pulled the pasta from the pot and drained it in a colander, any sound from the dining room has disappeared. I dump the noodles into a bowl and drizzle a little olive oil over them. Once I've finished, curiosity pulls me back to the room to find out why things have gone silent.

Oh, damn.

Alex is kneeling beside my chair at the head of the table, her position a carbon copy of the one she took in the club. As I step quietly into the room, she doesn't look up but keeps her eyes focused on the floor in front of her, hands palm-down on her thighs, her breathing smooth and measured. She's dressed this time, but even still, a hunger flows through me, a possessiveness I shouldn't be feeling because—*Christ*—this is only the second time we've been together.

One thing is certain... this woman is pressing all my fucking buttons right now.

Before, at Black Light, it was a challenge, a game. But now? Now, this is just *right*. Where both she and I belong. And while I shouldn't assume she feels the same, as I stare down at the light reflecting off the rich, silky strands of her hair, I'm positive she wants this as much as I do. I have to believe it. If not, what other reason would there be for her to arrange herself the way she has?

Rather than dwell on it, I simply accept what she's done and pick up our plates from the table. Alex doesn't move, maintaining her pose even as I brush past and head into the kitchen. I plate our meals and grab the bowl of salad, carefully balancing all three as I return to the dining room.

She's still kneeling in the exact same position when I step in. Steady as a stone, unmoving, a poised picture of submissive perfection. I slip past her and set her plate down before moving back to my chair where I pause to drink in the sight of her. God, I'd forgotten the sheer power of this, the heady feeling of this type of power exchange. It comes back now with a rush, and I want to grab on and hold it as if it's a physical, tangible thing.

I tear my eyes away from her to look back at the table. She found the napkins and—at some point while setting the table— placed her wine glass beside her plate, so everything appears to be just where it should. I cross back to her chair and pull it out.

"Sit," I order quietly.

She rises and does as I commanded.

I push the chair in until she's in place and then move to sit in my own. Glancing over, I see she has her face tilted down, staring at the setting in front of her, hands neatly folded in her lap.

I pick up my knife and fork and slowly cut into the chicken, then I take a bite, looking at her from the corner of my eye. She remains perfectly still, gaze down, eyes blinking yet never wavering to look in my direction. She waits without question even as I take a second bite.

"Look at me," I say firmly.

Her head snaps up.

"Is this what you want, what we've been doing? Is *this* what you've been looking for?"

She blows out a sigh. "It's a start. It's a better beginning than any I've had so far. And I'm not going to lie; I'm trying very hard to believe and not focus on waiting for all this to come crashing down."

Fuck yes. Okay, Galen, you know what to do here. Alleviate her fears. Make her feel at ease. But for God's sake, don't pressure her or you'll fuck this up.

"I propose a truce to that line of thinking. Let's just accept this for what it is, enjoy what we have, and see where things go. Let's not overthink it. Let's just let it… happen."

"Not overthink it." She gives me a wry smile. "That's asking a lot from me because I have a tendency to do just that."

"Same."

We stare at each other, and in the gaze there's a connection being made. A moment of trust shared that eases the anxiety, a sense of lowering the shield between us just a little.

"I want you to know I have expectations," I say, breaking the moment of silence. "I promise I'll tell you what they are if they're important to me because it's unfair to expect you to read my mind. You are always welcome to ask at any time too, or you can choose to discover them on your own if that's what you want. But understand this: I'll only tell you once. I expect you to remember these things because you've made it clear you're an incredibly intelligent person, and I won't insult that intelligence by constantly reminding you. That's a sign of arrogance I abhor." I take another bite of my meal. "Besides, I hate repeating myself." I stare at her, trying to gauge her reaction. "Does that seem fair?"

"Yes, sir."

"Rather than go through a list of them right now—which would be incredibly tedious for us both—I'll do my best to provide them to you organically as they arise. Again, you're allowed to ask for them at any time. In fact, I would encourage it. However, if I've already provided you with an expectation and you forget, you'll earn a punishment for doing so. Clear?"

"Yes, sir."

"Very well then." I point to her plate. "Eat your dinner."

She smiles, taking up her silverware. I wait as she cuts a bite of the chicken off and puts it in her mouth.

"Whoa." She finishes chewing and swallowing while looking over at me. "That's good, sir. Really, really good."

I grin. "It's a simple recipe, honestly, but if I do it right it can impress."

"Well, consider it done." She takes another bite, and I follow suit.

"Thank you. I like cooking. I'm no gourmet chef, for sure, but I'd like to think I can hold my own."

"I think you underestimate your skills."

"In cooking?"

The fork pauses halfway to her mouth. "In that. And perhaps other things, too."

"I'll have to make sure I don't disappoint."

Her eyes twinkle, and we continue to eat.

"So, your parents are French?" I ask.

She looks confused for a moment. "Oh! No, no, no. My parents are from Quebec."

"Ah."

"My father's an engineer. They moved to Virginia when he took a job at the North Anna Nuclear Station."

"But they taught you French growing up?"

"They are Quebecois. It speaks for itself, *n'est ce pas?*"

I grin. "I suppose it does."

The dinner continues to flow, and it's amazing how natural it feels. Alex is warm, witty, intelligent, and I find myself falling into a mindset I haven't been in for a long time.

"I try, I swear to you," I say, pointing my fork toward her. "But... it's just part of my personality. I mean, I can look back and see I'm doing it, but in the moment..."

Alex laughs lightly. "Well, at least you're self-aware about your mansplaining. So many Doms aren't, and while it's kind of expected, as a submissive it can be more than a little irritating at times."

"I promise I'll try and keep it to a minimum."

"You'll try. But it's still going to happen."

I pause mid-bite. "Careful, young lady," I say with a growl. "Forgetting an expectation isn't the only way to earn a punishment."

"Duly noted, sir," she replies softly, but the gleam in her eye doesn't escape me.

A short time and another glass of wine later, we're more comfortable than I expected in one night. I'm leaning toward her, pointing my finger as I try to maintain my stern expression. "But you *are* a brat."

"I am not, sir! I swear!"

"To paraphrase you: 'so are you saying sex with you would be bad, or you're just bad at sex.' And then that crack about me not being able to keep myself from mansplaining, I think—"

"Those two comments don't make me a brat!"

"Okay, fine. You're a smartass."

"Well, you did say I was obviously intelligent," she says with faux haughtiness.

"And clearly you need that intelligence channeled in the proper direction. *Not* baiting a Dom into blistering your ass."

"Speak for yourself," she mumbles.

"I beg your pardon?"

"Nothing, sir!"

Soon we've both finished our meals, but we continue talking, and I don't want it to end. The conversation is so easy, and we've discovered mutual interests beyond high protocol. She's shared a little about her job, and I about mine.

However, the one thing we both seem to avoid talking about is past relationships, which I'm fine with because the focus needs to be on us, not our past.

When the wine is finally gone, she leans on her elbow, chin cradled in her hand, staring at me, and I'm just as happy to observe her back, but she breaks the silence. "This is nice. I... I wasn't sure there was a place for this"—she makes a back and forth motion between us—"in a dynamic."

"If there hasn't been in the past, then your Dom was an idiot. It's ludicrous to think you can have a truly fulfilling high protocol experience if all I ever do is order you around, and all you ever do is kneel and say 'yes, sir.'" I hold up my hand. "At least in my opinion. I know others out there will tell you different, but I find the idea of being with someone in that fashion incredibly limiting." I stare at her for a second. "Is that what you were expecting or... hoping for?"

"Expecting? Maybe a little. Hoping for?" Alex shakes her head. "No. Not in the slightest, sir."

"Good. I'm glad to hear it." I worried I may have come on too strong at the club, so to hear her say she's enjoying our conversation this evening is a relief. Because what I've told her is true: I've never accepted the notion that high protocol needs to be a 24/7/365 Master/slave situation. In fact, in my opinion to demand that is a sign of weakness. A fallback position for an ineffectual Dom to retreat to so they can cover their inexperience or mask their abuse.

"Did you enjoy your dinner?" I ask, motioning to her empty plate.

"Yes, sir. It was wonderful. Thank you."

"Good. I'm glad you enjoyed it. Now, if you'll clear the table, please."

She smiles, rising smoothly. "Of course, sir."

I remain seated as she gathers both our plates and takes them into the kitchen. She comes back a moment later and removes the salad bowl, her glass, and mine.

"Shall I bring you something, sir?"

"No, I'm fine for now, thank you."

Alex dips her head, then moves into the kitchen once more.

Okay, Galen. Now what? Things have gone well so far this evening, but what's my next move going to be? It's frustrating I even have to ask myself the question, but the reality is it's been a while since I was in this situation, and I'm not completely sure what to do next.

To be fair, there's one part of me that knows *exactly* what it wants, but I didn't invite Alex here tonight for a fucking booty call. This dinner alone proved there's something to be explored and nurtured here and I'll be damned if I'm going to ruin it just because my dick wants to get wet.

So… yeah. What next?

I'm still mulling that over as I get up and head to the kitchen where I hear her moving about. I told her to clear the table, but I'm not at all surprised when I step through the doorway and find her rinsing the dishes in the sink and stacking them neatly to the side. I stand and watch her in silence for a moment, and she smiles as I do.

More of that initiative you praised her for. You better come up with something worthy of her.

"Those will need to be cleaned by hand," I say quietly, motioning toward the china. "Not the dishwasher."

She nods. "Yes, sir."

Moving to the stove, she gathers up the pasta pot and the small pan I prepared the piccata sauce in. Back at the sink, she rinses those out before returning to the stove and picking up the cast iron pan I used to prepare the chicken.

"Stop."

She halts immediately. Turning to face me, she drops her gaze to the floor in front of her. "Sir?"

"What were you about to do?"

"Wash this pan, sir."

"No, you're not. It's taken me twelve years to properly season that skillet."

I guide her away from the sink and over to the counter. Reaching to one side, I open a drawer and pull out a stainless-steel section of chainmail meant for scrubbing. I set it on the counter next to the pan, then cross the kitchen and pull a box of salt from the pantry. Once I've got it, I join her again.

"You never wash cast iron. Ever." I sprinkle some salt in the bottom of the skillet, then gather up the chainmail and place it in her hand. Then I gently guide her to scour the inside, using the salt as an abrasive to scrub away the stuck-on pieces of breading.

"Grab a paper towel," I order, and she stretches from within the cage of my arms to comply. She tugs off several sheets, and again I take her hand in mine and we wipe the inside of the skillet out, going back to the chainmail afterward when a few more spots are uncovered.

As we continue, her hands tremble slightly. She hasn't turned to look back at me, but she hasn't pulled away either, and though I'm not one hundred percent sure, I swear her breath has hitched at least once.

Fuck, Galen. Don't do this. Remember what you said: be patient, don't press, nurture this, don't fuck it up.

Except I can't. I give in. I give into want, desire, lust, all those things which I've held back on so many times tonight because I was so sure she was going to give up and run away. This time my dick wins out over my brain, and I slowly push forward with my hips, letting her feel my need, waiting for her reaction.

She presses back.

Leaning in, I trap her against the edge of the counter, my breath grazing her shoulder before tracing a path up her neck until I'm poised over her ear. "This is how you clean cast iron."

The rise and fall of her breath brushes against my chest as I wait for her to answer, to thank me, to say anything that ends in 'sir.'

She does none of those things. Instead, she gives me the best response of all.

She purrs.

CHAPTER 8

ALEX

Oh, God.
    I didn't mean to moan but… *Jesus…* there's no way I could stop the sound from escaping as Galen presses me against the counter.

I feel him. I feel *it*. And I don't want him to stop.

I want more.

For a moment he just holds me in place, bearing down on me in a way I hunger for. Our fingers are entwined, but our hands have stopped moving, the cast iron forgotten. I feel his breath on my ear, and if my heartrate is elevated so is his. The rhythm of his breathing gives him away. I shift my hips ever so slightly, and the low, rumbling groan I tease out of him sends an electric arc of thrill shooting through me.

"Alex." My name comes out as a growl filled with need.

"Yes, sir?" I whisper back.

Galen takes a deep breath then lets it out slowly. Instead of answering, his hands move mine again and a pang of worry cuts through me. Did I do something wrong? Offend him? Move too quickly or in a way he didn't want?

I don't understand how that could be the case. He wants me.

He's erect. I can *feel it*. So why is he back to cleaning this stupid pan instead of taking me to his bedroom and fucking the life out of me?

Okay, Alex, remember what he said. Don't overthink this. He's a Dom. He has his own plan for how this is going to go, and you need to let him handle it. Isn't that what you want? Someone who takes charge, provides direction, gives you the structure and order you crave in your personal life that you don't have in your work one?

Yes. So much yes.

Before I spiral any deeper into self-doubt, Galen takes my hand, and we wipe the skillet one last time. He steps back once it's finished, and the sudden separation is palpable in more ways than physical. I turn to look at him because I need to see him, to look into his eyes, and when I do, all I see is the burning heat of his desire.

Thank God. I wasn't wrong. I did feel what I did.

He stares at me, waiting.

I glance around quickly. There's a black pot rack hanging over one end of the island, and I move to it and hang the skillet on a hook next to the others.

"Good girl," he says quietly, and I can't help but beam.

"I'll be in the living room. When you've finished cleaning"—he points to the remaining dishes and utensils—"come find me. We can enjoy an after-dinner drink and continue our discussion."

"Yes, sir," I reply, lowering my head.

Once he's left, I move with quiet determination to finish what I started. As he directed, I clean the plates by hand, drying them with a towel I find folded in a drawer. I put the silverware in the dishwasher, then glance at the other pots. They're copper bottomed, and I seem to remember something about not washing those in a dishwasher either, so I hand wash them instead. As I'm doing all this, I steal quick looks toward the living room to see if he's watching me. Every time I look, his face is down, staring at his cell, so unless I missed it he appears to trust me to finish these tasks without him hovering. I'm prouder than I probably should be because it's only dishes, but... still.

By the time I finish wiping the wine glasses clean, I've noticed a bar tucked into one corner of the living room, and I have a gameplan for my next move. I step from the kitchen into the room, immediately crossing to the bar. Galen looks up as I do, and his gaze tracks me as I step behind the counter.

There are four shelves, each of them holding an array of expensive liquors. I'm not a connoisseur by any stretch of the imagination but I recognize some of the names and, armed with the crash course Klara gave me the other night, I pick out the Weller bourbon he ordered and one other.

"Would you prefer the Weller tonight, sir, or the Buffalo Trace?"

He says nothing for a moment, running a finger across his lip. "Bring me the Buffalo Trace."

Heh. A test. Klara warned me what to do if he asked for this. With the Weller he was very specific about two cubes of ice, no more, no less. But Klara's voice rings in my head.

Do not put ice in the Buffalo Trace if he asks for it. Find room temp water, even from the tap, and add about three to five drops of that, no more. And for God's sake put it in a Glencairn glass, not a shot glass. Don't worry, he'll have them.

She showed me what the glass looks like, and I find four of them neatly arranged beneath the lower shelf. I grab one and pour two fingers of the bourbon into it, then open the tap at the small sink nearby and carefully let four drops fall in. When I'm done, I walk from behind the bar and move to the side of his chair and drop to my knees to offer the glass up the same way I did at Black Light.

"Thank you," he says, taking the drink from me. Dropping my hands to my thighs, I take up the same position I did before dinner. I hear him take a sip, then the room goes silent except for the sound of our breathing.

He's watching me; I'm positive of it. I keep my gaze focused on my lap, but he's staring at me, and the sensation is both exciting and disconcerting at the same time. Our conversation at dinner was so much more than I'd expected. I wasn't lying, in any other so-called high protocol experience I've had to date, *nothing* like that ever occurred. The more I'm with Galen, the more I realize what I experienced before may have been a *type* of high protocol, but it wasn't the type *I* was looking for. I want the structure he's spoken about, the guidance inherent in his expectations. I want to *serve* him, not be enslaved by him.

And then what he did in the kitchen... *hoo boy.* Every growled command or fierce grip of my arm meant to bring me to my knees pales in comparison to what Galen made me feel simply guiding me as we cleaned a stupid pan. I want to say I feel dirty for the way I reacted, but I don't. I want more.

I want to do things that'll make him rumble the way he did, use my name in the tone he did as he pressed against me. I think back to the club, and what it felt like when he stood behind me, running his hands over my skin. That was hot, but the kitchen? The kitchen was the thermostat turned all the way up, and I'm ready to peel out of everything just to keep it there.

Oh, crap.

I was undressed by the time I crossed the club that first night, and we went into the private room together. I took off my clothes after he asked why I was still wearing any. Is that... was I supposed to...?

"Sir," I whisper gently.

"Yes?"

"May I ask a question?"

"Of course."

"Should I have undressed when I arrived?" I want to look up to see his face when he answers, but I force myself to keep my gaze down.

There's a long moment of quiet before he replies. "Typically, from the moment you step through that door, you shouldn't be wearing any clothing at all, unless it's something I assign you specifically. There *will* be nights I do, either before or after you arrive. Tonight, however, is our first real time together and, as I told you, I don't expect you to be able to read my mind. I'll inform you when I have a specific expectation."

Then his finger is under my chin, tilting my head up until I'm staring into his warm eyes.

"That being said, understand this: when you do come back, that *will* be my expectation. For now, I'm enjoying this as it is." His finger slips away, but his gaze keeps me trapped in place. "Do you understand?"

"Yes, sir," I whisper.

"Good girl." He boops my nose, surprising me as he smiles. "I want you to know how proud I am of you for asking."

God, I shouldn't feel the warm flush that runs through me at his praise, but I do. That's probably why he didn't mention it before—he was waiting to see if I would take the initiative on my own. He encouraged me to ask questions, and if this is how my body's going to respond, I'm going to follow him around the house and pester him incessantly.

Great plan, Alex. He also *told you there were easier ways to get your ass smacked.*

That thought sends another little shiver running through me, and I suppress a smile.

I lower my head again, and Galen returns to his drink. For now, there's no talking as we each relax into the mood of the moment. I could ask him another question—there's only about a million of them racing through my mind right now—but it's so quiet and comforting here at his side I let the questions settle into a pool then drift away until they fall beneath the surface. I calm into the moment, and simply *am*.

I hear when he takes another sip, feel him move as he shifts in the chair. I'm aware of his presence, focused on it, but I don't feel any of the anxiety I did previously. It's weird: on the one hand everything that's taken place so far feels to have happened almost too fast, and yet it also seems so natural I can't help but lean into it. When he reaches with his free hand to gently stroke my hair, it shouldn't make my pussy wet, but that's exactly what it does. Minutes pass in a dreamy tug-of-war drifting between languorous peacefulness born of letting the world fall away as I offer Galen my complete submission and an aching desire to show him my obedience in a completely different, *physical* way.

"So," he eventually says, breaking the quiet, "would you like to see my home?"

"If that would please you, sir."

His fingers tighten in my hair, and the needles from my scalp race straight down my spine and turn me into a soaking mess.

"It would."

He rises, pulling me up with him. It takes every ounce of effort not to mewl, but maybe I should. If it'll drive him half as crazy as what he's done to me, it'd be worth it.

Once he has me up, he releases the tension in my hair, and his hand moves to rest at the base of my neck. "So, let's start here." He turns me in a half circle until we're facing the opening to the dining room. "Living room, dining room"—he gestures behind us —"and of course the kitchen back there." With the slightest pressure, he directs me forward. "This way."

We travel through the living room into a hallway. A room branches off to the left, and he stops in the doorway. "The study. You'll become very, *very* familiar with this room."

I glance inside. It has the same clean lines as the rest of his house, three of the walls lined with asymmetrical bookcases that mimic the style of the Mondrian painting hanging in his living room. After a moment he squeezes my neck again, and we continue. "My office, a guest bedroom, another guest bedroom, the guest bathroom." He ticks off each door as we pass. When we come to the end of the hall, he stops, nudging the door open. "The master bedroom."

We step inside, and my eyes dance across the space. Every room in his house has been consistent thematically, and his bedroom is no different. Clean, simple, straight lines dominate, just as he said he preferred. The walls are oddly empty; there are no cabinets or chests of drawers to be seen anywhere. Wherever Galen keeps his things, the storage spaces are cleverly hidden. Instead, the walls serve only to highlight several additional large Mondrian lithos, and other pictures of a similar style. The one object that overshadows everything, however, is the bed.

It's huge.

It's square, easily king-sized if not larger, and it commands the space. My gaze lingers on it, my body tensing in anticipation. It's neatly made, the covers pulled taut, yet all I can imagine is the mess we could make of it as he throws me around while we're—

"Master bathroom there, behind that door," he says, pointing to the lines of a doorway I missed. He guides me forward until we come to the outline of another opening. He pauses for a moment, looking back at me. It feels as if he's hesitating, contemplating something. Whatever it is, he comes to a decision, turns away, and opens the door.

"And through here… the playroom."

Playroom.

Oh, damn.

Of course, he built one into his custom-made million-dollar home. Did I really expect he wouldn't?

He motions me inside, and I step through, my pulse racing. I've seen rooms like this before in videos and in pictures online, but I've never been in one that wasn't at a club. I stop just inside the door, slowly looking around.

There's a lot to take in: a spanking bench, a wooden horse, a set of stocks, a St. Andrew's cross. From the ceiling a series of chains are clipped to eyebolts, and from one set of those there's what looks to be a spreader bar of some sort hanging suspended just above head height.

Whereas the rooms I've often looked at were industrial-looking found spaces, or dungeon-like with stone and dark wood, Galen's playroom mimics the style of the rest of his house. Everything metal is either brushed gray pewter or painted black. The few wooden pieces are finished in a weathered gray tone. Along one wall is a series of staggered racks holding a slightly disconcerting number of implements, the layout of the brackets mirroring the bookcase shelving in his study.

The door closes with a soft thump.

Turning slowly, the gaze I find on his face is the same I found when I looked back after we finished cleaning the skillet. A hunger that tells me exactly what Galen Harmon is thinking about, and one I want to stoke until it becomes an all-consuming inferno.

Silence electrifies the space between us.

"Remove your clothes," he says firmly, and I want to yell in triumph.

I do as he orders, keeping my gaze down as I unzip my dress and peel myself out of it. Folding it and my underwear neatly, I place them on the bench because even though I haven't asked, I have a strong suspicion neatness is one of his expectations. Everything about his home is precise, and I doubt tossing my clothes on the floor in a heap would be acceptable to Galen, no matter his current state of mind. I place the last item down, then begin kneeling.

"No. There."

I stop and look where he's pointing. A bead mat? He wants me to kneel on the bead mat? I'm about to turn back to him but I stop myself. I've no idea what I've done wrong, but he's told me where to kneel, and instead of questioning him I move forward and drop into position on it.

Shit! This is the first time I've knelt on one, and I did not expect the spikes of pain it sends shooting up my legs as I settle upon it.

Galen's at my back now, and I lower my head, gritting my teeth against the torture those insidious little balls send through me. What the hell did I do wrong? I'm trying to think of a clue I missed, a signal he gave that I let slip by, but... nothing. I can't think of a single thing that warrants me being here. I could ask him, and maybe I should, rather than just blindly submitting to—

Oh.

This isn't about punishing me. No. No, if this was about Galen disciplining me for some infraction, he would've told me by now what it was. No, this is about something else entirely. This is about submission. The simple act of submitting to him without question.

The minute he stands behind me in silence feels like forever, but eventually he moves, his hand gently stroking my head. "Good girl," he says quietly, and God do I want to lean in and draw comfort from his touch. However, he wants my submission right now, and I'm going to give him just that, because I'm absolutely certain when the time comes, Galen Harmon will provide the aftercare I'll need.

For now? I let my mind release everything, focusing solely on being the perfect submissive.

His hand leaves me, and I struggle not to whimper at the loss of contact. I see him for a brief second as he moves past before disappearing from my limited range of view.

"Alex."

I snap my head up.

He locks his gaze to mine as he slowly moves from piece to piece in the room. First the bench, then the St. Andrew's cross, then past the spreader bar until he comes to the wooden pony.

He stops. "Do you like the wooden pony?"

Oh, God. What did I... how did he...

"No, sir."

"Perfect, hop up."

I rise from the mat and stagger slightly, the blood rushing back into my knees with a pins-and-needles sensation on steroids. Galen takes me by the elbow, steadying me.

"Sorry, sir," I whisper.

"You've no need to apologize. Now, come on. Up you go."

Again, I want to whimper but I bite down on the response. I've been on a wooden pony once before—which looks more like a sawhorse and nothing like a pony—and I wasn't lying when I said I did *not* like it. But I understand now what this is about and so I simply follow Galen's lead as he helps me straddle the wooden bar, centering me on the ridge of the pony.

"Balance yourself with your hands. I'm going to let go in a moment. I need to gather some things."

Great. I can only imagine what *that* means. It's clear now that like some of the other Doms I've met, Galen has a bit of a sadistic streak in him. How deep that runs remains to be seen fully, but as my labia spread and settle over the tapered beam of the pony, I find myself falling deeper into a submissive headspace than I have with any other man, ever.

Galen is at the implement rack, and I watch as he collects what he wants. The small crop I recognize, but I can't see what he's got in his other hand and for a moment his back hides the last item he picks up.

"This should do nicely," he says, turning around.

Oh, crap. That's a Hitachi. I recognize it because there's one very similar to it sitting in the drawer at my bedside about twenty-five miles from here.

"Comfortable?" he asks as he steps up to me.

"No, sir."

"Well, let's see what we can do about that."

The item I couldn't see in his hand resolves itself to be a pair of nipple clamps joined by a small silver chain. He sets the Hitachi and the crop to the side and holds the clamps up where I can see them clearly.

"Know what these are?"

"Yes." I grimace.

"Ever had them used on you before?"

"Once."

Galen grins. "Well, I like to switch things up a little."

I watch as he pinches them open, but instead of moving toward my nipples where I anticipate, he moves downward until he has the open jaws positioned on either side of my pussy.

"Oh, God," I whisper, and he pauses.

"Not what you were expecting?"

"No, sir."

"Have you ever had your labia clamped before?"

"No. Sir."

"Excellent. I'll be your first."

As the teeth dig into already tender flesh, I do everything in my power not to react. A hiss manages to tear its way out of me anyhow, but Galen doesn't seem upset; he simply chuckles as he leans back up.

"Nice?"

"No."

He pats my cheek. "It will be."

Turning, he reaches back and picks up the Hitachi. It's a cordless one, unlike mine, and it hums to life as he turns it on.

"So, I saw this during an event at Black Light back in February. A Dom had his sub up on a Sybian and he was doing everything he could to make her come while she was resisting. Now, I'm not *quite* the sadist he was. I *am* going to let you come. But only after you beg me to, and only after I tell you that you can. Understood?"

"Yes, sir."

"How long you choose to resist is entirely up to you."

"You're so kind, sir." I try to keep my voice neutral.

Galen pauses, then turns away from me. "And here I was

thinking I might not need this," he says, picking up the crop. "Silly me."

Dammit, Alex. Did you need *to pour gas on the fire?*

No, and yes, and even though this hurts like hell, I feel a tiny shiver of pleasure hidden deep within, and Galen's going to bring that to full bud, clearly.

"Let's start slow." He lowers the intensity on the wand, then brings it up to graze my clit with gentle pressure.

I grip the edges of the pony as tight as possible, bearing down on the gasp that wants to tear itself free of me. He tenderly massages my hood, and a little spark of pleasure bursts to life.

"*Mmnngh.*"

"See? I told you."

How long he continues working at my clit with the wand becomes irrelevant because time ceases to matter. Everything happening narrows to a microfocus on my pussy, and the pain blends with carnal decadence until the two are inseparable. At some point he ramps up the vibration of the Hitachi, then increases it again, then again until any hope I had of withholding reaction flees and I cry out.

"Okay, okay, okay, oh God, please, please, please..."

"Please what, Alex?" he asks quietly.

"Please, please, please, that feels so good.!"

"It does?"

"Yes!"

I've got my eyes closed, but a sharp burst of pain on my right nipple makes them snap open.

"*Ahhh!*"

The bastard's grinning. "Wouldn't want to be *too* kind, now would I?"

Before I can respond, he rains down a series of strikes on my nipples with the crop, switching back and forth between them. Now I'm pleading '*please, please, please*' for entirely different reasons. In total it's maybe a half dozen smacks, then suddenly he stops. The stinging burn from my breasts spreads downward until it reaches my pussy, joining with the slow return of heat to my engorged clit as the wand picks up where he left off. Tears have tracked their way down my cheeks, but despite it all my body is literally burning with desire. Screw my resolve: what I'm going to do is exactly what he told me I would.

Beg.

It doesn't take long. "Please. Oh, God, please, please, please..." I'm writhing atop the pony and even though I didn't notice it, at some point Galen moved closer, bracing me as I smear arousal across the ridge of the wooden torture device.

"I know you want to come, Alex."

"Yes, oh, God, yes, yes. Please... please sir."

"Am I making your pussy feel good?"

"Oh my God..."

"Is your beautiful little clit swollen? Have I made that little clit feel good?" he purrs.

"Please, sir. Please... I'm doing what you asked. I'm begging..."

"What do you want, Alex?"

He's going to make me ask for it. Begging alone isn't going to be enough.

"I want to come, sir," I whimper.

"Good girl." He continues to circle the Hitachi in a tight little pattern, and I swear if he doesn't give me permission soon, I'm going to explode into a thousand little pieces and he'll have to glue me back together before he can punish me.

"Please..." I whisper.

"Come."

The word barely caresses my ear before I fall apart. My body arcs, and I'm pressing against him as the cry bursts from me, turning my vision white. For a second there's nothing but a wall of blinding sensuality engulfing me, then slowly I come back to the reality of the room, the pony I've curved up from, and the *vrmmm* sensation of the wand held to my sex. A moment later, that stops as Galen turns off the Hitachi and pulls it away.

"Good girl," he whispers at my side and lifts me from the wooden pony... that I might hate a bit less now.

I can't do much of anything but cling to Galen as he carries me from the playroom into his bedroom. He lays me gently on the bed, and a moment later my labia throb with a stinging sensation as the clamps are removed. The pain is dulled by the lingering aftereffects of the orgasm he just gave me, and I curl on my side as he rises from the edge of the bed and walks back into the other room.

The sound of him moving around is a soft background noise to the warm, pleasant buzz that suffuses my body as I lie there. By the time he returns, I'm floating in that dreamy half-space between being in full-blown subspace and just feeling incredibly well fucked.

Galen comes back to the edge of the bed, looking down at me with a warm smile. "Hello, Alex."

I stare back up at him, a smile of contentment pulling up the corners of my mouth. "Thank you, sir."

He doesn't ask for what. He knows. "You're welcome."

For a moment I just stare at him. And then, like an insidious little worm, a thought intrudes, interrupting my languor and bringing me up off the bed to drop into a kneel at his feet.

I stare down at the floor. "I'm sorry, sir. What can I do to please you?"

Galen laughs. He slips a pair of fingers under my chin and lifts my face up. "Well, to start with, you're naked and I'm not, so you could work on that."

The words barely leave his mouth, and I'm reaching for his belt. The thought of undressing Galen has gone through my mind more than once tonight, and now that it's actually happening, I'm doing everything I can to savor the moment. At the same time, my eagerness betrays me as I struggle to get his pants over his shoes—

the ones I failed to remove— and as I fight with the mess I've created, he chuckles.

"Here, let me help."

Together we get them off, and I carefully fold the khakis and set everything in a neat pile. He's unbuttoning his shirt as I finish setting the pants aside, which leaves only one other piece of clothing.

I reach for his underwear.

It's clear I'm not the only one enjoying this because Galen's cock catches on the fabric as I work his briefs down. He's full, hard, and *damn*, the man is definitely sexy. He hands me his shirt, and I place it with the rest of his clothing. Then he's standing in front of me. Naked.

Oh, yes. Yes, yes, yes, yes, yes.

I start to reach for him with my mouth. He's right there, erect, beautiful, perfect, and it seems the most natural thing in the world to do. It's something I've done for men in far less arousing circumstances than this, and yet...

I stop.

"May I, sir?"

"Yes." His voice is husky with need.

I take him at the base with my hand and slip my mouth around him.

"Fuck." The hunger in his voice turns fierce, and the sudden grasp of his hand at the back of my head sends tendrils of delicious pain mixed with pleasure swirling through me.

I work his shaft with my mouth, letting my tongue trace patterns of decadence over skin heated by the blood filling him. I taste his precum, feel the slight jerk as I swirl my tongue around the tip before taking him as deep as I'm able. My throat constricts as he hits the back of it, but I don't stop, instead pulling back before plunging down once again. Where I fought to suppress showing him my need, Galen doesn't. He peppers my actions with growls and 'fucks' that let me know exactly how much he's enjoying this.

Until he tells me, "Stop."

I look up at him. Slowly withdrawing his cock from my mouth, immediately relieved and thrilled when I stare deep into eyes that flame with desire.

"On the bed. Now."

I scramble up and shift onto the mattress as Galen follows close behind me. Before I finish turning, he has me by the hip and flips me onto my back.

"Don't. Move." He pins me in place with a fingertip, then slides so he can reach the end table at the side of the bed. A moment later I hear foil tearing, then he's back, pushing my legs apart as he moves between my thighs.

"Do you want this inside you?" he growls, positioning his cock at my entrance. "Do you want me to fuck you?"

"Yes, sir. Please."

"Good girl. Right answer." And he drives himself into me.

I arch my back into the thrust. Galen has me by the hips, and the first plunge becomes a second, then a third, until it becomes a steady rhythm as he fucks me into a molten pool.

"Oh, God"—I gasp between the words—"that feels so good."

"Yes, it does." He brings his hands up from my waist to plant them on either side of my shoulders as he continues pounding into me.

When I first arrived tonight, I wasn't sure this is where we'd end up. God knows I thought about it enough times since Black Light, but Galen hadn't fucked me then, and a part of me thought he might not this evening. I was definitely wrong about that, and I've never been so glad. The slap of Galen's sweat-soaked hips to mine,, his cock swelling inside me, is everything I've dreamt of, the reality even better than I could have hoped for.

"Are you going to come?" His eyes bore into mine, his body slamming me into the mattress.

"I… I'm trying not to, sir," I whimper.

"Don't," he orders.

Don't? He's out of his mind if he thinks I'm not going to fail that command if he keeps this up.

"Don't, Alex. Don't hold back. Let me feel you. Let me feel you come when I do."

Oh.

"Yes, sir," I whisper, and I almost do.

He's close, I'm close, and one of us is going to be first to fall over the edge of the precipice we're both teetering on, and a part of me wants it to be him. But he's pushed me almost to the point of that beautiful oblivion, and if he doesn't come soon I will.

"I'm going to fucking fill you." His voice is heat, and even though there's no chance he will with the condom he's wearing, I understand what he means. A part of me wishes the latex wasn't there so I could feel it, feel his cum spill inside me and maybe next time he will if there's going to be a next time and oh God, he feels so good and—

"FUCK!"

Galen comes.

I match him two seconds later, and the room disappears as I slam my eyes shut and dig my fingers into flesh that soon disappears until there's only the sound of blood in my ears and the feeling of him inside me.

My ass comes up off the bed, or tries to, as I lift against him while he rams me back down on the mattress. A second thrust pulls me up from the aurora my mind has spiraled into, and I clench my fingers into warm, sweat-slicked flesh before I gasp and let them open. For a moment we lie unmoving, my body trapped beneath his while he remains sheathed inside me, rigid.

"Holy shit."

He opens his eyes now, gazing down at me with a look that mirrors everything I'm feeling. I swallow and look back, wanting to capture this moment.

'*Holy shit*' is right. That was better than good.

He shifts, rolling to my side. My heart's still pounding, chest rising and falling rapidly. I should move, do something, *say* something, but nothing will come out. I'm completely lost in the moment, and all I'm able to do is lie here staring at the ceiling in blissful exhaustion.

As my breathing finally slows, Galen slips off the bed and heads into the bathroom. A minute passes, and then he returns. I see his dick bobbing as he approaches, the condom gone. I'm about to thank him for everything he's given me this evening, but before I can he's scrambled across the mattress, reaching for me.

"Come here." His low tone brooks no argument, and he grips my arm and pulls me to him roughly.

"Oof!" He drags me across the covers until I'm cradled against him, my head resting on his chest. He's sweaty, I'm sweaty, but with his arm curled around me there's no place I'd rather be right now.

"Alex." His voice is a comforting rumble as it comes up through him.

"Yes, sir?"

"You're spending the night here." It's not a question. It's not an order. It's a simple statement of fact, and there's not a single part of me that thinks to say anything against it.

"Yes, sir."

He pulls me in tighter, and I burrow into place.

So?

I don't hear the question in my own voice. I hear it in Terry's.

Yes, you were right, I respond to myself. *Next time I see you, I'll be sure to let you know.*

I can lie here and analyze this, contemplate what transpired, what will potentially take place moving forward, and I can worry this to death like I do a thousand other things in my life. Or...

Let's not overthink it.

I choose that. I choose to remember what Galen said.

I let my eyes drift closed. He's the first Dom I've met who truly listened to me and understood what I've been looking for—*is* what I'm looking for. And while it's clear somewhere in his past there was a woman who also recognized what he offered, for whatever reason she's gone now. I may never know what happened there, but that's okay. I'm here. *We're* here, together.

Galen said something else too and his voice echoes in my mind as I drift off to sleep.

Let's just let it happen.

CHAPTER 9

GALEN

"*H*ere. Taste this."

I turn to where Alex is kneeling on the kitchen mat behind me. She brings her face up, opening her mouth obediently. I blow on the ladle, then gently hold it above her tongue, letting her take some of the sauce off the spoon.

"Too salty?" I ask, enjoying the casual comfort we've developed over the last three weekends together.

She swallows, shaking her head. "Not in my opinion, sir. It's salty, but I wouldn't say too much so."

I nod, returning to the stove. "It's difficult to control the saltiness of puttanesca sauce. You've got the capers, the olives, then you add in the anchovies… it's easy to overdo."

"I'll take your word for it, sir. I've never made it before."

I stir the sauce, then replace the lid, letting it simmer. Laying the spoon on a nearby towel, I turn back to Alex and kneel, bringing my face in line with hers. "Well, I know how much you like salty things, so I thought this would be the perfect dish to make for you."

"Like… salty things?" She gives me a perplexed look for a

85

moment before her eyes widen in recognition. "Oh my God, Galen... seriously?"

I grin, reaching forward to tweak her nipple.

She gives a sharp yip of pain then lowers her head, her voice tight. "Sorry, sir."

"It's okay. It *was* a terrible joke." I chuckle, still not releasing her.

Instead, she mewls, and I massage her bud as she pushes her chest forward into it.

I let go of her nipple and caress her breast. She keeps her eyes down, but I appreciate the hitch in her breath. "Do you like that, Alex?"

"Yes, sir," she says breathily.

"So do I."

I've indulged myself in Alex, spending most of our time together exploring every inch of her body several times over. It's been hedonistic gluttony, but I regret nothing, and Alex doesn't seem to either. Watching her orgasm is a drug I'm happily addicted to.

Which is why I keep thinking about peeling myself out of these clothes and fucking her right here on the floor or up against the kitchen counter again, but the dish I'm preparing is one of my favorites, and I'm genuinely curious if Alex will like it as much as I do and if I burn it, I'll be pissed—but she makes it so difficult to pay attention. "You've become a serious distraction around here."

I hear the grin in her voice. "Sorry, sir."

"No, you're not. But that's okay. I like being distracted by you." I tweak her nipple again, and she squeaks as I let go and stand up. "Okay. Be a good girl and go and set the table."

"Yes, sir," she says, rising beside me. I swat her ass as she moves past me, and she shoots me a playful little glare over her shoulder.

This shouldn't feel this good. There's no way after a few weeks together I should feel this comfortable, this *natural* with Alex, and yet it's been a recurring worry that I'm moving too fast. Maybe my assumption she's enjoying this half as much as me is conceit on my part. But if that's not the case, why is she here?

She's an incredibly strong-willed and intelligent person and—unlike what some people might think—her submissive desires in no way diminish that strength, nor do they make it impossible for her to say no. She could have easily left me two weeks ago and never returned, but she didn't. Instead, she came back the following Friday and stayed until late Sunday night. When I ordered her to pack a bag for this weekend with appropriate clothing to wear to work on Monday morning, she simply responded 'yes, sir.'

I've spent a fair amount of time the past few days going over what I hope to accomplish this weekend. I gave into an excess of greed with her body the last time we played, and there's a part of me that wants me to give in once again. But rather than let my little head govern my big head, I'm controlling my urges because there are things I need to discuss with Alex. There are conversations to go over the rules and expectations I conveniently ignored last weekend so I could give in to my rapacious desire to fuck her on every available surface, and that can't happen this time.

Jesus Christ, Galen. Exaggerate much?

Okay, so it might not have been *that* bad, but I did spend more time exploring her body than I did trying to discover if what I want and expect aligns with what she does.

I'm determined to correct that tonight.

I move into the dining room with the pan of chicken puttanesca and pasta and set it on the table. As she's done several times now, the table is perfectly set, everything arranged just as it should be from silverware to napkins, and Alex is kneeling by my chair, exactly where I love to see her. Once I have the pan settled, I move behind her chair and pull it out.

"Up," I say quietly, and she rises with poised grace to take her seat. Then I take mine and carefully serve each of us a portion while she waits patiently, her face angled down.

"Parmesan?"

"Please, sir," she says politely, and I grate some over her serving.

Unlike other meals, I don't eat first this time. Instead, I motion with my fork to her plate. "Try it."

Alex picks up her silverware and cuts off a small portion of the chicken, then swirls a bit of the pasta in the sauce before bringing it all to her mouth.

"So?"

She chews the mouthful slowly, keeping her face angled down so I can't read her expression the way I wish I could. When she finally finishes, she looks up, but her face is more thoughtful than thrilled, which is why I'm a little confused when she says, "It's really good, sir."

"Are you sure? A lot of people can be put off by the bolder flavors."

"I'm sure, sir. It's… it's not what I expected at first, but it's really, really good."

Even if she's just saying it to please, the compliment still warms me. "So, it's not what you expected, but let me guess… you were anticipating something more like a standard Bolognese sauce?"

She nods. "Exactly. The olives and the capers and the other ingredients… it's a much sharper flavor profile, and the sauce is less heavy than what I've had before on, say, a chicken parm or spaghetti."

"Yes, exactly. That's probably why it's one of my favorite dishes."

"You liking bold dishes absolutely fits your personality," she says, and it's clear she means it as a compliment.

"Does it?"

"Absolutely." This time when Alex peeks up from her plate,

she's smiling in a way that makes me feel even better than if she'd raved about how puttanesca was her favorite sauce.

I'm sure I'm preening as we talk about different foods from different cultures, and then fall into a comfortable silence as we eat. We're about halfway done when I speak again. "Can I ask you a question?"

Alex looks up. "Always, sir."

"Are you enjoying this?"

Am I enjoying this? Of course, sir. Very much so. Are you?"

"Yes, Alex," I say quietly. "I am."

"Good. Thank you, sir," she responds, her voice equally as soft.

"Now, that being said," I continue, "I believe I also told you I have certain expectations. Some I'd tell you what they are, some you'd discover organically, others you could ask for on your own. I know last weekend I let myself get carried away"—her head snaps up, and I hold my hand up—"and I don't regret that. But as much as I enjoyed every moment fucking you, I've equally enjoyed seeing how you've anticipated and responded to my rules and expectations. We played a game that night at Black Light, and I know I said we both won, but you *really* did. And you've only increased your lead since."

Alex bites her lip. "I still think we both won, sir. You've certainly showed me my desires could be more than just fantasy."

"You deserve that, Alex. Believe me." I take a sip of my drink. "I've been thinking a lot over this past week, and I want to share some specific expectations I have for you, if you want to continue this."

"I do. And I want to hear what I can do better."

"Stop." I give her a stern look. "You can't do better at something I haven't given you direction for. I told you that your first night here, and as far as I'm concerned, you're still exceeding all the expectations you've known about."

"Sorry," she says, giving a slight shrug. "Sub's prerogative."

"And Dom's prerogative to provide corrective reinforcement

when a submissive gets sassy," I counter. "But that's a discussion for later. For now, I know I talked about consent with you on your first night here, but I want to revisit it before I talk about expectations. Has there been anything I've done or asked you to do since then that crossed a boundary?"

"No! Absolutely not, sir."

"But you would've told me if there was?"

"Yes, sir. I swear."

"Good. That's all I need to hear. I trust you, Alex. I want you to understand my trust is implicit, and from this point forward I won't bring the subject up again unless you give me reason to."

"Thank you, sir."

I wait for a moment before I ask my next question. "What are your feelings on Master/slave?"

She flinches.

"Ah."

"Sir. Sorry, I..." She stops, her fingers clenching. "If that's something you want, I'm more than willing to explore it. It's... if I had a bad reaction, sir, it's because past Doms I've dealt with have soured me on that form of high protocol. But with *you*, I'm willing to try."

"That won't be necessary," I say, holding up a hand. "Based on what you've told me, I was more curious than anything else. Master/slave is a style of high protocol a lot of people try to claim is the only *true* form of it. The Gorean Philosophy, or subculture, or whatever other term they want to couch it in."

"One Twue Way," she says with an eyeroll, and I nod. "I take it you're not a fan?"

I sigh. "It's... I try not to judge those in the lifestyle regardless of their philosophies or the rules they establish in their own dynamic, and that includes those who adhere to the Gorean concepts. I know some couples love it and can make it work. That being said..." I let out a deep breath. "In my experience it's a dynamic that's easily misused. I've personally seen far too many Doms who use it as a shield to mask their weaknesses or who hide behind it to cover their proclivity for abuse. Worse, in my opinion, are the subs who buy into the exploitation and claim it's the only way they can truly experience being a high protocol submissive. That unless they're treated like an object, a thing, a 'slave,' they can't fully express their true submissive selves."

"You don't believe that's true, do you?"

I blow out another breath. "It's not for me to say, really, but…"

"But seeing someone being abused, even if they claim that's what they want, is not something you can stand by and tacitly approve, is it?"

"No, it's not." I stare at her. "What about you, Alex? What's your opinion?"

"Well, as I said, my personal experiences regarding Master/slave have not been good. I wouldn't know about Gorean because the one and only time some Dom tried to spring that on me I safe-worded out immediately."

"You did?" I interrupt her.

"Yes, sir."

"Interesting," I murmur.

"Honestly? I can see the appeal for some submissives, though. It takes those feelings of wanting to serve your Dom unconditionally to the ultimate level. If you accept that all choice has been removed, that your only option is to serve without questioning, it can be very freeing." She drops her gaze to her plate. "I'm not entirely immune to the desire myself. I mean, with you, I crave your control. I *want* your direction. I don't want to make the decisions; I want *you* to provide them. And when I succeed, when you confirm I've met an expectation of yours and pleased you, it's incredibly fulfilling." She stops, then gives her head a frustrated little shake. "I'm sure it probably doesn't make any sense to a Dom, but those are the very things I've been looking for, and to be able to fall into a headspace where my only concern is to obey you, to please you..." She looks up. "It's very liberating."

"I can see that," I say quietly. "I mean, you're right, I don't *truly* understand because it's not my personal mindset, but as an outsider looking in..."

"Can I ask you a question?" Alex asks after a slight pause.

"Of course."

"I said 'One Twue Way' a moment ago. Do you ever feel so firm in your convictions that perhaps in your own way you're doing the same thing those people do, but just coming at it from a different direction?"

"I would, except for one thing"—I stab my finger into the table top—"I've never tried to convince others my idea of high protocol is the *only* version of it and I've never tried to recruit someone into accepting my concept of the lifestyle just because I wanted to fuck them."

The words must come out harsher than I intend because Alex suddenly looks down. "Sorry, sir."

"No, no, don't," I say, waving my hand. "You don't need to apologize. You didn't do anything wrong."

"There's a story there, though, isn't there?" she asks quietly.

"Yes. But that's a conversation for another time."

We finish dinner and I tell Alex to meet me in the study once she's finished with the dishes. I don't bother following her or checking on her; she knows what my expectations are and she's met them flawlessly so far. I move to the other room and sit in my chair, thinking about what we discussed over at dinner. I meant the conversation to focus on specific expectations and rules, but instead it went off into territory I'm not fully ready to open up to Alex about. Some of the subject matter we talked about was definitely needed, but when it comes to...

No. No, I'm not ready to talk about that part of my life yet. Maybe someday, but that'll be in the future, assuming there'll be a future for her and me. For now, I'm not about to let my past color the present or what may be. I'll simply stay true to what I said before and let what's happening happen.

Alex comes into the study a short time later with my drink in hand and kneels beside my leg, offering the bourbon up to me. I take it from her and gently stroke her hair as she remains sitting with her hands on her thighs, face bent to my touch.

"When we go out together, I expect you to wait for me to open the door for you."

She starts to turn her head up but stops herself. "Sir?"

"When we go out together, which we will, you are not to open your own door for yourself. I will open the door for you."

"Okay..."

"That includes getting into and out of the car. You will always wait for me both ways."

"Sir?"

"Yes?"

"What... why are you telling me this?"

"I told you earlier I wanted to discuss specific expectations I hadn't brought up before. Now we're having that discussion."

"Oh!" She pauses for a moment. "I just thought... the discussion we were having at dinner... you might want..."

"That's a conversation we'll continue another time."

"Yes, sir," she whispers.

I go on. "You will never walk behind me in public. You're to be by my side at all times, so that there is no question who you belong to."

"Even in the club?"

"Even in the club. You belong to me. There should never be any doubt of that in anyone's mind. Now, when we're walking on a sidewalk together, you will always walk to the inside of me, away from the curb. You should never be closest to the street."

"Yes, sir."

"At breakfast, you will always prepare my coffee for me. You will add one, one"—I hold up a finger—"teaspoon of sugar, and then you will pass the cup to me with both hands."

"Wait," she says, concern tinging her voice, "even in public?"

"Most importantly in public."

"Yes, sir," she says with a quiet gulp.

I go on with more examples as we sit. They're mostly simple, mundane tasks, but I explain to Alex the very ordinariness of them is part of what makes them so important. Large, bold expressions of high protocol—such as her nakedness the moment she comes through the door—have their value, but the subtle nuance of those common expressions, ones most people would never even notice, are the very reason they carry the weight they do for me.

I've almost finished my drink when I tell her to look up at me. "This might be the most important of all, Alex. When we're in public together, whether it be at a large gathering or in a small social setting, you will never, *ever* act obsequious to me. You are to speak your mind always as the incredibly intelligent person you are. You can be deferential at times if you so choose, but I cannot stand toadying, sycophantic behavior from a sub. You are not merely a piece of furniture when you're with me, and I want everyone to see how smart and gifted you are. I want them to be jealous it's not them you're with but me. Am I clear?"

"Yes, sir," she answers serenely. "Sir?"

"Yes?"

"Earlier you said I belonged to you."

"Does that bother you?"

"No, sir, it's just… do you think of me as *your* submissive?"

And there it is. "Are you not?"

"I…" She presses her lips together for a second. "I didn't want to presume, sir."

"You're enjoying what we're doing together, aren't you?"

"Yes, sir."

"Are you planning on doing this with someone else in the near future? Did you intend on going back to Black Light to check out some other Doms and see if one of them would be a better fit for you?"

Alex shakes her head emphatically. "No, sir."

"Are you bored? Have you decided to stop coming here on the weekends?"

"No, sir."

"Have I talked about going back to Black Light myself to seek a new sub? Did you think I laid out all the rules I did tonight because I was just in the mood to hear myself talk, or that I wanted to test them out on you and see what your response was before I went off and tried them on someone else?"

"No, sir," she whispers.

There's a sheen to her eyes, and a part of me recognizes I'm being a fucking asshole. The thing is, though, I need her to understand we've passed a checkpoint here, and we both need to be thinking of what's happening between us as more than just *'testing the waters'* as I'd commented our first night together. Because for me that ship has sailed, but if it hasn't for her...

"Good. Then let me be perfectly clear: you're *my* submissive and I'm *your* Dom. And if that's not the case, then tell me right now, Alex. Because if that's true, there's a completely different conversation we need to have."

"No, sir," she says in a choked voice.

"Good girl." I bend and capture her mouth with mine.

When I lean back up, I feel where her tears have brushed my cheeks and I reach with my thumb to sweep them from her own. "Sorry if I was harsh, but this was important and needed to be said."

"I understand, sir. It's just... I didn't want to assume anything or say something which might jeopardize what's been going on, so I just... didn't."

"Alex, it's important you respect my rules and obey me, but you should never fear me. You should never be afraid to speak your mind, no matter what the subject matter." I cup her face in my hand. "I need you to understand that."

"I do now, sir," she says, leaning into me. "In all my 'fantasies' about what a high protocol relationship would be like, I never really thought it could be... would be... like this."

"What do you mean?"

"Well, that we'd be having conversations like this. I only thought of it in terms of you setting the rules and me obeying them. I mean, you *do* set the rules, sir, but..." She shakes her head slowly. "There's a lot more to it than just that. I never realized high protocol could be the way it's been between you and I."

"Some people make it that simple. And if that works for them, who am I to judge? But I admire intelligence. I've always sought out partners who are smart because I need that in a relationship. Otherwise, the time we spend together becomes stagnant, boring. I love the structure and rules and formality of high protocol, but without allowances for the personality and intellect of the sub to shine through, I might as well just hire a maid."

Alex narrows her eyes, the corners of her mouth twitching. "A maid who doesn't mind cleaning your house naked, you mean?"

"I'm sure something could be worked out to accommodate that side benefit."

"Side benefit?" She reaches slowly and cups her tits. "Is that what these are?"

I rise from my chair swiftly and scoop her up into my arms. She squeals as I do, wrapping her arms around my neck, her legs circling my waist.

"There is *nothing* about you that's a side benefit, Ms. Carre."

"Well," she says, grinding against me. "I'd like to think that you come with a very *substantial* side benefit, sir."

"How many, Alex?"

She scrunches her brow. "How many... what, sir?"

"How many swats do you think that deserved?"

She giggles, and my cock grows even harder. "I dunno. You're the Dom, after all. I'm just the meek little submissive..."

I land the first and she gives a yelp.

"That one doesn't count," I growl, raising my hand. "And as for me being the Dom..."

"With you, sometimes I'm not so sure."

CHAPTER 10

ALEX

"*D*inner?"

"Yes. Dinner."

We're in bed, and I should be enjoying this moment of post-coital bliss, but Galen has no clue he's just yanked me out of it by the roots.

"You want me... to make dinner... for you?"

His hand stops stroking my back. "Yes," he says, drawing the word out. "You did tell me once you could cook."

I nod my head slowly. "Yes, sir, I did."

"Okay, so...?"

"It's just... you're such a good cook, and I've grown accustomed to being with you in the kitchen while you do, and I've learned to set the table perfectly, right? And I know how to clean the cast iron, and put everything away the way you—"

His fingers dig in, stopping me. "Alex. Answer me: can you cook?"

"Yes, sir," I whisper.

"Then next weekend you'll cook dinner for me. Friday night. Understood?"

Oh, shit. Shit, shit, shit, shit, shit.

A sudden thought occurs to me. "Sir... do I have to... am I going to have to do it naked?"

"What are the rules, Alex?"

"Once through the door, no clothing," I say softly.

"That's right. And so that means...?"

"Naked."

A moment later Galen kisses the top of my head. "I've got an apron. You can wear that."

"Great."

I've prepared and planned multi-million-dollar talent acquisitions. I've coordinated the staff integration of corporate mergers involving thousands of people. In the fifteen-plus years of my career, I've done these things and so much more and barely broken a sweat. But this...?

It's dinner, Alex! A simple meal! What the hell is wrong with you?

It shouldn't make my stomach lurch every time I think about it, and yet it does. Galen's barely drifted off to sleep, and all I can do is stare at the plane of his chest as I contemplate whether fleeing to Antarctica might a viable exit strategy to get out of this.

The remainder of the weekend I do my best to hide my anxiety. If Galen notices he chooses not to say anything, whether out of deference to me, or whether he's making it clear he's not letting me dodge this bullet.

Monday morning on my way from his house to work, the reality that I have exactly one week to prepare a dinner for my Dom begins to settle in. In his home. In his kitchen, with him probably standing there, watching and critiquing me because why wouldn't he; he's practically a fricking *chef,* and then when I fail, he'll take me into the playroom and make me kneel on that stupid mat and tell me if I can't prepare an edible meal with *five full days* for preparation, then I'm clearly not the right submissive for him.

It's complete nonsense, but I'm as close to a panic as I've ever been in my life, even though *there's no rational reason to be.*

By Monday afternoon, after several Google searches only

increase my anxiety, in desperation I go to the only person I can think of to help me.

"Bri?"

"Hmm?"

"Can you come into my office? I need your help with something."

"Sure."

By the time she arrives I've talked myself out of it because not only does she *not* know about Galen, but I've also convinced myself telling her why I'm panicking will only make her question my sanity.

She won't listen when I tell her to never mind. In fact, she's relentless, closing the door and pestering me until she wears me down and drags the details out of me.

"Ooo! Wow, how did *you* manage to keep this a secret? I'm impressed!"

"What's that supposed to mean? I've got plenty of secrets."

"Uh huh, sure, sure. You're a veritable Kim Possible of intrigue."

"Bri!"

"Listen, Alex, all I'm saying is you're a pretty open person. Sure, you're not hanging around the breakroom telling everyone how you got laid over the weekend like Dale or Clint, but you aren't exactly a blank page either. Most of us don't pry, but it's been pretty clear you're married to your job, and except for that one guy who didn't last long…"

I shudder. She has to mean Dalton. The online Dom from New York who I'd lasted less than a month with.

"…you've given no one any indication there's been anyone in your life. And now this…"

I hold up my hands, shrugging.

"So?" she says.

"So?"

She rolls her eyes. "Oh my God. Who is he? What's his name? What department does he work in?"

"Umm... His name is Galen. I met him at a party a few weeks ago."

"Annnd?"

"He doesn't work here."

"Okay, even better. Annnd?"

I groan. "And I'm supposed to make him dinner this weekend. Listen, are you gonna give me the fifth degree or are you going to help me!"

"Both."

"*Arrgh!*"

Bri sighs. "Fiiiine. I'll help you, but in payment you need to give me more deets than just 'I met him at a party' and 'I've got to make dinner for him.'"

I give her a *very* brief background on Galen because no one, including Bri, knows anything about my lifestyle outside of GSR, and I've every intention of keeping it that way.

"Ooo. He's got a home in Laurel, huh? And you're sure he doesn't work in HR or finance?"

"Yep. He owes his own expediting business, and that's all I know."

"Well, he must do pretty well for himself to have digs out there."

"So, it would seem." I give her an imploring look. "Look, it's almost four. Are you helping me or not?"

"Yes, yes, calm your tits." Bri grins as she reaches around me, taking my mouse. "We're going to plan this dinner using the KISS Principal. Keep It Simple—"

"Stupid. I'm familiar with the term."

"Says the woman who's had to come to her favorite co-worker to figure out how to cook a simple dinner for her boyfriend."

Telling her Galen's not my boyfriend would open up a whole

host of questions I don't want to answer right now, so I let it go. "Will you *pleeeease* just help me!"

"Fine! Quiet down and listen."

Forty-five minutes later I have three new bookmarks, four places saved on Google Maps, and a written list of instructions in hand.

"Thank you," I say quietly, gripping Bri by the shoulder.

"You don't need to thank me," she says, getting up out of my chair. "You could have done this on your own, and we both know it." She stops and looks at me, and even though she's smiling, there's a look in her eye. "This guy... he's different, Alex. I don't know what it is, but he's definitely got you wound up."

It's a little hard hearing her say it because while everything Galen and I have been doing has been incredible, I'm still thinking of it in terms of us finding our way as a Dom and submissive. But what Bri's talking about is something far more than just that, even if she's completely unaware of our dynamic.

And that's a thought I'm not sure I'm ready to confront just yet.

"I... it's just been a while since I've done something like this for someone. I shouldn't be freaking out; we've only just started seeing each other. But... I want this to be right, you know? I don't want to screw it up."

"I can tell." She pats me on the shoulder. "Don't worry. You'll be fine. Just make sure to stick to what we outlined there"—she points to the paper on my desk—"and you'll be golden." She steps around me. "Oh, and one more thing: make sure to send me a wedding invitation when you guys set a date."

I start to retort, but she's past me and out the door before I'm able to.

Wedding date. Oh, no. No, no, no. Galen's not said anything to indicate he's thinking our relationship is trending in that direction. We're just two people with a mutual kink who have finally, *finally*, found someone who gets it. Nothing more than that.

Right? Right?

~

SHOW TIME.

It's Friday evening, six-thirty, and I've literally got a wheeled cart full of supplies I'm trying to haul up the pebbled walk to Galen's house. I've gone on vacation in Europe with less stuff than I'm schlepping into his home for a simple dinner, but I'll be damned if I get caught short-handed. Galen must suspect something because he opens the front door before I reach it, then comes out to take the handle of the cart from me before I make it halfway up the walk.

"What the fuck?" I hear him murmur as I rush ahead to the bedroom to undress.

When I'm done, I head immediately to the kitchen, and he's there, unloading everything I brought. Some he sets on the counter and the remainder he transfers to the fridge. I find my spot and drop to my knees, head down, waiting.

For a minute there's nothing but the sound of him unloading, until he gives a drawn-out sigh.

"For fuck's sake, Alex, seriously?"

I don't look up, and he comes over to me.

"Olive oil? You've seen me use olive oil. I know you have." He wiggles the dark green bottle in front of me.

"I... I wanted to be sure, sir."

I don't need to see him shaking his head to know he's doing it. Stepping away, he moves back to the counter, and another minute passes before I hear the rustle of a sheet of paper.

"Please, sir. Don't..."

He doesn't respond, but the room is silent.

"You don't want me to read this?" he asks quietly.

"Please."

"Very well."

He finishes putting things away, then approaches. An object lands at my feet, green fabric pooling over my toes.

"I'll be in the study. Come get me if you need me."

"Yes, sir," I whisper, and he walks away.

When his footsteps fade, I get up, grabbing the apron as I do. I slip it over my head, knotting the ties around me. I go to the counter and find where he's set down Bri's instructions. Whether he read them fully or not I've no idea, but I don't have time to worry about that right now. I have a dinner to prepare.

'Sprinkle both sides of the scallops with salt and pepper. Heat 2-3 tablespoons of the EVOO in a large skillet over medium-high. Pour in oil to coat the surface & heat until you see little wisps of smoke. DON'T LET IT BURN!'

We picked this recipe for two reasons: it adhered to Bri's KISS principle, and because Galen once told me how much he enjoys seafood. On paper it seemed easy enough, but as the oil sizzles in Galen's cast iron pan, I wonder if I've taken on something I should have thought about more thoroughly. Because even though I'm wearing the apron he gave me, when the oil pops...

"*Shit!*" I hiss, trying to choke off the word as a needle-like point of fire burns what feels like a hole through my arm.

"Everything okay?" his voice drifts out from the study.

"Perfect, sir," I say through gritted teeth.

As if.

As the scallops sear and the butter melts to make the sauce, I put the water for the pasta on to boil, adding salt as I've seen Galen do even though Bri didn't mention it, and God I'm so glad I let the guy at the counter shuck the oysters because if I had to do that along with everything else right now I swear I'll end up burning the scall—

"Dammit!" I whisper the word as I grab the tongs and turn them over before they do just that. The idea was for this meal to come together quickly and easily, but I'm discovering a fatal flaw to my best laid plans: I'm literally sweating like I've done twenty minutes of cardio, and how the hell does he mange the flow of these things so everything comes out at the same time?

Macaroni and cheese. I should've stuck to macaroni and cheese. I can do macaroni and cheese.

It's an exaggeration, but right now I'm a little overwhelmed, and it feels more like the truth than I care to admit. A part of me deep inside says I'm overthinking this; I'm doing fine, but another part looks at the scallops and says, "They're overdone, you burnt them," and another that chides, "Shouldn't the sauce be a little browner? Oh, and by the way, how are you going to finish this *and* get the table set at the same time, hmm?"

If Galen isn't able to read my mind, he does a damn good impression of it as I look up to see him standing in the archway.

"Almost done?"

"Yes, sir," I say tightly because my brain's decided to destroy what little confidence I have left reminding me of details like setting our dishes in place.

"Okay." He tips his head toward the dining room. "I'll go and set the table."

"I can do it!" I start moving around the counter, but Galen's voice brings me to a halt.

"I said I'll do it, Alex. You finish cooking."

I dip my head. "Yes, sir. Sorry."

He doesn't say anything more but moves off.

Okay, this is coming off the rails. I mean, the scallops do look pretty much like what Bri showed me, and the pasta is *al dente*, and the sauce looks like it's starting to brown to the right color, so at this point I shouldn't be freaking out but I'm forgetting something, and—*Christ!*—if I could just get my head screwed on straight and figure out what it is...

Calm. Down.

I take a deep breath. I use every trick in the book to clear my mind. This is ridiculous. It's just *dinner*. Why the hell am I overthinking this. Just take the damn meal out and serve it. If he doesn't like it, he doesn't like it, and he'll let you know, and you can take your punishment like you deserve.

I turn the burner under the scallops down to low, then scoop a little of the sauce over the pasta to keep it from sticking. I grab the oysters from the package and arrange the shells in a circle on the plate like Bri showed me. I tug off the apron, then grab the little bottle of hot sauce from the counter where Galen left it. Taking a deep breath, I turn and march toward the dining room.

Galen's sitting in his chair as I enter. I walk to the table and set the oysters down in front of him, placing the little bottle to the side. Once everything is arranged, I take a step back, then kneel at the edge of his chair.

"When you're ready for the main course, I'll bring it in, sir," I say, face down.

"You won't be joining me?"

"When you're ready, sir."

He gives a barely audible sigh. "Go get the rest of dinner, Alex."

I nod, rising. It takes two trips, but I arrange the scallops, pasta, and the salad in front of him neatly. As I finish, Galen comes up from his chair and behind mine, pulling it out. I'm about to sit when I notice it.

The chives. The garnish for the scallops. They're still sitting in a small bowl on the kitchen counter.

I let out a tiny cry of frustration. "Sorry, sir! Sorry, sorry..." I exclaim as I sideslip from the chair's edge and nearly run back into the kitchen.

Way to go, Alex. You had one job...

I scurry back into the dining room to find Galen waiting behind my seat, a wry grin creasing his face. I quickly sprinkle the chives over the scallops, then hurry back into place.

"Anything else?" Galen asks, amusement tinging his voice.

"No, sir," I whisper dejectedly.

He pushes my seat in, then returns to his own. I keep my face down, frustration tensing my muscles because the only way this is going to end is with me in the playroom on my knees or straddling the pony because it's a simple fricking dinner and I couldn't even get *that* right.

Simplicity. Form. Structure. All things Galen's told me he admires, and the trainwreck I've presented is none of them.

The thoughts warring inside me are counterpoint to the quiet sounds of Galen plating the meal. He prepares mine first, then his own. When he's finished, he says, "This looks wonderful."

"Thank you, sir," is all I'm able to mumble, despite the tumble of apologies that want to spill out.

He stares at me for a moment but says nothing further and begins eating. An oyster first, then a bite of his scallop, then a swirl of the pasta. The food on my own plate might as well be ash for all the appeal it holds right now.

For God's sake, Alex. Overreact much?

I am but knowing that does nothing to stop it from happening. I wanted this to be perfect, and it's not. It's a mess. I'm a mess. And what makes it all the worse is it's just dinner. Of the thousand things I could be obsessing over, why this?

Doesn't matter. Galen continues eating, and I'm hoping he won't give me permission to do so because right now I'm not sure I could.

A minute passes, the silence only broken by the sound of his silverware and my breathing. He reaches for another oyster, applies several drops of the sauce, but instead of bringing it to his mouth, he holds it hovering above the plate.

"These are excellent. What type are they?"

"The man at the shop suggested them. They're called Miyagis."

"Hmm. I've never had them before. Good choice."

"Thank you, sir," I mumble.

"Alex."

"Yes, sir?"

"Look at me."

I bring my face up slowly. Galen's staring back with a neutral gaze, but the corners of his eyes are narrowed.

"Open your mouth."

I do as he orders, and he gently, smoothly brings the shell to my lips, tipping it in. The oyster slips past, and the slightly briny flavor punctuated by the sharp vinegary bite of the hot sauce he's applied meld together inside my mouth. The flesh is creamy, velvety and I can't help but savor the taste as I swallow, my current anxiety notwithstanding.

Galen returns the empty shell to the plate, never taking his gaze from me. I've no idea what he's thinking, but my brain is more than happy to fill in the gaps. He leans back and picks up his silverware once again.

"Eat your dinner, Alex."

I don't answer but simply nod, picking up my knife and fork. I cut a small piece of scallop off and bring it up to my mouth.

Okay. Okay, so it's not *that* bad. It's actually pretty tender. The sauce does go really well with it, and the capers work with everything like they did in the dish he made last weekend. But, still...

My brain reminds me of the forgotten chives and a hundred other little things, and as quickly as I enjoy the bite it's forgotten as I go over a mental laundry list of everything I did wrong.

"Alex?"

I snap my head up. "Sir?"

"You're not eating."

"Sorry, sir."

"Do you not like it?"

"I..."

"What?"

"I made a few mistakes."

"News to me. As far as I'm concerned, it's perfect."

"I... there's things I could have done better. I should have added—"

"Alex."

His tone makes me bite off my words.

"Are you about to tell me I'm wrong?" he says quietly.

"No, sir," I whisper.

"Good girl. Now finish your dinner."

I do as he says, though it's not easy, despite his praise.

Galen finishes before I do. I'm still picking at the last of my pasta when he stands and gathers his plate.

"I can get it, sir!" I start to scramble up, but his voice claps me back into my seat.

"Finish. Your. Dinner, Alex."

"Yes, sir," I answer meekly and go back to doing just that.

He leaves me sitting at the table as he clears everything away, and I just know I'm in more trouble than I thought. I don't often catastrophize, but I'm doing it now because he's taken from me the one chore I've done since the first evening I arrived here, and there's no doubt in my mind that signifies a mistake I've made greater than any I've considered.

The kitchen! Oh my God, the kitchen's a fricking mess! He has to be livid.

A minute passes, and I've taken maybe another two or three bites when he returns. He comes and stands beside me, his eyes tracking from the plate to my face and then back again.

Shit. I shovel the last of the pasta into my mouth, my cheeks bulging.

"Soddy, suh." I hold the plate up, and he frowns as he takes it from me and turns away without a word.

I am so screwed.

My hands clench and unclench in my lap and I sit here and listen while he moves about the kitchen. I contemplate whether I should go in to help, but Galen didn't give me permission to get up. I worry whether this is another choice of my own I need to make, much like following him across the club floor that night at Black Light was. But there's been a look in his eye the last half hour, a tone in his voice that convinces me to keep my butt in this chair until he tells me otherwise. I can make this situation better or worse, and I'm certain staying put will do the former rather than the latter.

Time drags as I sit in silent dismay while he repairs the damage I've done. Eventually the noise tapers off, and Galen reappears, wiping his hands on a dish towel.

"Follow me."

I get up silently and trail behind him. We move past the living room, past the study, down the hall and through the bedroom. As we cross toward the far wall, I'm certain of where we're headed, and every fear I've taken counsel in this evening is justified.

Well, you deserve it. He's made it so simple and clear for you, and you couldn't even handle that.

Galen motions me through the door and closes it behind us. I stand at the attention position, my face down, waiting.

"On the mat, Alex."

I don't need to ask why. I screwed up, and I deserve whatever punishment is coming my way. The mat I've come to hate more than the pony waits on the floor, and I move to kneel upon it.

Galen stands behind me for a moment, then comes around and drops into a crouch in front of me. He cups his hand under my chin, lifting it until I face him.

"Do you know why you're here?"

"Probably for a lot of things, sir," I say miserably.

He tilts his head. "Give me one."

"I forgot to put the chives on the scallops before I brought them in for dinner."

He closes his eyes, shaking his head. "Do you seriously think," he says slowly, "I would bring you in here and put you on the mat for something like that?"

"I…"

"Give me another."

"I left the kitchen in a mess."

"When you clean up after me, do I leave the kitchen spotless?"

"That's... well... that's one of my tasks, and you cook the meals, so it only makes sense I have to—"

"Did I cook dinner tonight?"

"N... no."

"Do you think I hold you to a different standard than myself?"

"I..."

Galen pinches my chin in his hand. "The night I made you piccata I forgot to check to see if I had chicken stock in the cupboard before I started cooking. I didn't. So, instead I opened a bottle of white wine and used it. The same one I poured you a glass of when you arrived. To have made chicken piccata *properly* I should have used stock to create the sauce. Instead, I deglazed the pan with wine and made a slight rue with some flour. Now"—he gives my chin a little tug—"if I hadn't told you that just now, would you have ever known?"

"No, sir," I whisper.

"You think you made mistakes with dinner tonight or by not cleaning the kitchen? No. Dinner was perfect. You could have left the chives on the counter and never brought them out, and I'd have never known. And as for cleaning up afterwards: you cooked, I clean. That's the way it works. A simple, clean division of tasks. Shared effort. Balanced results."

"But I..."

"But you what?"

"I feel like I failed to live up to your expectations."

"Did I tell you that? At any point this evening did I say you did something wrong?"

"No..."

"What was one of the very first things I told you when we started this? That I wouldn't expect you to read my mind. Last weekend I asked you to make me dinner. That was my *only* expectation. Not what to make for dinner, not how to make it, what ingredients to use, what pots and pans you could dirty. Just make me dinner. Did you do that?"

"Well, yes, but I mean—"

"No, Alex! No. You do *not* get to second guess me. I told you: if you have questions about an expectation, you always have permission to ask. Always. I meant that. I told you I'd let you know my expectations, and last weekend I laid out a whole list of them for you. I told you to ask when you felt you needed to, or you could discover them on your own organically. And I know I also told you I don't want a slave; someone I'd set up to fail then punish arbitrarily. I want an equal. A partner. Someone who wants to be here doing these things we do on equitable terms. Not me getting everything out of it while you get nothing in return."

"Galen, that's not the way I feel…"

"Then for God's sake tell me why you were so anxious tonight? Tell me why you were wound up tighter than a watch spring. And don't tell me you weren't, Alex, because I'm not an idiot. I could see it from the moment you dragged that cart up the walk."

"I just wanted to please you," I whisper.

"Oh, for the love of God."

And Galen Harmon kisses me. Hard.

At first the intensity startles me. Not because Galen's never kissed me this way before, but in the past, it's always seemed a function of the passion of the moment. This is different. This is a message he's sending me, and at first, I'm confused.

However, the longer he holds me the less it matters. I lean into it, draw comfort from it because even if I've completely misunderstood his intention, one thing is clear: Galen's not angry with me. There's not a single thing about this kiss that indicates displeasure. In fact, it's the exact opposite.

A minute passes and he finally pulls back, resting his forehead to mine. "Do you know why I put you on the mat tonight?"

"I thought I did."

"Do you now?"

"I..." I let out a deep sigh. "I'd rather not guess, sir, but I'm pretty sure it's not for the reasons I thought."

"Pretty sure you're right." He leans back and cups my cheek. "I put you on the mat because you didn't trust me."

I scrunch my eyes. "What?"

"You didn't trust me. Tonight, instead of remembering what I've told you in the past about my expectations and believing what I said, you chose to decide for yourself how you'd failed me." He gives me a gentle smile. "You didn't communicate with me. Instead, you assumed."

I may not agree with everything he's just said, but I can't deny the gist of it. He's right. I *had* assumed. Even when I knew I was overreacting I still did it because I really wanted to make tonight special for Galen. I wanted to please him. I wanted him to be proud of me. So instead of making the same mistake he's just accused me of again, I tell him those things.

"Oh, Jesus Christ, Alex! Of course, I'm proud of you. You've gone way beyond what I could ever have expected. For God's sake, have I not made it clear enough how much I care for you?"

Oh, shit.

"Care for me?"

"Yes, Alex. I care for you. Very much."

I can't help but laugh nervously before I find myself in his arms.

"You talk about me assuming," I say as he holds me to his chest. "I definitely didn't want to assume what's been going on between us was anything more than two people fulfilling each other's kinky needs."

"And that means we can't care about each other? That we can only have feelings as long as they're tied to fulfilling our desires?"

"Well, okay, when you put it like that..."

"Come on, Alex. I know you know better than that."

"We've both been burned."

"True," he says quietly. "But I'm pretty goddamn confident by now we're beyond worrying about whether we're going to burn each other."

"Maybe."

"Maybe." The sigh he lets out melds into a chuckle as he releases me and stands up.

"Give me your hand."

I stare up at him, then reach forward.

Galen doesn't immediately pull me up. Instead, he gently massages my fingers. "You worry about displeasing me? Let me make it simple for you: you can't. Unless you're going to tell me everything you've done to this point was some sort of Oscar-worthy acting job, there's no way anything you do can upset me."

"Galen..."

"You've met my expectations, Alex. In fact, you've exceeded them, including dinner tonight. You are something I'd thought long gone from my life, something I'd been ready to give up on completely. Telling you all of this is a calculated risk, but I can't go on pretending what's going on between us is nothing more than a high protocol version of Friends With Benefits. Because, at least for me, it isn't. And if there's one thing I need from you at this point, it's simply this: trust me when I say I'm not about to walk away from you, because I'm not. I care for you too much to do that."

Oof.

"I'm not sure what to say."

"You don't feel the same?"

"No! No, I didn't say that. It's just... I've been telling myself similar sorts of things, but I've been afraid it wasn't the same for you."

"Well, looks to me like we've cleared that up, so... problem solved."

Gazing up at him, I can't stop the smile that tugs the corners of my mouth up, despite the pain still shooting up my legs from my knees. "I guess so," I say appreciatively.

"Good. Now, that being said, there's one more thing we need to attend to."

Galen pulls me up from the mat, and I hiss as blood flows back into my knees.

"Bend over the bench, Alex," he says, pointing.

My mouth comes open to protest. I want to ask what I've done that merits me being punished further, but instead of questioning him, I close it and simply move into position.

"Do you know why I'm going to spank you?"

"Honestly, sir, no."

"Ah. Well, let me explain..."

He leans over the back of me, one hand cupping my ass while the other rests on my shoulder. His breath caresses my ear while another part of him presses into me, both in ways that are becoming familiar.

"Because I like to," he whispers.

I shouldn't laugh but I do. For some reason it's so damn funny right now, especially coming on the heels of what we just talked about. And though I'm positive my laughter will only serve to fuel the fire I've stoked inside him, it's a fire I want to feed.

Ten swats later I'm up on my toes, counting out the last one just before Galen scoops me up in his arms and carries me back into the bedroom. He tosses me on the bed, and I watch as he takes off his clothes. Though I've grown more than accustomed to his body over these past three weeks, it still takes nothing away from the heat that pools in me as he strips. When he's done, he scrambles up and pushes me back until my head comes to rest against the pillows. He slips up the length of my body, caging me in his arms, hands to either side of my shoulders and...

"*Nnnngh!* Dammit, Galen!"

"I thought you liked that?"

"I do. But... give a girl a moment to get ready, okay?"

He laughs. "You were plenty ready. I could feel it when I slipped in."

"Yeah, well you were clearly ready too."

"Never said I wasn't."

"So not fair," I mumble, biting my lower lip as he falls into a smooth pattern which only confirms how much each of us are enjoying this.

"Life is pain, princess. Anyone who tells you different is selling something."

"Wait, wait..." I press my palms against his chest. "Did you... did you seriously just quote *The Princess Bride* while fucking me?"

"Language, little girl!" He grins down at me, thrusting past the pressure I'm applying with my hands. "And for the record, yes, I did."

"I'm so not ready to be in a relationship with a man who'll quote *The Princess Bride* during sex," I murmur.

"Say that again."

"I'm so not ready—"

"The next part, Alex."

"In a relationship?"

"Yes." Galen stares down at me. "Are we in a relationship, Alex?" he asks calmly.

Oh, shit.

'I care for you...' He'd said that, not me, but the fact is I care for Galen too. Very much so. And if that doesn't put us in a relationship, then...

"Yes, sir. I think we are."

This time he bends slowly. When his mouth captures mine, it's warm, sweet, caring.

Perfect.

"Good girl. That's what I wanted to hear."

I shouldn't feel so warm inside. And if I do, it should be because Galen's returned to driving his cock into me. It shouldn't be from those last six words of his that now ring through my head.

Sex with Galen has always been good. After the first night, we ditched the condoms because I'm on birth control, and I love the feeling of him releasing inside me. Tonight is no different, except for one tiny detail: he doesn't just fuck me. He makes love to me. And though neither of us has dropped the L-bomb, the thought of it hovers in the background, a silent unspoken word that may still be too early to invoke, but something that'll need to be addressed if things continue the way they're going.

At least for me. Because I'm beginning to feel it.

"Oh, *fuck*, Alex! *Fuck*, I'm gonna..."

Oh, God. He's about to come, and even though I'm close, I've let my thoughts pull me out of the moment. Shoving them aside, I dig my fingers into him as the pace of his thrusts quicken. I clear my mind and I give myself over fully to the sensations of Galen filling me.

"*Fuck!*"

The pulses of his release are the final push I need, and I tumble into my own orgasm. The white envelops me, and tonight I fall into it with reckless abandon. An hour ago, I was convinced this evening was a complete, unmitigated disaster. And now?

Now it's the furthest thing from it.

Galen pulls me to his side, wrapping his arm around my shoulder so I have no choice but to nestle onto his chest. We're both sweaty and still breathing a little heavy, but I don't think I'd trade where I'm at right now for the finest accommodations anywhere in the world. He's brushing his fingers through my hair, and the soothing feeling has my eyelids growing heavier by the second.

"Sir."

"Hmm?" Galen's voice is heavy.

"Thank you."

"You're welcome." He kisses the top of my head.

"Oh, there *is* one more thing."

He says nothing as he turns his face to mine, eyes blinking.

"Did you make sure to clean the cast iron properly? Because there's a right way and a wrong way to do it, sir..."

Galen shakes his head, closing his eyes. "The pony's just beyond that door, Alex."

I smile, closing mine too. "I know."

And I do. But I'm smiling because even if he were to take me back in there, I'd be okay with it.

In fact, I don't think I'd mind at all.

CHAPTER 11

GALEN

"You own a plane?"

I pinch the bridge of my nose. "I don't believe I said I own a plane."

"Well, you did say, 'my plane,' sir." Alex reminds me.

Well, fuck.

"Okay, you're right, I did. What I meant by that was, the plane I regularly use in the course of my business."

"So, you fly? You're a pilot?"

"Okay, hold up. First things first: I need you to answer my original question."

Alex looks up from where she's curled on the floor beside the edge of my chair. "Of course, sir. I'd love to go to the airport and meet your friends."

I grin down at her. "Okay. Now, as to your other question: no, I'm not a pilot. I've never gotten my license. I have Mia for that."

"Mia?"

"One of my friends I'd like you to meet."

"Ah." Alex looks back down, leaning her face against my leg.

Damn, she makes it so hard lately not to carry her back to the bedroom and spend the day tossing her around the bed. In the past two weeks these subtle little gestures have grown in number —leaning her face against my leg as we sit here in the study, nuzzling me when I stroke her hair as I pass by while I'm cooking in the kitchen, and a dozen others like it. I'd told Alex once before she was a distraction, and that has only multiplied tenfold since.

Oh, boo fucking hoo, Galen. My, how you suffer.

Okay, so maybe I don't have any reason to bitch, but this meeting today is important for several reasons. One, I want the two people I work closest with—Deacon and Mia—to meet Alex. Of the handful of people I call friends, they're the most important to me, and I want Alex to get to know them. Plus, I am not above the conceit of vanity and I'm so damn proud of Alex I want to show her off.

Not that I'd tell her that. There's no need for me to press my luck.

"Galen?"

"Yes?" She's used my given name, and that's become a clear way to tell she's stepping out of our dynamic for a moment.

"You've told me you're an expediter, and I can infer a bit from that. But you don't work for a specific company, do you?"

"Nope. I'm a freelancer."

"Sooo... Who contracts you to deliver things for them?"

Ugh. I knew this would eventually come up, but I'd been avoiding it for as long as possible. Alex works deep in the corporate world and she's incredibly intelligent, so being perfectly forthright with her is the best course of action, but... there are some things I'm still not comfortable telling her in their entirety. So, I'm going to hedge my bets here.

"Well," I say slowly, "I have some contacts in commercial trade, mostly in supply-chain circles. Private firms who hold and store things for people that then get moved about through private transactions. I actually do some work for museums and private collectors."

"Transporting works of art?"

"Exactly. High value pieces where the parties would rather the transfer be kept as lowkey and below the radar as possible, for insurance purposes. And it's not always works of art. Sometimes it can be rare or valuable items. Jewelry, antiquities, wine, things of that nature."

"Ah."

"Then I also have some government contracts. Moving small quantity items that agencies don't want to contract out to larger commercial firms. Sometimes we even transport people to highly secure... places."

None of what I've told her so far is a lie, but it's vague enough to hide the full truth I'd rather shield her from.

"It all sounds very interesting," she says mildly.

Uh oh.

I've come to recognize *that* tone. It means she's thinking, and this isn't a subject I want her sharp-as-a-tack mind dwelling on.

"Honestly, to tell the truth, it's really rather boring. The bulk of what we're contracted to move is pretty mundane, even if it's considered high value by the owners."

"Ah, I see. I'm sure to *them* it's all very dull."

There's a warning there, but right now I don't have the time to focus on it. I told Deacon I'd be out today just after lunch, so taking Alex back into the playroom and distracting her from pursuing this train of thought won't work. I need to think of something else fast.

"Listen, we need to head out soon to get to the hanger on time, but there's this place I want to take you to lunch before we get there, so we need to get moving."

Alex looks back up at me. "We aren't eating here?"

"Nope," I say, shaking my head.

"Oh." She looks taken aback.

"You don't want to have lunch out with me?"

"No, no, it's not that, sir. It's just..." She drops her gaze. "This'll be the first time we've been out in public together since our first night at Black Light."

"Yes... what about it?"

"It's just... I wasn't sure you *wanted* to be seen with me in a public setting."

I reach down and grip her face and turn it up to mine. "I don't have the time to correct that statement right now," I say firmly, "but rest assured once we're back I will." I let go of her. "Now go and get dressed."

"Yes, sir." She gets up smoothly and crosses the room, looking back only once before disappearing toward the bedroom.

I thought a minute ago not to tell her how much I want to show her off. I'm rethinking that notion now. If she thinks for one second I want to keep her hidden...

When Alex comes back, I lead her out into the garage. If I thought she might have forgotten my rule about entering and exiting the car she puts it to rest as she stands by the passenger door, waiting patiently.

"Good girl," I say, opening it and waiting until she's seated and buckled in.

"You thought I'd forgotten, didn't you?" she asks as I pull down the drive to the front gate.

"I'll admit, that was foolish of me."

She laughs. "I'm not perfect, sir."

"You're damn close."

I haven't seen Alex blush before, but she does now. "That's very kind. Not sure I totally agree, but it's still very kind."

I open the gate then drive through until we hit the main road. Once we're on it I pick up the conversation I'd promised to come back to.

"I'm curious why you think I wouldn't want to be seen out with you? You're incredibly intelligent, beautiful, and any man would be a fool not to want to be seen in your company."

Alex sighs. "I don't know much about your life beyond the

time we've spent inside your home, Galen. Maybe you had reason to want to keep things private. I'd understand if you did. I just didn't know for certain, so... all I could do was guess."

"You know you could have—"

"Galen, stop. Not everything requires me questioning you for an answer. That's not fair, sir. You have a right to some privacy. I get there are things you're not ready to talk about yet, and maybe this was one of them. You've shown me repeatedly how much you respect my wishes, the least I could do is return the same courtesy to you."

Shit. She's right. And the shot across my bow doesn't go unnoticed.

"Point taken. I'm sorry, Alex."

"It's okay, sir. I'm not trying to be difficult. But... this is something we need to clarify. I'm *always* trying to anticipate your needs and what you want from me. It's part of what I like about our relationship, especially when I get it right. But there are some things I need to trust you to tell me about when you're ready, and not before then. Sure, there are some things I'm willing to take a guess at and pay the price if I'm wrong, but others... not so much."

I chuckle. "'Try high protocol,' they said. 'It'll be easy,' they said."

Alex laughs. "Exactly. I once had a fellow sub tell me 'kink can be so goddamn messy sometimes.'"

"Smart woman."

"Yeah. I hadn't realized before just how right she was."

We make our way westward toward the airport where Deacon and Mia are waiting. It's about a forty-mile drive, which gives us plenty of time to talk.

"Can I be honest with you about something?"

"Isn't that what we've promised we'll do with each other?"

"Touché." I glance over at her. "Part of why I'm taking you to meet my friends today isn't just so I can introduce you to them."

"Oh?"

"Yeah. I want to flex a little, show you off."

"Oh, *really?*"

"I've never said I'm not vain, Alex. You're a beautiful woman, and the fact you're with me makes me proud. So… yeah, there you go. I hope that doesn't make you feel uncomfortable."

"I mean, what woman in her right mind would want to hear the man she's with finds her attractive and wants to boast about her to his friends?" She rolls her eyes. "The very idea."

"Remind me, I did tell you you're a smart-ass, right?"

"You may have mentioned it."

"Good. Because I'd hate to think I hadn't." I glance across again, and Alex looks as if she's trying and failing to hide a smile. "I'm serious, though. If anything about this makes you feel uncomfortable, please say something. I never want to put you in that position. And if you want to keep our relationship private, just say so and I can introduce you as my… financial adviser. Or my secretary."

Alex snorts. "Oh, you'd like that, wouldn't you?"

"Well, admittedly it does play into certain fantasies."

"Yeah… I'll bet," she says, chuckling. "Save that for the private booths at Black Light, sir."

I put twenty miles behind us, and Alex and I fall into easy, comfortable conversation. I'd been concerned about how today might go, but if this is any indication, I didn't have any reason to worry. At noon I stop for lunch at a little hole-in-the-wall place I know that serves some of the best *trompo* tacos on the Eastern Seaboard.

"Umm… a gas station?" Alex says with reservation as I pull in.

"Looks can be deceiving. Trust me."

"Ookaayy," she says, her tone clearly dubious. A half hour and a half dozen tacos later, her attitude has changed completely.

"Okay, never in a million years would I have expected that. Those were fantastic!"

"I know, right?" I grin. "Like I said, looks can be deceiving."

I get back on the highway for the remaining twenty miles, and Alex spends most of it watching the scenery pass by outside. When I exit the freeway the next time, it's to pull off and head down a side road deeper into the Virginia countryside. Finally, the edge of the airport comes into view, and I turn off the road and in through the front gate. Alex looks around as we drive past the small building that serves as a terminal, squinting at the row of Cessnas and Beechcrafts as we pass.

"This is a private airfield," I say as I steer us toward the largest hangar visible.

"So, I gathered."

I pull the car up to the large metal building. The tall bi-parting door at the front is cracked open, and I park just to the side of it. After helping Alex out, I do something I haven't done before: I take her hand in mine.

"Come on. They'll be inside." I give her hand a squeeze, and she grips me back as we head in.

It's surprisingly bright inside the hangar. The roof has a lot of acrylic panels that let the outside light in, which makes it easy to see everything. Squatting square in the middle of the floor, taking up much of the space, is the plane Alex had called mine. Beyond it there are two shipping containers positioned to one side near the wall. They're part of the reason I'm here meeting with the team today. No one seems to be around, so I head toward the back where the offices are.

"About time you showed up."

The voice brings me to a halt, and I turn to find an indistinct figure sauntering toward us from around the rear of the aircraft. An orange glow lights up the face for a brief second as smoke curls up, but I don't need that to know who it is. I'd the voice recognize anywhere.

"I did say we were going to have lunch first, Mia."

"Yeah? Didja stop by Hector's?"

"As a matter of fact, we did."

Mia comes into view, stepping up to Alex and me. She's got her flight suit on, the one she wears most days like a second skin. The camouflaged Nomex fabric is faded, the double black bars of a captain sewn onto one collar tab almost blending into the uniform's pattern. She takes another drag on the ubiquitous thin cigar she's rarely without. "Cool. So, where's mine? I'm hungry."

"Pretty sure there's a vending machine over in the terminal. *Bon appétit.*"

"You're a dick, Galen." She blows out another cloud of pungent smoke and turns her gaze to Alex. "Who's your friend?"

I let go of Alex's hand and bring it the small of her back. "Alex, this is my friend, Mia. Mia, this is Alex."

Mia bites down on her cigar, glancing at me with a mischievous grin. "Ooo, so I'm your friend, just not friend enough to warrant *trompo* for lunch." She sticks her hand out to Alex. "Pleasure to meet you, Alex."

"Likewise," Alex says, returning the handshake.

"I'll be sure to bring you and Deacon with me next time."

"Promises, promises," Mia says, her eyes never leaving Alex.

"Speaking of Deacon, where is he? In the office?"

"Yeah. Probably asleep."

A door bangs from across the hangar, and we all turn toward it.

"Sorry!" Mia calls out. "Hope we didn't wake you!"

"Fuck you," a voice rumbles as it grows closer. "If I didn't have to do ninety percent of the fucking work around here so your bitch-ass could just sit in the seat, maybe I could—" His voice cuts short as the three of us come into view.

"Gawddammit, Mia," he growls, shooting her daggers.

"Alex, this is Deacon. Deacon, this is Alex, Galen's friend." Mia steps close, throwing her arm over Alex's shoulder. "Deacon here's a Rhodes scholar, as you can clearly tell from his extensive vocabulary."

"Shut it," he mutters as he steps forward, extending his hand. "Pleasure to make your acquaintance, ma'am."

Deacon's a big man. A *big* man. He's six-foot-three and just over three hundred pounds, his arms a Louvre gallery of tattoos. He's got a bald head and a stomach that arrives a minute before the rest of him does. He's a formidable presence even after you've known him for a while, and I give Alex full marks—she doesn't blink an eye as his hand swallows hers.

"The pleasure's all mine, Mr. Deacon," she responds smoothly.

"Ah... it's... it's, uh... just Deacon," he stumbles, pulling his hand back.

"Of course." Alex smiles warmly. "Thank you, Deacon."

Deacon glares at Mia for a second. "There's some people 'round here I know could learn a few things 'bout courtesy from you."

Mia snorts. "Yeah, afraid that ship sailed a *loooong* time ago."

Deacon rolls his eyes.

"So," I say, motioning to the containers against the side wall. "Those them?"

Deacon directs a pointed glance to Alex before coming back to me. I give him a quick nod of approval.

"Yeah, those are them," he says. "Colbie called me again yesterday wanting to know when we're gonna get them moved."

"Well, hopefully we'll have the answer to that after the party."

"Did you tell him about the other thing?" Mia interjects.

I glance over at her. "What other thing?"

"Yeah, 'bout that..." Deacon heaves out a sigh. "Colbie's got another delivery for us."

"Okay?"

"It's..." Deacon rubs his forehead.

"It's fucking Trey. And his team," Mia says tightly.

"Fuck. No." My voice is harsh, and I catch a look of concern flit across Alex's face. "I said last time was the last. Not again."

"Colbie didn't make it sound like it was open for discussion."

"Yeah, well Colbie's got a way of assuming things are his to decide. I'm not inclined to agree."

"Maybe you should give him a call," Deacon says impassively.

"Oh, I'm fucking going to." I blow out an aggravated sigh. "Where did he say they need to go?"

"Landing strip at some *rancho* down in Sonora."

"Insertion and extraction?"

"Yep." Mia nods.

"I'll call him." For a moment they all stand watching me. "Okay," I say, "enough of this. I'll handle Colbie later. I didn't come here to get caught up in a bunch of his crap."

"Yeah. This is a bullshit way to introduce us to your new girlfriend." Mia blows out another cloud of smoke, a wicked grin peeking through.

I should say something, tell them Alex isn't my girlfriend, but… honestly, I don't want to. The sound of it has pride swelling inside me. Before I can say anything, though, Alex cuts me off.

"I mean, I'm not following everything you're talking about, but I'm still enjoying the conversation." She motions to the aircraft behind us. "I will say, though, I'd love to get a tour of Galen's plane, if someone has the time."

There's an abrupt silence, and Mia's smile turns deadly.

"Galen's plane," she says pointedly. "Oh, yes, we should most definitely give you a tour of *Galen's* plane." She tugs on Alex's shoulder, turning her away.

"I'll come—"

Mia whips her head back toward me. "You'll stay right the fuck where you are, Galen Harmon. I'll take Alex on this tour *by myself.*" She's still smiling, but the cobra's venom in her tone freezes me in place.

"I'm sure we'll be fine, sir." Alex's voice is almost cloying, but the look she gives me is one hundred percent pure sass. "It'll be a chance for Mia to fill me in on all the details about *your* plane, and maybe a few other things, too."

Oh, I am so *putting you on the pony when we get home.*

Deacon claps me on the shoulder. "Tactical retreat time, brother. Mia won this one. I got a bottle back in the office. Let's go have a drink, discuss some business, and maybe you can explain what the fuck possessed you to tell your girl Mia's plane was yours."

〜

BY THE TIME Alex and Mia finish their tour of 'my' plane and join us in the office, I've called Colbie and hashed out a compromise. It's going to require Mia, Deacon, and me being out of town for a few days next week. And while I'm not entirely happy having to concede anything to the man, it's not the first time it's happened, and it won't be the last.

"I like your girlfriend. You can bring her here anytime." Mia gives me a broad grin, one arm slung over Alex's shoulder.

"I'm so glad you approve." I glance at Alex, and she smiles back enigmatically. "I take it you had a good time?"

"She did," Mia says. "And I promise I didn't corrupt her too much."

I pinch the bridge of my nose. "I knew I should have waited until you were out on a job to bring her here."

"And make me miss the chance to show her *your* plane? I don't think so."

I sigh in resignation.

Deacon and I take a few minutes to give Mia a brief overview of the discussion we had with Colbie, including the job we're going on this coming week. She listens quietly, nodding when we've laid it all out.

"Those guys are assholes, but… a paycheck's a paycheck, I suppose."

Even though I don't want to agree with her, it's the truth. The final thing we talk about is the party next weekend.

"You'll be coming, won't you?" Mia gives Alex's shoulder a tight hug, but her gaze is laser focused on me. "I'd hate to think Galen would show up without my new best friend."

"That's entirely up to him," Alex says innocently.

"Oh, I'm sure he can be convinced. Can't you, Galen."

"Am I not the boss here?" I look over at Deacon. "I could swear I was the boss here."

"Man, did you like, take a blow to the head or something recently? 'Cause if you really believe you've ever been Mia's boss..."

"Point fucking taken." I give Mia a placating smile. "If Alex would like to come to the party, I'd be honored to have her there."

"Then it's settled." She gives Alex another tight squeeze, and Alex's eyebrows shoot upward.

"Okay, is there anything else we need to go over? If not, we're going to head home."

"Nope, I think we're good here, brother."

"Thanks, I appreciate it." I take Deacon's hand, shaking it firmly. I turn toward Mia, and she slips her arm from Alex's shoulder, slowly, deliberately closing the short distance separating us. She makes an elaborate production of taking out another of her cigarillos, biting off the tip, then lighting it up. When she's got it glowing, she blows a cloud of smoke in my face, her eyes narrowing almost to slits.

"I like you, Galen, I really do. But if you *ever* tell anyone my plane is yours ever again, I will cut your balls off slowly, roast them over the number two engine manifold, and then hang them in the cockpit as my own personal good luck charm." She pats my chest gently. "We clear, boss?"

"For God's sake, Mia, all I meant—"

Her fingers suddenly dig in. "I said, we clear?" The words come out soft, almost seductive.

"Yes," I answer through gritted teeth.

"Good boy." She gives my chest a final pat, then turns and strolls away, a single plume of smoke trailing in her wake.

"Told you we shoulda hired the old man," Deacon says under his breath as she disappears.

I sigh. Not for the first time, I think he might be right.

CHAPTER 12

ALEX

"*S*he said what?"

Galen's voice is incredulous, and it's hard not to smile, especially considering the story I'm relating.

"She said once they'd stripped you out of the remnants of the uniform, it was just... there, and so curiosity got the best of them. They needed something to use to measure it, and..."

Galen closes his eyes briefly, his jaw working. "And, what?"

"And a dollar bill was all they had."

"That is complete and one hundred percent utter bullshit." Galen stares grim-faced out of the windshield at the freeway slipping by as we head home.

"If you say so, sir."

He doesn't take his eyes from the road, but the low growl that rumbles out of him doesn't go unnoticed. I can't help but grin because Mia was right: winding Galen up is a sport that's addictive.

"For the record, I'd been up for forty-eight hours straight, I was covered in fuel, *and* I'd passed out."

"Mia said as much."

The road noise fills the cab with a muted hiss as I sit with my hands folded in my lap, trying not to burst out laughing.

"What other nonsense did she fill your head with?"

"Not much."

"Not much?" He shoots me a jaundiced look. "That's not encouraging."

"Well... she did tell me one more thing."

"Oh, God. What?"

"She said you're the best boss she's ever had."

Galen doesn't say anything for a long moment. "Yeah," he says evenly. "More bullshit." We both go silent, but he's smiling.

The afternoon has been wonderful. Mia, Deacon... Galen clearly has a tight group of friends surrounding him. Deacon is still a bit of an enigma because I didn't spend much time with him, but his appearance aside, he's obviously a decent man. Mia...

Mia is the archetypical *one-of-the-guys* woman. However, when we were alone inside her plane, she'd shown herself to be bright, kind, with a razor-sharp wit, and though I'd never tell her, she's downright sweet. Busting Galen's chops whenever she was around him was clearly her way of leveling the male-dominated playing field, and despite her parting shot when we left, she made it clear she was fiercely loyal to him and Deacon, both.

The truth was, though, my teasing aside, what Mia and I had discussed mostly was Galen. Mia had been polite but blunt: was this thing between him and I just casual, or was it more serious than that? I was honest with her about where I saw things, and when I questioned her about Galen's past, she was honest with me.

As I'd long suspected, there'd been another woman in Galen's life. Her name was Charlotte, and she and Galen had been together for years. When I asked Mia what had happened, her answer was cryptic: *'That's not for me to say. If and when he wants to tell you, I'm sure he will.'* I didn't press further because she was right. When Galen's ready to talk about this woman, I trust he will. Until then, I'd at least confirmed my suspicions there *had* been someone else, and whatever had happened was a contributing factor to his guarded nature when we first met.

"Alex?"

His voice pulls me out of my reverie. "Yes, sir?"

"You did catch that I'll be gone for a few days next week?"

"I did. For that man you called Colbie."

"Yeah," he says, his voice going tense. "For him."

"Can I ask what you'll be doing, sir?"

Galen glances over at me. "Do you remember when I said I sometimes do work for the government?"

"Yes."

"Colbie *is* the government." Galen's fingers tighten around the steering wheel. "Let's just say he's a part of it that takes care of things people don't want to talk about."

"Oh."

For a moment the cab of the SUV goes silent. "Listen, I'm not trying to make this out to sound more serious than it actually is, Alex. Colbie, and the men who work for him... they're not good people. They're necessary people, but they're not good."

"Are a lot of the people you work for 'not good people?'" I ask gently.

Galen sighs. "No. But there are enough."

I don't ask him to elaborate, but I can put two and two together. This man Colbie is probably military or CIA or something similar, and the news stories about civilian contractors working for those organizations to keep things off-the-books have not escaped me.

I have a suspicion some of the work Galen does for his commercial clients skirts the edges of legality, too, but I'm equally certain nothing he does runs along the lines of drug-running or human trafficking or anything of that nature. Over the course of my career, I've learned I'm a fairly good judge of character and, while I'm betting Galen has a moral compass that's flexible, I doubt it bends far enough to include those things.

"Thank you, sir." I say quietly.

"For?"

"Trusting me."

He glances my way but doesn't say anything. "You're welcome," he finally says with a nod. A moment later he continues, "I wanted to ask you a favor."

"Okay."

"I want you to stay at my home while I'm gone."

I cock my head. "W—why?"

"I was afraid you'd ask me that." Galen opens and closes his fingers around the steering wheel. "It's hard to explain exactly. It's... there's just a level of comfort and familiarity when you're in my home that goes beyond our power exchange. I don't want you to feel like I'm trying to keep you there like some object I own, or that you're some kind of service sub I also just happen to like fucking." He blows out a deep sigh. "I'm sorry, I'm doing a shitty job of explaining this. I wish I could describe it better, but... it's... it's just important to me." He glances in my direction. "If you're uncomfortable with it, I totally understand. This is *not* an expectation, Alex. This is... a desire."

A hundred thoughts are racing through my head right now, but I narrow them down to a single question I need to ask. "Galen?"

"Yes?"

"Today, when Mia called me your girlfriend, you didn't correct her."

He doesn't look my way but keeps his gaze fixed straight ahead.

"*Am* I your girlfriend, Galen?"

His jaw moves without any words coming out. I wait for him to answer because I *need* him to and I won't do it for him. Finally, he works out whatever's going on inside that head of his because he looks over with resolve in his eyes.

"Yes, Alex. You are."

No, 'would you like to be?' or 'are you're okay with that?' Galen simply tells me I am, and he has no idea how much I need to hear it.

"Okay," I say serenely, "I'll stay at your place."

He reaches across and squeezes my hand. "If you're upset I didn't ask, I under—"

I can't help but chuckle. "Don't overthink it, sir."

"Wow. Hoisted on my own petard."

"Happens to the best of us."

"Well," he says firmly, "just so we're clear, this doesn't mean you're getting out of your time up on the pony when we get home."

I turn my head toward him, dropping my mouth open slowly. "What did I do?"

"'Ooo, Mia please give me all the details about Galen's plane, and how big his dick is and *all* the things!'"

"I did not say that!"

"In so many words."

I huff. "Okay, maybe, but..." I point my finger at him. "You're keeping track."

"Damn right I am."

"That's not fair." I cross my arms over my chest. "My boyfriend's a sadist."

"I like that."

I glance over and find a broad grin creasing his face. "You like being a sadist?"

"No. I like hearing you call me your boyfriend." His grin turns wicked. "And, honestly, the sadist part too."

I shoot him a side-eye glare that has zero sincerity in it. "Should've told Terry I was doing my hair that night."

We smile at each other until it turns into laughter.

~

"*PLEASE, SIR, PLEASE, PLEASE, PLEASE, PLEASE!*"

Galen was true to his word, and I'm straddling the pony. The bastard has me worked up to the point my body is shaking, but still he won't give me the one word that'll let me tumble over the edge into the sweet oblivion I so need right now.

"Do you want to come, Alex?"

"Yes, sir," I pant. "Please..."

"Are we going to tease our Dom again with his friends?"

I want to say yes. I want to have the strength to do it because it would be the perfect comeback, worth whatever punishment Galen might dole out. But my body feels as if it's been plugged directly into a wall socket, and the delicious energy shooting through me balances on that knife's edge between pleasure and pain. If I goad him, he'll likely deny me the orgasm I crave so badly, so the reward for saying no outweighs the reward for saying yes.

Maybe next time.

"No, sir, no, sir, I promise I won't."

He places the stim back on my clit and moves it in a light circular pattern, and I swear I'm going to explode.

"Okay. Then come."

I do.

My body has only just stopped shaking by the time Galen gets me off the pony and curled up in bed. I expect him to fuck me, but instead he just wraps me in a cocoon of warmth that sends me off into a dreamy land hovering just at the edge of subspace.

"Hey," he murmurs into my ear. "You still with me?"

"Mmhmm."

"You're sure about this coming week, right?"

"Yes, sir," I mumble, smiling.

"Good girl."

For a moment I just let him hold me tight, purring each time he kisses the top of my head. There's been a question perched at the back of my mind since we began playing tonight, so before I drift off completely, I ask. "Sir?"

"Yes?"

"You know I wasn't trying to be disrespectful."

He kisses me again. "I know."

"If I went too far, please let me know."

"You didn't, Alex." He runs his thumb along my cheek gently. "If you can make Mia call you her best friend after only one meeting, you clearly didn't go too far."

"Your friends are nice."

He chuckles. "So are you."

"Do you think they liked me?"

He kisses me once more, holding it for a long second this time. "I know they did. Now go to sleep."

The rest of the weekend goes by in a warm, comfortable blur. Galen and I go over some details of my stay while he's gone, and we map out the best ways for me to make the commute to and from work on a weekday. Galen will be leaving early Tuesday morning and he won't be back until late Wednesday night, assuming nothing goes wrong. I'll only be here two days and three nights without him, but it's that latter part—without him—that's both intriguing and disquieting in equal measure.

"You'll be fine, trust me. Just remember the rules."

"Wait…" I look up from the edge of the chair into his eyes. "Do I… do I have to be naked even when you're not here?"

Galen stares back with a chiding look. "What do *you* think, Alex?"

I drop my gaze to my lap, pursing my lips. "I think I should have kept my mouth shut."

On my way home from work Monday evening, I stop at my condo to pick up a few things. Over the month we've been together, I've migrated some personal belongings to Galen's house, but for this stay I want a few others. It's not much, but a few things that'll make the stay a little more comfortable,

We spend most of Monday night in bed, but I sleep fitfully when I do manage to drift off. Nervous energy keeps waking me up. It's four-thirty when Galen's alarm goes off, and even though he tells me to stay where I am, he doesn't seem too upset when I defy him and join him in the shower.

"You really are a distraction," he murmurs against my wet skin.

"Good. That means I'm exceeding your expectations."

He laughs, and then he makes me hiss in pleasure, and then…

I'm afraid I've made him late, but as I towel him dry, Galen tells me he planned for this possibility. We finish, he dresses, and then one minute I'm kneeling in the kitchen looking up at him as he takes the mug of coffee I've prepared, the next the house is silent, his presence gone.

I could go back to the bedroom and slip on a robe, or one of his shirts, but I don't. There's no chance I'm going back to sleep, so instead, I go to the study and lean against the edge of the chair. I swear I can smell him, feel his presence in this room so uniquely him, and it's calming. I look around at the muted gray of the walls, the contrast of the white bookcases and the rainbow pattern of book spines, the feel of the soft leather of the chair brushing my cheek. I've come to look forward to the time he and I spend here, whether talking or simply sitting in silence as he strokes my hair. He's been gone less than an hour, but the room feels emptier than it should, and I roll my eyes at myself for the moment of drama in the sentiment.

When I come home from work that evening, I do as I've always done when I come here. I go to the bedroom, remove my clothing, and putt it away. I go back to the kitchen and fix myself a salad and eat it at the counter rather than the dining room. It feels more appropriate, and I scroll through texts and emails on my phone, hoping he might have left me a message. He warned me it might not be possible, but I still feel a pang of disappointment when there's nothing.

When I've finished eating and cleaned and put everything away, I migrate back to the study. There's still a little of the lonely feeling I'd felt this morning, but it's not as pronounced, and there's none of the uncomfortable or awkward feelings I was afraid I might have. I've only been spending weekends here for a little over a month, but in many respects, I've grown as comfortable here as at my own place.

It occurs to me Galen's never been to my condo. Most of the time we've spent together has been here. To be fair, I've never thought to invite him to my home, and I wonder if he's been waiting for me to ask. It's not that my place is crappy or anything —for the money I've spent, it damn sure shouldn't be. But it's not nearly as big as Galen's, and we've established certain patterns here which wouldn't be possible at my place. Still, it's something to consider for the future.

When I step into the study, I move toward my spot next to his chair but then stop. Since Galen's not here, I indulge in something I haven't before: I move to the bookcases and begin looking through the shelves. Glancing at the titles on the spines, it becomes apparent Galen has eclectic tastes in reading material.

There are books I expect: manuals on packaging, handling, and shipping. There are others which are clearly focused on other aspects of the running of his business. But then I find a section on national parks, world wonders, all sorts of travel Galen's never spoken about. It's clear we have so much more to learn about each other, and I'm warmed by the idea of the time we'll spend doing it.

The more I scan his bookcases, the more intrigued I become. He's got cookbooks in one section, which isn't terribly surprising. But then there's a small section of graphic novels, and I pull some of them out and flip through them in fascination. There's a series called *Saga*, which seems to be about a family in some sort of post-apocalyptic sci-fi world. Another is a space opera using Russian themes as its basis, and the final series I pick through is called *Sunstone* and I...

I kneel on the floor in front of the bookcase and become totally absorbed for a half hour. It's a love story between two women enmeshed in a BDSM relationship, and while I've never been a comic book person, the story and themes are so well-written, so perfectly developed, and so totally relatable, I'm not even aware how much time has passed when I finally stop.

"*Sunstone*," I murmur, looking back at the cover one more time. I move to put it away, then change my mind and keep it. *Just some light bedtime reading to pass the time.* I'm sure Galen won't mind. He did tell me to feel free to explore, and this... this has been a fascinating peek into parts of him that haven't come up in the time we've spent together.

As I'm getting up, I notice the box. It didn't catch my eye at first because it's innocuous looking, tucked away on a lower shelf. It's the only thing I've seen so far that isn't a book, and my curiosity is piqued, so instead of heading off I move toward it.

The box slides out with ease, and I take the lid off carefully. The only thing visible at first is a stack of papers, and at a quick glance they appear to be documents relating to his business. This is starting to feel like prying, so I begin putting them back. As I do, however, further down I see the corner of a picture poking out, and I work my way down until it comes into view.

"Oh," I whisper as the last page lifts free.

It's a young Galen, and he's in uniform. I'm not much on military things, but the little black lettering over his left breast spells out 'U.S. Army,' so it's clear what branch he served in. It's a posed shot, obviously taken after he completed training of some sort. He looks so young, so serious.

He never told you he served. Yet another thing he's kept hidden

There's another picture underneath the first. This time he's standing by some gigantic Army vehicle, the tire of it nearly as tall as he is. His sleeves are rolled up, and Galen's in good shape right now, but here... the muscles of his arms are whipcord tight, his skin bronzed. Wherever this was taken is somewhere in the desert, and it doesn't take a rocket scientist to guess where *that* might be. He's got goggles pushed up on the front of the helmet he's wearing, and though he's smiling, there's strain around his eyes that doesn't go unnoticed.

There are two more pictures of him in uniform, and I expect the next to be another, but it's not.

It's a picture of three people. Two men standing with a woman sandwiched between them. They're all smiling, looking directly at the camera, casually dressed in jeans and shirts as if they're outdoors at a park or hiking somewhere. The one man is dark haired, with an aquiline nose. A handsome man, European-looking in that way you see and immediately assume sometimes. He's standing close to the woman but not touching her, well enough within her personal space to clearly be a friend and not some random stranger. The woman... the woman is beautiful. Her blue eyes are piercing, and her hair frames her face in a whorl of wheat-gold swirls, clearly natural and not dyed. Her cheeks glow, making her smile a brilliant sunburst of happiness that leaps from the photo.

The other man is Galen.

I swallow as I stare at him. Galen has his arm wrapped around the woman's waist, his hip pulled tight against hers. Her hand disappears behind his back, and from the angle I'd guess she's got it stuffed in one of his pockets or his waistband. His face is turned to her, and the look on it...

Fondness can sometimes be mistaken for devotion as devotion can be mistaken for love. But there is nothing to be mistaken about the look on Galen's face. As I stare at the picture, I'm positive who the woman is, and another piece of a puzzle I didn't know I was putting together falls into place.

"Charlotte."

I flip the picture over to see if there's anything to prove my suspicion, but the back is blank, whatever watermark there might have been long since faded. I set this picture aside and pick up the next. This time it's just Galen and the woman. They're obviously at a party somewhere and they're sitting close together. The woman looks like a model: poised, sophisticated, perfect. Again, Galen's not looking at the camera, but toward her. If I thought I was mistaken about his look in the first picture, that notion is driven away with this one.

Galen Harmon was in love with this woman who I'm almost certain is the Charlotte Mia spoke to me about.

There are two more pictures of them together, and it's always the same: she's smiling or laughing as she stares into the camera, and Galen's always looking at her, enraptured. I knew Galen had been in a high protocol relationship before we met, and Mia had spoken to me oblique about the woman he'd been involved with, but nothing in any of these images suggests a strained relationship.

Looks can be deceiving.

A thought occurs to me, and I go back through each photo, flipping them to the reverse sides. It takes a second, but I find what I suspected. At some point, all these pictures were trapped in picture frames. There are little indentations in the paper I recognize from having done similar to pictures myself. I imagine these placed in simple, elegant frames, the kind you might find scattered around your house to remind you of the person you love.

I pick up the next photo, and this one is like the first: it's Galen and Charlotte with the same dark-haired man. This is another party picture, both of the men looking chic in expensive black suits, Charlotte elegant in a deep crimson dress that highlights everything about her. Galen once again has his arm around her, his face turned toward her. The other man is standing just behind and to the left, his hand lightly touching Charlotte's shoulder. Whoever he is, he's clearly a good friend in some capacity.

I gaze at several more shots until I come to the final one. Again, it's of the three of them. This time I recognize where they are. It's a room I've spent time plenty of time in myself. The depth of field of the shot blurs the Mondrian print in the background— his picture was taken in the living room less than fifty feet from where I'm kneeling. If it's a party, it's a casual one, and again Charlotte is gazing into the camera, her face turned as if she's just finished saying something to the other man. Galen is staring at Charlotte as before, and I almost miss it.

He's not smiling.

He doesn't look angry, but in every other picture he's been smiling in a way that makes it clear how much he's in love. Something's happened in this pic. He looks relaxed, comfortable, but there's a tension to the set of his face. A tightness at the corners of his eyes I recognize because I've tried to make sure nothing I ever do warrants it. There's no way to know what's happened prior to this, but the signs are unmistakable. Galen isn't pleased.

There are more papers below this last picture, but I've seen enough. I put everything carefully back into place, then return the box to the shelf where I found it. I could—maybe should—feel uncomfortable having gone through it, but I don't. I abandon the bookcases and move back to the study. I kneel in my familiar spot by the chair and sit and think.

Charlotte. I don't know her last name, but I don't need to. All that matters is Galen was clearly in love with her, and she a large part of his life who now isn't. Terry once told me they'd been longtime members of Black Light. Like Mia, he didn't go into details, he only told me something had taken place and they were no longer together.

It's not unusual for couples in the lifestyle to split up. I'd seen my fair share of it. But something about this seems different. There's more than just one piece of this puzzle missing. I've given Galen the space he's asked for to discuss his past with me when he sees fit, but now I'm really. Something intense definitely took place to turn the look on his face from the first pic into the one in the last.

Sleep doesn't come easy once I crawl into bed. With Galen here, the bed had always seemed big, now it's an ocean of sheets and covers, and it feels as if I'm fighting to keep my head above them. When I finally do drift off, it's with the image of Galen's face in that final picture. Collected as always, but beneath the surface something is simmering, and it's a gaze I never want directed at me.

And as sleep overtakes me, I realize what I really want is the one I saw in all the others.

Galen hasn't returned home by the time I arrive the next evening. He told me he might be late, but a part of me hoped he might make it back first. I fix myself a simple dinner, clean up the kitchen after I finish, then go to the study and kneel beside his chair to wait. When the security alarm chimes it's almost ten, and I move to my spot in the kitchen when he's here.

The door from the garage closes with a *thunk*, and the sound of Galen's boots on the entry tile draws close until it comes to a stop.

"Perfection," he says quietly, dropping his bag to the floor.

He approaches until he's beside me, reaching with his hand to stroke my hair.

"Welcome back, sir," I say, my head still bowed.

His fingers tighten, and he tilts my head up. "It's good to be back."

It takes effort not to suck in my breath. It's not delicious spikes of pain running across my scalp. It's Galen's face. He looks drawn, tired, and there's a tightness around his eyes that mimics the creases I saw in that picture. Whatever's taken place on this trip has not been all fun and games.

"Are... are you okay, sir?"

He stares down at me. "Yeah. I'm... I'll be fine."

"Please tell me what I can do."

"A drink would be nice," he says in a weary voice, and I'm scrambling up even before he's fully let me go.

I go to the bar and prepare his bourbon, and when I return, I find him not in the kitchen but in the study, collapsed in his chair. I kneel at the side and offer up the glass with both hands. He takes it, and I listen as he takes a long drink.

"Rough trip?" I finally say.

"It was fine."

"You seem tired."

"I said I'm fine."

He doesn't raise his voice, but the snap of his tone is clear.

"Sorry, sir."

"You don't need to apologize."

I open my mouth to apologize again but bite off the words before I do.

We sit in silence, but unlike every other time we've been in here, Galen doesn't reach to caress me. Instead, he sits with his drink in one hand, rubbing his temple slowly with the other. Finally, the silence—and Galen's reticence, which is unlike anything I've experienced from him until tonight—get the best of me.

"Are you sure everything's okay, si—"

"What did I tell you about making me repeat myself, Alex?"

"I'm sorry, it's just—"

"It's just what? I've told you three times now I'm fine. I'm a little tired but otherwise…" He lets out a deep sigh. "Everything's fine."

"Yes, sir. I'm sor—"

"Don't. Fucking. Say. It," he growls roughly, and I clamp my mouth shut.

The room goes silent once more, and for the first time since I've come into Galen's home, I don't feel welcome here. I feel like an intruder. Whatever happened over the last two days can't have been good to put Galen in this mood, and rather than leaning on me to help him through it, it feels as if he's keeping me at arm's length.

He must sense some of my tension because a moment later he blows out a deep sigh. "Sorry. I know I'm not the best company right now."

"It's okay, sir," I whisper.

He grunts, and I hear ice tinkle in his glass as he finishes his drink. Left to let my own thoughts, they spin off into a million directions until coalescing into a sudden apprehension. Galen looks fine from all outward appearances, but... could something have happened to...

"Sir?"

"What?"

"Are... are Mia and Deacon okay?"

He's pushing up from the chair. "Jesus fucking Christ," he mutters and begins stalking from the room.

"Galen." I scramble up and move after him, my anxiety turning into full-blown fear. He's halfway down the hall before I catch up. "Galen. Are they okay?"

He doesn't answer or break stride to look back at me. Instead, he ignores me and pushes through the door into the bedroom before coming to a stop.

"Galen..."

He whirls. "You're my submissive, right, or did I just fucking dream all that up? You're the one who claimed you wanted my guidance, my direction, to serve and obey me because it's so freeing. And now you do this? Alex, if I tell you things are fine then you need to fucking stop pestering me and trust that things are fine!"

"Oh, yes, sir. Because the way you're acting right now certainly proves nothing could possibly be wrong."

He takes a step toward me, stabbing a finger in my face. "Don't you fucking dare accuse me of lying. I have *never* lied to you. Ever."

"But you've withheld, haven't you? You kept me in the dark about the truth."

I've never seen Galen truly angry. I see it now. A cold fire that turns his eyes almost black, the muscles along his neck whipcord taut, and what I saw a tiny bit of in that photograph from last night is increased here in front of me tenfold.

I don't like it. Not one bit.

"If I choose not to tell you about something it's because it's my fucking choice, not yours. And you may also rest assured if I don't tell you about something, it's for your own fucking good. What you need to do is respect those choices and obey me."

"Is that right?' I say tonelessly. I'm drawing on every skill I've learned over the years negotiating with difficult clients, and it hurts all the more I'm having to do it with Galen right now.

"Yes, that's right."

"I think I'm going home." I turn to head for the door.

"The fuck you are." In four large strides, he sidesteps his way around me to block my path. "You're not abandoning me. You're staying right here."

'Abandoning me.' There's something about the way he says it, the tone of his voice and the way he's looking at me that makes me stop. I recognize with absolute clarity there's a piece of the puzzle buried within his statement, and I pick it up. "Okay, Galen. I'll stay with you tonight, but I'm not sleeping with you."

"Fine," he growls. "Sleep on the floor." He points to the foot of the bed.

It's a power move, pure and simple, and not a pretty one. I can stand here and argue with him about how wrong what he's telling me to do is, how much it violates everything we've negotiated in our dynamic, but that's clearly what he wants. He *wants* a fight with me. He wants to believe I'm disobeying him because, wrong as it may be, that would justify his actions, at least in his mind.

So instead of giving him that, I turn wordlessly and move to the end of the bed. Keeping my gaze glued to his, I kneel, then slowly position myself until I'm wrapped up in a curl on the carpet.

Galen stands and stares as I do, hands clenched at his sides. "Fine," he eventually mutters, then stalks off to the bathroom.

I hear him banging around, slamming doors and further muttering. Hot tears streak my cheeks, but I don't really cry. I've heard couples reminisce about their 'first fight,' but this doesn't feel like any of those descriptions. Mostly they've been explained as 'it was over the stupidest thing,' but nothing about this is stupid. Something's happened, Galen's in pain and, instead of looking to me for comfort, he's lashing out. And *that* hurts far more than it should.

Several minutes pass before it grows quiet. I don't look up, but I feel his eyes on me. He huffs out a low burr of irritation but says nothing as he crawls into the bed. A moment later, the lights go out, and then there's silence.

I've no idea how much time passes. Sleep's not going to come easy tonight if it comes at all. I've little doubt Galen's intention is to try and outlast me and I'm betting he'll expect me to be the first to break, to ask or beg or plead or something. He's an idiot if he thinks I'll do it. I may be his submissive, but I'm not weak. If he wants a fight from me, he's gonna need to bring it. I *do* care for him, but I refuse to be walked over, and I won't do his dirty work for him.

The first crack appears. He turns over in the bed, twisting in the covers, and grunts out a sigh. The room stills, but ten minutes can't have passed when he does it again.

Ball's in your court, sir.

I wait as it happens a third time, then a fourth. I can do this all night, but Galen obviously can't.

"Why the fuck are you down there?" he finally asks, his voice gruff.

"Because you told me to, sir."

"Well, I'm a fucking idiot. Get up here."

I could push and tell him no, tell him if he has anything to say to me that doesn't start with an apology, he can say it while I'm down here. I don't, though. Instead, I simply get up from the floor and move to the edge of the bed to sit across from him.

Even in the darkness I can see Galen's sitting with his back braced against the headboard, and a second later the lights come up as he turns them to low.

"This isn't the homecoming I'd planned."

In any other circumstances I'd have my head down, but not right now. I may be his submissive, but there's nothing submissive about how I'm feeling at the moment. "It certainly isn't what I envisioned either." I glance over at him, and his face is still drawn and now even more weary looking. It stabs at me, but there's no justifying what he said or did. "Can you at least tell me one thing?"

"What?"

"Are Mia and Deacon okay?"

Heat flares in his eyes briefly, and his mouth comes open for a second. He closes it slowly, and his gaze cools before he finally speaks. "Yes, Alex, they're fine."

"Thank you."

"I shouldn't have snapped at you."

"No, Galen, you shouldn't have."

I'll give him credit; he doesn't look away or try to argue he had reasons. He just nods, and we stare at each other for a long moment.

"It… it was a rough trip. I'd rather not go into it right now, okay? Just give me a little time. Please."

I dip my head in recognition. "Okay. If you need time to process, I can wait. However, let me be clear about something: I won't be an emotional punching bag for you to work your anger and frustration out on when you come home like this."

"Goddammit, Alex, that's not what I meant—"

I raise my hand. "It doesn't matter what you meant. It's what you did. And I know you didn't do it intentionally, but it *did* happen. Believe me, you're not the first person that's done this. I've dealt with situations like this in my career plenty of times. Here's the thing, though: while I might have to accept it from a difficult client, I don't from a lover. I'm willing to obey you and follow your rules because those truly are parts of what I crave in our dynamic. But there are rules *you* need to follow too, and one of them is you will never, ever treat me like you did tonight in a fit of anger."

Galen has always looked so confident, so in control and self-assured. He doesn't look that way right now. He looks defeated, and if I wasn't so upset, I'd reach out and pull myself to him. But I don't. Instead, I sit on my side of the bed, arms wrapped around my knees, gazing at him.

"I'm sorry, Alex," he says gloomily.

"I know you are. So am I."

Running a hand over his head, Galen scrubs at his hair as if the gesture alone might clear away some of what's taken place this evening. "I was serious, Alex. Yeah, things were rough this trip, but everyone's okay. I'll be okay. I just need a little time to decompress." He looks at me with a smile I'm certain he wants to be reassuring, except it isn't. "You have to trust me, okay?"

"You keep demanding I trust you, but are you exempt from that, Galen? Trust is a two-way street. If you can't trust me, how am I supposed to trust you?"

"I do trust you."

"Do you? Do you really?"

"Yes, of course I do!" he says in exasperation.

"You have an odd way of showing it."

"What's that supposed to mean?"

"Like I said earlier, you withhold. That's not a sign of trust, Galen."

"I'm protecting you."

"I'd rather you trust I can handle whatever it is that's going on." I stare at him pointedly.

151

He groans. "It's not that simple."

"Because you can't trust me?"

"Don't twist my words."

"I'm just saying..."

We both fall silent. Galen leans back against the headboard, tilting his head to stare at the ceiling. He looks more tired now than he did when he arrived, and that sends a pang shooting through me.

"I'm sorry, Galen. I swear this wasn't how I wanted this evening to go."

"I know."

I move up onto the bed and lean back against the headboard beside him. There's less than an arm's length separating us, but it feels like a mile.

"Sure would be a whole lot easier if you could just order me to obey rather than have to deal with this, wouldn't it?"

He turns his head to stare at me. "Would that work?"

"No," I say, shaking my head. "No, it wouldn't."

"*Pfft.*" He turns his head back, closing his eyes. "Just my luck I'd find a beautiful, intelligent, *and* strong-willed submissive."

I smile at the compliment. And though it does lessen a bit of the sting of what's taken place, it doesn't wipe it all away.

We lay quietly together, and I think maybe he's drifted off, but he finally speaks. "I suppose after my bullshit tonight going with me to the party on Saturday is out?"

"Did I say that?"

"No. I just assumed."

"Right this moment I honestly *don't*, but I *would* like to see my BFF Mia, and since you're my plus one..."

Galen chuckles ruefully. "I guess I should count my blessings you're even willing to go with me as your plus one, all things considered."

"Yeah, you should." I smile at him, and for a second he looks back in a way I remember from before he left.

He rolls to his side to face me. For a moment we just stare at each other, and a part of me wants to slide across the covers and slip into his arms. To feel him draw me in tight and forget any of this has happened. But I won't do that. I want things to go back to being the way they were, but that can only happen if he understands this can never happen again.

From our first night at Black Light, I played his game by his rules, and I loved it. But tonight, he needs to make the effort. He needs to show me he understands that even for a submissive who craves his dominance and control, I won't be taken for granted.

"Alex, I know we're not done, but I'm exhausted. Can we continue this in the morning?"

It's fair. I'll give him credit: at least he's not pretending to think just because we've talked and he's calmed down, this is over.

"I understand." I give him a gentle smile and start to turn to my side.

"No." His voice is firm, but it's not the same commanding one he's used on other occasions. It's a request, an expression of desire, and I suspect it's tied to those two words he used early. The ones I'm not sure he even realized he said.

'Abandon me...'

I roll back. "What, Galen?"

"Please."

He reaches and pulls me to him. I try not to stiffen because it's clear he needs to believe this is behind us, at least for tonight. But it's not. I'll give him what he's asking for because I *do* care for him. He's a good Dom, a good man, and this one instance can't completely erase every incredible thing that's happened between us. But I won't demand he tell me what happened on his trip, nor will I pressure him to talk about Charlotte and everything I found in that box, either. He needs to come to me. To take stock and realize I didn't abandon him when I had every right to. He needs to step up and play by the rules, whether his or mine.

He needs to *trust me*. We're not just playing BDSM games

anymore; we're in a *relationship* now. And if he won't trust me, if he simply can't, then there's no future for us. And if that's the case, I won't just stay here just for the sake of continuing the high protocol dynamic we're engaged in, no matter how good it's been. We're beyond the fuckbuddy stage here, and if that's all this relationship is ever going to be...

I'm out.

CHAPTER 13

GALEN

"Oh my God, Galen!"

I've no idea what she expects. You can't look as fucking gorgeous as she does in the shower and just assume I'll not take advantage of the situation.

I spin her around and grip her wrists, pinning them to the marble tile. She squirms beneath my grasp, and I step into her, making sure she feels exactly what she's done to me and what I plan on doing. "Be. Still."

"Sir," she whimpers, wiggling her butt against the pressure of my hips. "We're going to be late!"

"Fashionably late," I growl into her ear as I take her lobe between my teeth.

"Oh, God," she moans as I maneuver myself into position. "Sir... Mia... I told her we'd be there..."

"Well now you'll have something to talk about."

I push into Alex's pussy, and it's clear for all her protesting she's as ready for this as I am. She wraps me in slick warmth that makes my cock jerk. I press up into her until my thighs connect with her ass, then I just hold her there, hilted inside.

Alex gasps, tilting her head back.

"I think someone forgot who's in charge here," I rumble.

"No, sir. Never, sir."

"Then what are you going to do, Alex?"

"Take your cock, sir."

"Does it matter what time we get to the party?"

"No, sir."

I reach down to the apex of her legs, drawing my index finger over her clit, flicking up over the hood to drag a hiss out of her. "Whose pussy is this?"

"Yours, sir."

"Whose cum do you want?"

"Yours, sir. Always yours."

"Who's going to fuck you?"

"You, sir," she whispers.

And I do.

I'm cognizant Alex and I are still working through what happened the other night but I'm arrogant and self-absorbed enough to take her at her word this morning when she reminded me not to 'overthink' things.

"*Nnngh...*" she groans as I swirl my thumb over her clit. It's not as easy as they make it look in porn. Both of us are slippery with water and keeping one hand cupped to her ribcage while holding her in place as I tease her hood with the other *and* continuing to fuck her is a bit of a balancing act. The shower tiles are glossed with wetness, as are the walls where her hands are braced, and while shower sex is fun, keeping all the parts in the right places is entirely different than tossing her around in our bed.

Not that any of that is going to stop me.

"Oh, God, sir," Alex whispers as she clenches down on me.

"Mmm. Feels good, doesn't it?"

"Yes."

"Do you want to come?"

"Yes."

"I want to come in you."

"Please. Please..."

"Uh uh uh," I tell her reproachfully. "Not yet. Fashionably late..."

Alex hisses. "Oh my God, your timing is something else."

I chuckle, then drive hard into her. She gives me the exact gasp I was hoping for, and now this stops being a game and becomes something far more animalistic. The noises Alex is making are driving me toward the edge, and I won't be able to hold out much longer. However, teasing her is just as potent, and making her fucking come first before I give in to my own release is my priority right now.

"Are you close, Alex? Are you?"

"*Yeeesss,*" she cries in frustration.

"God, your clit feels so swollen." I slam into her, and she whimpers in response. "You want to come, don't you? Don't you?"

"Please, dammit... please..."

God, I shouldn't love this as much as I do. Torturing her like this shouldn't feel so good.

Except it does. It's a drug.

"Are you sure?"

"Yes, sir, yes, sir, *yessiryessiryessir...*" The words become a babble, and I need her to come *right now* because I'm fucking lost, teetering at the edge of a cliff there's zero chance I can stop myself from falling over.

"Then fucking come." I thrust hard and, for several seconds I have no idea if she has or not because my cock's jerking, my body rigid in orgasm as I give myself into it.

Alex is gasping when I finally come back to the present, and the wetness smearing my fingers is not just the wetter cascading the length of her body. She's come or made a damn good impression of it, and since being truthful to each other has been the main focus of our conversations the last twenty-four hours, I'm betting this isn't an act.

"Goddamn, Alex, you are incredible," I rumble against her ear.

"Thank you, sir," she responds in a breathy voice.

I pull her into my arms, holding her tight to my chest and, for a long moment, I luxuriate in the feeling of her body against mine. Right now, I could forego the party, screw over Deacon and Mia and let them handle the negotiations that need to take place, all to take this woman back to my bed and do this over and over again.

I could, but I won't.

"Okay, come on. We need to get ready for the party."

"Mmm," Alex murmurs, grinding her ass against me, and my dick twitches in response.

"Oh, you're a *very* bad girl," I say, chuckling. "Stop that. Finish cleaning me, and let's get going."

Alex turns in my arms, a wicked grin unfolding across her face. And to be fair, she follows the letter of the law, if not the intent.

I'd figured maybe forty-five minutes late is what we'd be. It's an hour-twenty by the time we're both dressed and in the car heading toward the hotel.

"*Grr.*" Alex slips her cell back into her clutch.

"What?" I already know what she's irritated about but I ask anyway because I find her little displays of frustration amusing.

"It's nothing, sir."

"Oh, really? Mia's not giving you shit for not being there already?" I hide my grin.

She wiggles in exasperation. "No offense, sir, but we're over an hour late."

"None taken. I'd have gladly made it two if I could have fucked you again after what you did."

She rolls her eyes. "I don't have any idea how I'm going to explain this."

"Don't worry. I'll take care of it."

Alex snaps her head in my direction. "You wouldn't, sir."

"Is that a challenge?"

Her eyes go wide before she looks down quickly. "No, sir."

"I thought so."

When we arrive at the party, Deacon and Mia intercept.

"Goddammit, brother," Deacon says under his breath, "I thought you were gonna bail on us."

"Blame her," I say, tilting my head toward Alex standing at my side.

Alex's mouth and eyes go wide in retort. "I—"

Mia cuts her off, punching me hard in the bicep. "I know you're an asshole, Galen, but don't be a *fucking* asshole. This has nothing to do with Alex and you know it."

"Maybe." Mia may be smaller than me, but she's still got a wicked slug, and the hit throbs. "Anyways, we're here. Have you seen Paul yet?"

Deacon grunts. "Yeah, he's around. He's already asked about where you were twice. I made up an excuse you were having car trouble."

"Good cover, thanks." I glance around the room. "Okay, let's get drinks for the ladies and then we'll see if we can find him."

Mia shakes her head, raising a finger. "Um, no. You get drinks for yourselves and go find Mr. Gaither. Alex and I will take care of ourselves."

"I'd rather—"

Mia doesn't even wait for me to finish. Hooking her arm through Alex's, she pulls her away, leaving Deacon and me standing alone.

"That's not gonna go well for you," Deacon says as the two of them walk away.

"Probably not." And knowing Mia, it probably won't.

Deacon and I head to the bar and get our drinks. Moving off to the side, both of us scan the room. The party isn't huge, but there are at least a hundred people here, most of them mingling. For the moment, I've lost sight of Mia and Alex, nor is there any sign of the man we're here to meet.

"Maybe he left," Deacon says, his head swiveling.

"He better not have. I know he's got the upper hand here, but we've done right by him in the past, and if he tries to play hardball now, I'll make sure people know it's a one-way street."

"Well, maybe if you hadn't been late…"

I turn my face to his.

"Just saying. Hope it was worth it."

"Don't start with me, Deacon."

"Lissen, Alex is a very attractive woman. I'm not blaming you."

"Does no one understand the concept of being fashionably late anymore?"

"Brother." Deacon gives me the side-eye. "There's fashionably late and then there's just fucking late. You were fucking late."

I sigh and take a drink. "Okay, maybe." I glance over at him. "And, yes, it was."

He grins, and we continue our watch.

I've made maybe a half dozen passes over the crowd and there is still no sign of Paul Gaither. There's also no sign of Alex and Mia. Deacon's warning aside, I'm not worried. Considering what Alex said she and Mia spent most of their time talking about the last time they were together—including that bullshit story about the dollar bill and my dick—I've a feeling she's likely bringing Mia up to speed on how our relationship is progressing. I put the two of them out of my mind for the moment because my irritation's growing that Deacon may be right, and Paul's skipped out on us.

A few minutes go by, and I see Mia and Alex weaving their way through the crowd.

"Did you find him?" Mia asks as they approach.

"Not yet," Deacon grumbles. "I told Galen he probably bailed, late as he showed up."

Mia shakes her head. "No. He's here somewhere. He can smell a nickel from a mile away and he's not about to let this opportunity pass." She looks around, then her gaze latches onto mine. "Deacon, let's you and I go see if we can find out where he's hiding. Alex and Galen can hold down the fort here."

Deacon glances at the three of us, then shrugs. "Might as well. Ain't turning up shit just standing here."

The two of them move off, leaving Alex and me alone.

"Mia looks nice this evening," Alex says diplomatically.

She does. The first time Alex met Mia she was wearing that ratty Nomex flight suit she's had since she got out of the Army. Tonight, Mia looks like a completely different person. The deep red, almost black dress she's wearing is beautiful. The color compliments Mia's dark, auburn hair cascading over her shoulders instead of being pulled back into the ponytail it normally is.

"Yeah, she cleans up well, doesn't she?"

Alex shoots me a pointed look. "Until tonight I didn't realize she had tattoos. You can't really see them when she's wearing that jumpsuit. I admire the fact that in a situation like this"— Alex motions to the room around us—"she doesn't try to *hide* them."

There's something about the way Alex emphasizes the word that sets alarm bells off in my head.

"Mia's never been one to take the opinion of others too much to heart. She pretty much has a *I-don't-give-two-shits* attitude about that sort of thing."

"Mmhmm. It's refreshing to have a friend who's confident enough to trust that others won't judge them even after they've exposed what was previously hidden."

Oh, shit.

I turn to face Alex. "What did she tell you?"

She stares up at me, and the look on her face is a mixture of apprehension and frustration. "You were shot at, Galen."

Fuck.

I pull Alex to the side of the room where we'll have a little more privacy. "Look, it's happened before. This wasn't the first time."

"I don't give a damn."

"See?" I say, pointing a finger at her. "This is why I didn't say anything. You're just getting yourself upset."

Alex's mouth drops. "Are you... are you seriously that dense? Of course, I'm upset! Galen, those men were *shooting at you*. You, Mia, Deacon... you could have been killed."

"Maybe. But we weren't."

"Oh. Well, that makes it all better." She turns her face away from me.

"Alex, can we please not do this here."

She whirls back to face me. "Galen, I've been giving you a lot of space and I'll keep doing it for now, mostly because Mia's asked me to. But I have to be honest with you—my patience is finite. You've been at me about trust, trust, trust, and we both know that's a big component to any serious BDSM dynamic. But if the trust in our relationship ends when we come out of the bedroom or the playroom, I think we need to seriously reevaluate where we're at with each other."

"I'm trying to protect you."

"Dammit, Galen." Her voice bleeds frustration. "I don't need you to protect me. I'm a grown woman and I can protect myself. I need you to *trust me*. I'm willing to give you time because I care about you, but if there are parts of your world where something like what Mia told me can happen, then keeping me in the dark isn't protecting me. It's just making me completely vulnerable."

Before I can respond I catch movement out of the corner of my eye. It's Deacon and Mia approaching, and they've got someone else with them.

"There you are."

Paul Gaither approaches us, his hand thrust forward.

"Paul." I shake his hand. "Good to see you." Motioning to Alex, I say, "Paul, this is Alexandria Carre. Alex, this is my associate, Paul Gaither."

Paul takes Alex's hand and kisses it, his gaze traveling the length of her. "A pleasure, Ms. Carre." He glances over at me. "Deacon said you had car trouble getting here."

"Just a little."

"I'm surprised you made it at all," he replies, and Alex's cheeks flush.

I smile, letting him have his moment. In the small world I travel in, Paul Gaither is a man who makes things happen. As I mentioned to Deacon, we've worked together before He's done things for us, and we've done things for him, and for everyone it's been mutually beneficial. Colbie has a task for us to deliver those two containers sitting in our hangar, and Paul is the one man I know who can get them where they need to be.

"Thanks for meeting with us tonight." I motion to the party going on around us. "Is there someplace we might be able to talk in private?"

His eyes narrow. "Business at a party? With such beautiful company?"

"'Fraid so."

"You're a foolish man, Galen, but I'll humor you." He gestures with his hand across the room, and all three of us follow.

Paul ushers us into a small meeting room. There are a few random tables spread about, most of them without chairs except for one that has several seats loosely arranged around it, a laptop set to one side.

"I try not to mix work with pleasure, but it never seems to escape me." He gives us a slight shrug.

"I understand completely. Sorry to intrude like this."

"Eh. You did mention in your email you had something you wished to discuss." He moves to the edge of the table and balances against it, crossing his arms. "So, what brings you to me tonight, Galen?"

Before I'm able to answer a brief *psss* cuts through the air, followed by an earthy, pungent aroma.

"Hope you don't mind," Mia says, releasing a small cloud of smoke.

I don't know where she's kept it, but it's there now: a cigar she's gripping between two fingers, a wisp drifting away above her head.

"Mia, how long have we known each other?"

"I dunno, Paul. Couple of years?"

"And in those 'couple of years,' have I ever been able to stop you from doing what you want?"

Mia shrugs. "I forget. Maybe once?"

"If I've been lucky." Paul shakes his head, muttering something I don't quite catch.

"*Pardon?*" a voice next to me says quietly.

I glance to my left, and Alex has her head tilted, her eyes narrowed. If Paul heard her, he chooses to ignore it, instead continuing with our conversation.

"As I said, how can I help, Galen?"

"We have an assignment from Mr. Colbie."

"How unfortunate for you." Paul's tone decreases in warmth by several degrees, and I haven't even told him where he fits in. I'm not surprised, though. We've both dealt with Colbie before, and as Deacon, Mia and I just experienced, working for the man is never easy.

"It's two containers. We need help getting them somewhere."

"Where?"

"Prymors'k."

"And how do you think I can help with that?"

I stare at him. "C'mon, Paul."

His eyes turn icy. "I'll remind you of what happened the last time I helped transport some of Mr. Colbie's goods for him."

"Listen"—I hold up my hands—"after the week I've just had, you're preaching to the fucking choir. But the CIA isn't someone you just say no to." I snap a quick glance at Alex because I've never used the exact agency Colbie nominally works for in her presence before. Her gaze is fixated on Paul, however, and if she's surprised, she makes no indication of it.

"Perhaps that's true for you, but I have my limitations."

"And you're saying Prymors'k is a limit more so than, say... Tin Daoulne?"

"That's a continent away and under a completely different political climate."

"So?"

"Let's just say I'm risk averse."

"You? Risk averse?" I cock an eyebrow. "Since when?"

"One gets older. One decides that the thrill of meeting a beautiful woman"—he motions to Alex—"outweighs the thrill of going where one shouldn't be."

Deacon sighs. "Come on, Mr. Gaither. None of us are buying that. What is it about Prymors'k that's got your nuts in a knot?"

"Deacon, you're a good man, but I've been dealing with people like Colbie for far too long to keep putting my neck on the line forever. As my father used to say, '*Ça'a pas d'allure.*'"

"I knew it." The sound of Alex's voice jerks everyone's gaze toward her as she steps forward. "*Vous êtes du quartier Limoilou, n'est-ce pas?*"

Paul's eyes go wide. "*Comment saviez-vous que?*"

My jaw drops. *What the fuck?*

A flurry of French begins flying between the two of them. I've known Paul Gaither for ten years, but he's always been a very private man, and I'd no idea he spoke French. Whatever he and Alex are saying is going far too fast for me to keep up with, so I just stare in bemusement as they continue.

Alex holds up her hand. "*Attends, attends, je dois appeler mon père! Il va être tellement surpris...*" She grabs at her clutch and pulls her phone free.

Paul comes away from the edge of the table and moves close to her while she taps on the screen. A second later, she has the cell to her ear.

I glance over at Deacon, mouthing the same words I'd thought just a moment ago. He shrugs, and I look toward Mia to find her gaze fixed on Alex and Paul, her look inscrutable.

"Papa, papa, tu ne le croiras pas! J'ai quelqu'un ici du quartier Limoilou." Alex turns her face up to Paul's, thrusting the phone toward him.

He takes it. *"Bonjour, ici Paul Gaither. Votre fille est assez persistante."* He listens for a moment before a broad smile creases his face. *"Ah, oui, cela suivrait la compagnie qu'elle garde."* He turns and begins walking across the room, continuing the conversation.

I wait until he's just out of hearing range before I grip Alex by the arm. "What the fuck is going on here?" I ask, keeping my voice low.

"Patience. You'll need to wait and see," she whispers back, her eyes tracking on Paul as he paces the room.

Everything's gone quiet aside from Paul talking. He's smiling, chuckling occasionally, nodding in agreement with whomever is on the other end. Finally, he begins walking back toward us, his gaze concentrated on Alex.

"Oui. Oui, je m'assurerai qu'elle comprenne que c'est dans son meilleur intérêt." He moves to stand in front of her, not sparing a single glance in my direction. *"Ce fut un plaisir, monsieur. J'attends notre rencontre avec impatience. Au revoir."* He hands the cell to her.

Alex takes the phone and, after a few additional comments in French, she ends the call.

"So, three things," Paul says in an authoritative tone once she's done. "One, when your parents are in town next month, we shall all be having dinner together. Don't worry about where: I'll make the arrangements. Two,"— Paul turns to look at me—"your delivery is handled. It may not go how you were originally thinking, but that doesn't matter, it will be taken care of. Better you don't know the details. Three," he turns back to Alex, speaking French once more. By the time he's finished, she's blushing furiously.

"Ne laissez pas cet imbécile profiter de vous. Semez votre avoine, puis nous parlerons. Comprendre?"

"Oui Monsieur," Alex says diffidently, her eyes cast down.

Paul bends to kiss her hand again, then turns to me. Where with Alex he'd been all smiles, now his face goes stern. "Take care of this young woman, friend," he says firmly. "If I find out you haven't, we shall have words." He reaches and grips my shoulder, leaning in. "Very, *very* serious words." He squeezes until his grasp becomes painful.

What the hell?

"May I assume our business here is complete?" he says, letting go of me.

"I guess so?" I glance over at Alex, but she's still got her face down, an enigmatic smile tugging at the corners of her mouth.

"Great. I look forward to dinner next month. I'll be in touch." With that, Paul turns and crosses the room, disappearing through the door back into the party.

For a moment none of us move.

"What the fuck just happened here?" Deacon breaks the silence first, his voice incredulous.

"That's a question I'd like to know too." I turn to face Alex. "Well?"

She looks up at me. "I was just trying to help. I thought I might be able to help smooth things over."

"Is that what that was?"

Her face falls. "I'm sorry if I overstepped a boundary, Galen."

"It's not that!" I run a hand over my head. "I... I have no clue what just took place."

Alex stares at me for a second. "He's Quebecois."

"Quebecois?" Deacon says, looking confused.

It takes me a second to put it together.

"Shit," I whisper.

Mia steps to Alex's side. "Are you from Quebec?"

Before Alex can answer, I say, "No. But her parents are."

"When he was speaking earlier," Alex explains, "I caught a trace of an accent. It's one I've only heard a few times in my life, but it's very distinctive. And then he made that little comment to Deacon." Alex looks toward him.

"What was that?" he asks.

"*Ça'a pas d'allure.* Basically, 'It makes no sense at all.'"

"Oh."

Alex brings her gaze back to me. "Your associate Mr. Gaither is from Quebec City, specifically the Limouilou district."

"And so is your father," I say, staring at her. "Isn't he?"

"Yes." She cocks her head. "How did you know?"

"Like I told you before, my French isn't the best, but I caught '*papa.*' That's who you called, isn't it?"

"Yes," she says in quiet acknowledgment.

Deacon glances between us with a puzzled look. "I still don't understand how you figuring out where Paul Gaither is from got us from 'fuck you, I ain't putting my neck on the line for Colbie again' to 'hey, let's have dinner and, oh by the way, your shit's taken care of.'"

"I think I do," I say, staring at Alex. She meets my eye, but the flush creeping into her cheeks does not go unnoticed.

"Did your father have something to do with it?" Mia asks, her gaze calculating.

"In a sense. I mean, not in the details, I'm sure, because that's not something he would know anything about, but..." Alex makes a vague gesture with her hand.

"Kinda like a Quebecois version of the Oath of Omerta." Mia says shrewdly.

Alex nods. "Yeah. Something like that."

Deacon elbows me. "Does any of that mean shit to you?"

"I get the gist of it." And I do. I may not know all the details, but I'm aware of what Alex does for a living, and even though I've never seen her in action at work, I just got a pretty good indication of how goddamn good at it she is.

I reach and pull her into my arms.

"Galen—"

Before she can finish, I kiss her. Hard. This isn't just a thank you kiss, a 'you done good' buss on the cheek. For me, this is a confirmation of everything she's just done, *and* a sign to Mia and Deacon of just what Alex means to me.

At first, she stiffens, but it takes less than a second for her to fall into it, her arms snaking up my back, fingers digging in as I hold her tight. I use my lips to convey what words would be insufficient to do right now. When I finally finish, I let my forehead rest against hers. The room has gone silent.

"Thank you, Alex," I whisper.

"You're welcome, sir," she whispers back. "I'm really sorry if I went too far."

I pull back to look into her eyes. "I told you before I never want you to pretend to be anyone other than who you are. Whatever you did tonight, you keep on doing it because it makes me so goddamn proud of you."

She bites her lower lip, smiling. "Thank you."

"Well." Mia's voice is thick with amusement as she steps close to us. "As touching as this Hallmark moment is, I think we all need to get back to the party before this becomes a threesome."

"Jesus Christ, Mia." I groan, pulling Alex to the opposite side from her.

"Oh, quiet, Galen. You know you'd enjoy it. Before we go, however..." She sidesteps around me to stand in front of Alex. "Here."

I've no idea where she's pulled it from, but she brings up another of her little cigars.

"A little something to celebrate with later because you, my friend, deserve it." Mia nestles the smoke into the vee of Alex's dress with a gentle pat. "You"—she says, turning to me and tapping her finger to my chest— "had better keep a close eye on your girlfriend. Because I warn you, Galen, if I ever find her out of your sight, I assure you you'll never see her again." Mia blows out a cloud of smoke, her smile predatory. "Come on, Deacon," she says, turning away.

Deacon gives us a shrug, then follows as she saunters toward the doors.

"*Ciao*, Galen," Mia calls back over her shoulder.

"That woman scares me sometimes," I murmur.

"I know. It's kinda hot," Alex says with a dreamy smile.

She starts to move to follow them, but I hold her back. Once the two leave the room, I pull her into my arms once more.

"I owe you," I whisper into her ear.

"You do not," she says, leaning into me.

"We can discuss arguing with me later. For the moment, I want you to tell me what you said to Paul."

Alex gives a slight shrug. "I told him I recognized where he was from. He confirmed it, then I called my father and let him speak to Mr. Gaither. You saw him walk away, so I'm not sure exactly what they talked about, except for what he mentioned when he came back."

"Dinner. With your parents."

"Sorry." She looks up at me meekly.

"Don't be. I'm not upset in the slightest."

Alex presses to my chest, holding tight. "At least he agreed to handle your containers," she murmurs into my jacket.

"Yes. He did." As I gently stroke her hair, my thoughts turn from pride to something far more carnal. "Alex?"

"Hmm?"

"At the end there? What was it he said that made you blush?"

She leans back, giving me a rueful grin. "I thought maybe you didn't catch that."

"Think again." I tilt her chin up. "What was it?"

Biting her lower lip, she pauses before speaking. "He said, 'When you're finished sowing your oats with this foolish man, please come find me. I know many suitable young men who'd be worthy of your attention. It will please your father and I both.'"

I laugh. "Oh! Is that what I am? A wild oat to sow?"

Alex gives me a look. "I didn't say that, sir. That was Mr. Gaither."

"Mmhmm. But it made you blush."

Now she looks flustered. "I've never thought of myself as someone who has wild oats to sow."

"But you're thinking of it now, aren't you. Perhaps with..." I glance toward the door where Mia exited a moment ago.

"Galen." Her eyes have gone wide.

"Uh huh." I shoot her a wicked grin. "I give you a little of what we've both been looking for and now I'm yesterday's news, a rag to be tossed aside."

"That's not true," she whispers.

"Maybe. But I heard the tone in your voice. 'Hot.'"

"Oh my God."

I kiss her again. Where the last had been to let my friends know what Alex means to me, this one is strictly for her. To let *her* know she is mine and so much more.

"Thank you, sir," she says when we finish.

"No, Alex. Thank *you*. I'm so proud of you. Everything you did this evening was perfect." I stroke her cheek, and she beams. "However, just so you're aware, when we get home, you're to go straight to the playroom."

Her mouth drops open. "Wha...? Why?"

"Because." I grip her chin, smiling devilishly. "You and I are going to have a little chat about 'sowing your oats.'"

CHAPTER 14

ALEX

"So, are you ready?"

A week has passed since the party, and I'm back in Galen's home. We're in the study, and I'm kneeling in my now normal spot alongside Galen's chair, looking up into his face. I've provided him his drink, moved into position, and there shouldn't be anything that remains to prevent us from beginning. "Yes, sir."

"Okay."

When he'd spoken to me earlier this week it was to say he wanted to have a conversation with me to 'go over some things' he felt I needed need to know. I wasn't sure exactly what to expect, though I had some suspicions. Now that we're here, I'm feeling both excitement and a little trepidation. I've been waiting for Galen to trust me enough to come clean about the things he's kept hidden, but now that he's ready to do it, I can't help but worry it might be more than I anticipated.

Well, whatever he's going to tell you, it's going to include being shot at, so how much worse can it get?

"So. My real name isn't Galen Harmon."

Oh my God.

"It's John Wick."

"Galen!"

He chuckles and takes another sip of his drink. "Sorry. Couldn't resist." He reaches and brushes a bit of my hair behind my ear, then continues. "Okay, seriously, here's the real story..."

I could bite his leg right now, even if it would earn me a serious punishment. Admittedly, though, the joke does ease a little of the tension that's built up inside me.

"Like a lot of young men, after 9-11 I joined the Army. I went in thinking I'd be fighting the Taliban, hunting down Osama, all that hero bullshit. I signed up for Special Forces, but instead of being trained as some badass *Zero Dark Thirty* operator, I ended up in Supply." He looks down at me, nodding. "Yeah, Supply. Even the Rangers need bullets and beans."

"Okay." I don't tell Galen I saw the pictures of him in the box I found on the shelf less than ten feet from me because I don't want to derail this conversation right now. And though I'm not big on military terms, I get the basic idea of what he's telling me.

"So, yeah, there I am, in Iraq, a supply sergeant with the 528th Sustainment Brigade. I was the biggest, baddest supply room clerk you could possibly imagine. I ruled the SOF supply chain."

"SOF?"

"Special Operations Forces. I was an enabler. That's what they called us, all the people who kept the guys in the field operational. It's what I did: enabled all the supplies a real soldier needs to fight the enemy to be moved from one place to the next so they could have them available when they needed them."

The self-deprecation does not slip by me, nor does the slight bitterness to his tone. "You served your country, sir. That alone made you a soldier."

"Yeah, so I've been told." He's being dismissive, but I don't interrupt. "Anyway, Iraq's where I met Colbie."

"Colbie was a soldier?"

Galen laughs contemptuously. "Oh, fuck no. No, Colbie was *never* a soldier. He's an enabler too, just like me, but his master is himself and the CIA, and not necessarily in that order."

"So, you worked with the CIA while you were in the Army?"

Galen shakes his head slowly. "You see, that's the thing. Even in the CIA, Colbie and his people are fringe players. Remember when I told you he's not a good person? That he's a person who takes care of things people don't want to talk about?"

"Yes."

"Well, that's what Colbie and his team were doing the night they showed up at our forward operating base. I happened to be the CQ on duty. He just came in through the wire with about ten beat-up old Iraqi cars and pickups, drove straight to our Conex and told me I needed to provide him with four HEMMTs and an MRAP."

"I don't understand what that means."

"Sorry. Specialized trucks. He needed five of our trucks."

"Okay?"

"Yeah, see, in the Army, especially if you're Special Forces, you don't just hand out equipment to anyone who shows up. So, this civilian coming up to me and demanding I turn over five vehicles from our motor pool got him a one-finger salute. I didn't even give a fuck he had five guys in uniform with him; I had no idea if they were legit, or just civilian contractors playing soldier."

"So, you turned him down."

"I tried to." Galen takes another sip of his bourbon. "Colbie just smiled at me and said, 'You seem like a decent man, Sergeant. Here's what's going to happen: you're either going to give me the five vehicles I need, or my men here are going to shoot you and we'll just take them.'"

I swallow. "Are you serious?"

"Yep. And he was too. There was just something about the way he said it, so calm, so matter of fact, I just knew he wasn't yanking my chain. So, I looked at him and said, 'Who the fuck are you, and how the fuck am I supposed to explain five missing vehicles to my CO?' He just looked me dead in the eye and said 'All you need to know is I'm the man who can either let you live or make you die. As far as your CO goes, you seem very resourceful. I'm sure you'll figure it out.'"

"Jesus."

"Yeah, that's pretty much how I felt. I had to make a decision real quick because the man gave off some serious 'I don't wait patiently for long' vibes. So, I grabbed a ring of keys for the vehicles and tossed them to him. 'You never fucking met me, and I never seen you,' I told him. Colbie just smiled and said, 'I knew my first impression of you wasn't unwarranted. Have a good evening, Sergeant.' And then he and his guys walked out and started loading up."

"Loading up... what?" There's a knot in my stomach as I ask the question. Like most people, I'd heard the stories about places like Abu Ghraib prison and the things that had gone on there. A lot of bad things had happened during the war, and a part of me is tense for what Galen's about to say.

"Well, at that point I was curious because... you know, you have someone threaten your life in one breath then compliment you in the other, it makes you wonder just what the hell is going on. And the really interesting thing was, he didn't try and stop me. He just let me watch while they were working."

"What did you find?"

"Gold."

I blink. "Gold?"

"Yep. More gold than I've ever seen in my life. All sorts of gold. Bars and chains and jewelry and statues, just about anything you could think of that could be made of gold. They were just loading it out of all these pickups and cars and piling it into the trucks."

"And where was this gold from?"

"I've no fucking clue. Even to this day, I have no idea. It was just there, and then... it wasn't. They loaded it up and disappeared."

"But... I don't understand. You're working for Colbie now."

"That's because he came back."

"He came back?"

"Yeah. Three days later the five trucks he'd taken the first night come rolling back into the compound. Colbie get out, tells the CQ duty officer to find me, and I hauled ass over. 'Here's your trucks back,' he says. I couldn't fucking believe it. And then he asked, 'I'm curious, how did you cover for them being gone?' I told him I typed up some fake orders releasing them to the armored unit we were scouting for. He just gave me this really long look, then smiled and said, 'I'll be in touch.'"

Galen goes quiet, the ice in his glass tinkling as he swirls it slowly.

"What happened then?"

"For the remainder of the time I was in, I never saw him again. I'd like to say I forgot about him, but you don't really forget a man like Colbie. When I got out, I went to work for a company that handled international freight, mostly really big machinery. That's where I met Deacon. One night after I'd been out for about a year, I was sitting in my apartment and there was a knock on the door." He looks down at me. "It was Colbie."

"What?"

"Yep. He asked if he could come in, and... I let him. He told me he'd finished his work in Iraq and he was stationed back in the US now. Then he told me he'd been thinking about me. He needed to set up a supply chain to handle 'special commodities' that couldn't be moved through normal shipping channels, even those the CIA already had established. A 'dark expediter,' he called it. He thought I'd be the perfect guy if I was interested. One thing led to another, he introduced me to Mia, I asked Deacon to come partner with us, we set the business up, and..." Galen shrugs. "Here I am."

"Wow." I rest my arm against his leg, staring up at him. "That's crazy."

"Yeah, I know, right? The truth is," he says with a shrug, "I've done well. Turns out I'm pretty good at it. Colbie's let me take on my own clients outside of the government work I do for him, and..." He motions to the home around us.

We sit in silence, and I reflect on everything Galen's just told me. It's a lot to absorb. In the D.C. metro area, it's not uncommon to hear 'oh, I work for the CIA' or the FBI or the NSA or a hundred other highly sensitive agencies and know there's always the potential there are things that person can't discuss. It's another thing entirely to find out your Dom boyfriend works for someone who claims to be CIA but does some awfully sketchy things.

"Sir?"

"Yes?"

"Do you... are some of the things you arrange to be shipped illegal? Specifically, things like... drugs. Stuff like that."

Letting out a sigh, Galen reaches and gently strokes my hair. "That's a fair question. I trust you, Alex, so I'll be honest with you: some of the stuff we do move stretches the boundaries of legality, but not in the way you might be thinking. So, no, we don't move drugs or traffic in humans or any of that sort of thing, if that's what you were worried about. Is everything we haul one hundred percent legit? No. I've handled art from questionable sources, Cuban cigars direct from the source, certain other commodities from countries we're technically not supposed to be doing business with. And, yes, some of the places we go, some of the people we transport and what *they* do... Let's just say there's no court of law in the world that'll give us a pass if we get caught. I'm sorry if that upsets you, but it *is* a part of what we do."

"And some of it involves you getting shot at," I say quietly.

His hand stops. "Yes. Sometimes it involves us getting shot at.

That's the price we pay for working with men like Colbie. The bill for the deal with the devil I signed."

"Do you regret it?"

"Some days. Other days, I look at what I've gained, where I'm at, what I'm able to do, and I think I made the right choice."

I nod. "Well, I work in the financial industry, even if it is HR, so I've been privy to my fair share of questionably legitimate things. I guess the big difference is anytime I've seen someone with a gun it's usually the police, coming to take someone away." I lean my head against his leg. "I don't judge what you do, sir, but I'd be lying if I said after what you and Mia have told me, I'm not a little concerned."

"I understand. All I can tell you is we're very careful and we do everything we can to protect ourselves. The men who work for Colbie may not be nice guys but they're very good at what *they* do, and we've all survived so far."

I don't tell him that's cold comfort, but it is. "Well, thank you for trusting me enough to tell the story. It puts a lot of things into perspective."

"In a good way or a bad way, Alex?"

I look up at him. "What do you mean?"

"In a 'I still want to keep seeing you, sir' way, or a 'I think we need to talk' one?"

I smile reassuringly. "The former, sir."

"Good."

I press my cheek to him, waiting to see if he's going to move onto a different subject. Specifically, about the woman in those other pictures, Charlotte. I wait to see if now is when he'll tell me what happened between the two of them, and why she wasn't a part of his life any longer.

It's not that I don't appreciate everything else he's told me because it does fill in some gaps, especially what he does for a living. And while our conversation tonight has established a certain level of trust that's been missing, what concerns me now is, what if this isn't everything? What if there's more involved? And what if it all plays into why Charlotte isn't the sub kneeling at his feet now and I am?

I'd hoped tonight would clear things up between us, establish that level of trust I'd found missing, but it hasn't entirely. I've learned a lot about Galen, for sure, but where one curtain's been pulled back, the others still closed are all the more frustrating.

Still, I'm holding firm to what I said to myself before: I'm not going to force his hand. When he's ready, he'll need to tell me what took place between him and Charlotte. For now, I'm going to let it go.

A short time later Galen pulls me to the bedroom, and we make love. Normally he's aggressive in bed, taking charge, securing his pleasure then pleasuring me as he sees fit. I love that about being intimate with him, and I've never complained.

But tonight, there's a slight hesitancy to his moves, an almost imperceptible check to his grip as he tosses me around the bed. Most often Galen's first to come, teasing and torturing me to withhold my own orgasm until he's fully enjoyed himself. Tonight, however, he pins me to the bed, using fingers and tongue to work me into a fever pitch. And where normally he makes me beg for release, this time I've barely started writhing when he orders me to.

"Come, Alex. Come for me. Let me feel you come."

His voice is insistent, demanding, and I don't deny him. His fingers and tongue push me over the edge, the incandescence of my orgasm shattering thought and driving away the unease I'd felt earlier. For the moment there's just pleasure, and everything else that's happened this evening falls by the wayside.

When he's finished giving to me, he takes for his own, and I revel in it. I've never shied from serving Galen, and I don't now. I exult in the looks and sounds he makes as he fucks me, and when he finally releases, the warmth of satisfaction washing through me is both decadent and self-indulgent. He doesn't need to pull me to him when he moves from on top of me; I crawl to him, wrapping my arms around him and snuggling in tight. It's more forward of me than I've been in the past, but I want him to know he doesn't need to worry about an 'I think we need to talk' conversation.

At least for now.

"This is where you belong," he murmurs, brushing his lips to the top of my head as I lie against his chest.

"I agree." I love the smell of him, of us, like this. The heady trace of sex a lingering reminder that makes the contentment of the moment sensual.

"When you're not here, the house feels empty."

"It does?"

"Yes." Galen takes a deep breath and lets it out slowly. "You know you can come here more than just on the weekends."

The comment startles me a little. Aside from the one instance when Galen asked me to be here while he was out trying to get himself killed, he's not mentioned me staying beyond the weekends we spend together. "Did you want me to come over more often, sir?"

"Alex, you can come here anytime you want. I hope by now you understand that. I enjoy our dynamic and being in your company. I like having you here."

He sounds a tiny bit annoyed, as if this isn't a discussion we should even be having.

"I'd like for you to think of my home as your home."

Oh.

"Okay. I mean, I do like being here with you too, sir. I hope I haven't given you the impression otherwise."

"No, no, that's not it." He blows out a tiny huff of irritation. "I just wanted you to know you're always welcome here. If I hadn't made that clear."

"Sir, you've always made me feel at ease in your home."

"Okay. Just making sure."

I'm not trying to irritate him, but he's making it feel like I am.

As if this was something he expected me to discern on my own. Maybe I should have? There's no doubt our relationship has been evolving, but the fact is just a little over a month ago Galen and I didn't even know the other existed, and we were both about to give up entirely on the idea of being in a high protocol relationship at all. And now...

"I mean, there's some nights I need to work late and driving here takes longer than just going home."

"I understand. But if you wanted me to come get you, you know I would. I'd be happy to take you back to work in the morning, unless you wanted to take off for a mental health day."

"'Take off for a mental health day,' huh?"

"Well, it'd do my mental health a solid, I can tell you that."

"And maybe this?" I reach and take his cock in my hand.

"Absolutely. That always improves my attitude."

"I'll bet it does." We both chuckle, and instead of pulling my hand away I slowly begin stroking him.

I wait to see if maybe Galen will ask about coming to my place to spend the night as an option. It's a question I've been waiting for him to propose. I mean, I understand his place is larger than mine, and it's also a home on this big piece of property secluded from prying eyes and ears, but... my condo is still nice. I like it. Much as Galen, I'm no interior designer but I'm still proud of the way I've decorated it, and with the exception of some of the sounds he's made me make in the playroom, we could have perfectly satisfying sex without waking up the neighbors. Probably. The only concession he'd have to make is to let me have a robe nearby in case I need to rush to answer the door.

I shouldn't feel disappointed he hasn't asked because when we're here, we're practicing a big part of what drives our dynamic. Here, there's zero doubt who's in control. He's taught me all the subtle nuances of what's expected of me the moment I walk through the front door, and him coming to my place would change that narrative. But it shouldn't.

Whether there's a study to kneel at his feet, a playroom for him to torture me in with the bead mat and pony, none of those things should ultimately matter. They're just things. As Galen pointed out, the core of our dynamic is based upon my willingness to submit to him fully. To learn his rules, obey them, accept punishment and correction when I fail, praise and affirmation when I succeed. Sure, they're on his terms as long as they don't violate consent or become abusive, but all those things could be done in my two-bedroom, fifth story condominium just as easily as they could here at his home in Laurel.

I get it. This is Galen's home turf, and I'm sure being here puts him in a much more comfortable headspace than adjusting to something completely new. But it would be nice if he made the effort to come to my home and see a different part of who I am than what he gets when I come here.

"If you keep doing that, we're not going to get any sleep," Galen growls.

"Oh, my. I'm so sorry, sir. All I need you to do is tell me to stop."

He growls a second time but says nothing further, which tells me all I need to know about whether or not to stop.

"Sir?"

"Hmm?"

"If I *were* to come during the week, would I need to announce it first? Call ahead to make sure it's okay?"

Galen reaches and stops my hand. With his other, he turns my face to look directly into his.

"Here. Let me make this as clear as I can, Alex. This home is your home. You can come here any time you wish. You have the gate code, and I'll give you your own key before you leave this weekend. You know my rules when you're here, and as long as it's still your intention to obey them, then as far as I'm concerned, you can consider this house your own as much as it is mine. Understood?"

Whoa.

Okay, there's a part of me that feels pleased Galen trusts me enough to make that offer, but at the same time it's a little disconcerting. I mean, our relationship has grown, and it's clear we care for each other, but… It's only been a little over a month. This, the way he's said it, feels like something more than just inviting me over.

This home is your home…

Except it's not. Yes, I'm comfortable here, I like being here, and I love the time we spend together engaging in our dynamic. It's become a familiar routine. But all that being said, this is *not* my home. Galen has to know that, and yet, if so, why did he say what he said? Why is he pushing for me to be here more often? Neither of us has dropped the L-bomb yet, but it feels like Galen is pressing for something awfully close to crossing that line. As if he needs me to be here to… fill a gap, maybe? And if that's the case, for what? Companionship? Increased sex? To take this to the next level?

"Alex?"

Shit. I've been spiraling down a rabbit hole and I haven't answered his question.

"Yes, sir. I understand."

"Are you sure? Is there anything you want to discuss?"

"I…" Jesus, he's putting me on the spot here, and there is a lot I *do* want to discuss, but what he's just dropped on me is a lot to unpack, and I'm not ready to do a deep dive into everything he might be intimating in that question.

Shit, shit, shit.

"No, sir. Not right now."

God, I hope that comes across the right way. I hope he doesn't think it insincere, or even worse, start trying to pull at threads I really don't want unraveled right now. What I need is time to sort this out. I care about Galen. There's a good chance I'm falling in love with him. But… dammit, this is happening so fast, and there are things I want to know, *need* to know, before I'm willing to even consider what he's clearly offering.

I'm not ready to move in. I'm not ready to take that big of a step in our relationship. I... I trust Galen. I really do.

Just not *that* much.

Yet.

CHAPTER 15

GALEN

"*They're gone.*"

I've been pacing the kitchen, but once I hear those two words, I heave out a sigh of relief. "Christ, that's fucking good to hear."

Deacon chuckles on the other end of the phone. "You ain't kidding, brother. Your girlfriend getting Paul Gaither to agree to the move was a fucking blessing, but having his guys actually show and haul them off was fire."

"Agreed. Now I just need to call Colbie and let him know they're on their way, and then wait for Paul to let us know when they get there."

"Hey, heads up," Deacon says, his voice low. "Mia's been bitchin' you ain't brought Alex back out here to see her. I'd look into that if I were you, otherwise you might find her camped out on your doorstep."

I roll my eyes. "I'm honestly surprised she hasn't shown up already."

"Yeah, after that night at the party…"

I remember what Deacon's talking about vividly. I also

remember Alex's reaction just as well. "We both know Mia likes… variety. But Alex is my girlfriend, not hers. And I don't share."

"Yeah, I remember you sayin' the same thing 'bout Char—"

A single syllable of her name, and my fingers clench around the phone.

There's a second of dead air before Deacon recovers. "Sorry, man. I… I didn't mean to bring her up."

I smile tightly. "It's okay. I'm… for the first time in a long time I'm actually in a good spot. What happened back then is over. Done with. I'm finally starting to feel like I'm moving beyond it now."

There's another short pause before Deacon's voice comes back. "That's good to hear, man. We been waiting for that to happen for a while now. Knew it would eventually when you found the right person, it's just good to hear it's finally coming 'round."

"Yeah. I know. And I appreciate the concern, Deacon."

"Hey. Like I told you, man, you're a brother from another mother to me."

I groan.

"Eh, you fuckin' bitch all you want, it's true. You done right by me, Galen. And Alex is good people. She's good for you. We can see it."

He's right. She is. The past two weeks we've spent together have solidified that. In fact, it's precisely because of how well things have been going that instead of heading straight home I'm driving the direction I am right now.

The name she uses on her Etsy shop is Gilded Angel, but in the years I've been doing business with her, I've come to call her just 'Angel.' I first met her at one of The Crucible's Leather Flea Market events, and her gear, especially her collars, was some of the finest I've ever seen.

'Oh, this isn't even the good stuff. Go to my page and check that out.

And if you're looking for something extra *special, I do take custom orders, as long as you'll give me the proper amount of time to deliver...'*

Which I always have. It's why I'm headed to her home today. I called in advance to see if she could spare some time to make another custom order for me, and she'd said yes. I want it to be something unique, something exceptional.

Something worthy of Alex.

"God, it's good to see you again, Galen." Angel pulls me into a hug, her head landing squarely in the middle of my chest. Her fiery red curls tumble across her shoulders, and for as tiny as she is, she's surprisingly strong as she holds me tight.

"Mr. Harmon," her husband Adam grins as he stretches his hand around her toward me.

I grin in return as I shake it. "Uh, you wanna take your sub back here?"

He chuckles. "She isn't done with you yet. I don't interrupt when she's greeting customers."

"Smart man," she mumbles from my chest before pulling away. "It's been too long, sir."

I give her a worn smile. "Yes, it has been."

Angel holds me at arm's length, staring into my eyes. "I saw Charlotte at Crucible the other night."

I stiffen, and Angel's fingers tighten in reaction.

"I hope she's well," I say brittlely.

"No, you don't, sir."

"I wish her no ill will, Angel."

"I believe you, but if you think for a second anyone who knew you two doesn't see what she did to you, you're an idiot."

"That's enough," Adam tells her calmly, and she snaps a look in his direction before bringing her gaze back to me.

"Yes, sir." Angel lets go and takes a step backward. She turns her frown into a tight smile, her gaze keeping me pinned in place. "So, you have a commission for me?"

"Yes, I do." I try and match her smile, each of us strained by the conversation we almost just had. "I think you'll be pleased."

"Oh, really?"

"Yes. I need a collar."

Her eyes widen. "A… collar?"

"Yes."

Now Angel's eyes narrow. "For a sub?"

"Yes."

She launches herself back at me. "For fuck's sake, why didn't you say something?" She wraps her arms back around me, squeezing tight.

I look at Adam over the top of her head, rolling my eyes, and he grins in return.

Angel pulls away and looks up at me. "Who? What's her name? Do I know her? Where'd you meet her? How long?" She tugs me to a kitchen table, and we sit while Adam makes coffee.

"Her name is Alex."

"Ooo. Let me guess: short for Alexandria?"

"Damn, you're good."

Angel grins brightly. "And?"

"And… we're dating."

Angel gives me an annoyed look. "Don't play games with me, Galen Harmon. You spill right now, or I'll make you a goddamn CBT cage rather than a collar."

I laugh and give her a brief history of Alex and my relationship.

"Wow. And it's just been a little over a month now?"

"Almost two."

"And she's asked you to collar her already?"

I stop short.

"Galen?"

"She didn't exactly ask."

Angel scrunches her brow, the smile slipping into a frown. "She didn't ask you? Okay, so you asked her, right?"

"I plan on it."

"Okay, I mean I know you've always been a very confident Dom, sir, but aren't you jumping the gun a bit here?"

I take a sip of the coffee Adam's dropped off. "Things have been going really well, Angel. I mean, really, *really* well. She's been staying at my place, and I think eventually she's going to move in. For the first time in a while, I really believe what happened with Charlotte is behind me."

Angel reaches across the table and grips my hand. "And that's great, sir. I mean that sincerely. You have no idea how happy all of this makes me, and how happy I know it'll make other people too. But..."

"But what?"

"It sounds to me like, in all the excitement and discovery of what's going on in this new relationship, you might want to take a step back and pause for a moment, especially where it concerns something like collaring her."

"Why? She's my sub, Angel. She's been burned too, just like me, and the dynamic she and I have created is something we've both been looking for. I can't see any reason why she *wouldn't* want me to collar her."

"Sir." Angel squeezes my hand before pulling back to bring her fingers to her lips. "For most submissives, myself included, being collared is probably *the* single most important commitment in the lifestyle you can make. In some cases, as or even more significant than marrying someone. It's not something you do on a whim."

"Okay? And your point is?"

"My point, sir, is this: I'm more than willing to discuss this collar with you. Jot down some notes, hear more about her, find out what you're looking for, and come up with some ideas. But Galen, before I cut a single piece of leather, I need to hear from you that you spoke to her about this."

"Angel, I think I know my sub well enough—"

"No." She doesn't raise her voice, but she cuts me off,

nonetheless. "I'm sorry Galen, even if this does cost me a sale, but my comment still stands. I believe you *do* know her. But you don't know her from a sub's perspective. Only from yours as her Dom."

Irritation wells up inside me but it dies before I let it be expressed. Because… she's right.

I *don't* know this from a sub's perspective. The first time I ever collared a submissive it was Charlotte, and she was the one to approach me, not the other way around. Alex hasn't even broached the subject of being collared, and even though I stand by my contention she'll say yes, Angel has a point. I should speak to Alex about it first. Then I'll put Angel's worries to rest so she can proceed as I've requested.

"Okay, Angel. I get it loud and clear. I'll talk to Alex."

"Thank you, sir," she says kindly. For a moment we stare at each other, then the serious look on her face morphs into a wicked one, and she leans forward, elbows on the table. "Now, let's talk about how you want to make her feel when she's wearing it."

An hour later I'm on the road, heading back home. Angel's gotten everything she needs from me for the moment, the only remaining item is my call to confirm Alex has agreed. I'm not worried about that. I know she will.

I should probably head out to the airfield, but the one thing above everything else that'd been hanging over our heads is gone now that those two containers have been picked up, so instead I drive straight to the house. Alex is working today, but a part of me hopes she'll be there later, after she's off.

I made it clear she should consider the house our home, and she said she was honored I trusted her with that. I'm hoping she took it to heart because I really do believe it's only a matter of time before she moves in, considering how well our dynamic has evolved, and our relationship is progressing.

Finally, after almost two years, everything that happened between Charlotte and me is fading away. I'm closing that door because the gaping hole she left behind is more than being filled by Alex. She's becoming everything I could ever hope for. So much like Charlotte, yet so different too. All the good things that were once a part of my life, except no indication of the bullshit that made things go south.

We just have a few more details to iron out, and then I'm certain things will be right where they should be.

I get home and prep a dinner for two. Six becomes seven, and there's still no sign of Alex. By seven-thirty, I start the meal, hoping she's just working late as she mentioned she sometimes does. By eight-thirty, there's still no sign of her, so I text.

Hey, just checking in. You okay?

Yeah. At home, getting ready to collapse.

Fuck.

Oh. Thought you might be coming here tonight.

Sorry. I worked until almost eight so just came home.

I shouldn't feel angry, but I do. I take several deep breaths because I've zero right to lash out at her. I didn't make it a command for her to come here every night, but I'll admit I assumed she'd take the hint and understand I'd like her to be here more often during the week. To be fair, she *did* just tell me she had to work late, so it makes some sense she went back to her apartment rather than drive here. I could have come and gotten her, but obviously she didn't think to text me to come—

Stop. Don't overthink this.

I'm trying, but between Alex and my conversation last weekend, my conversation with Angel earlier today, and now this, it's hard not to let irritation get the best of me.

Okay. See you tomorrow?

I wait for her to reply. And wait. As one minute becomes three, my impatience grows.

It's a simple fucking question, Alex.

Finally, I see dots appear on my screen as she types.

Hopefully.

Hopefully. A single word and my hands clench as I brace myself against the kitchen countertop. A second later I scoop up the dish of food I'd plated for her earlier and scrape it into the trash. When I'm done, I let the plate clatter into the sink.

Calm the fuck down, Galen. What the hell?

I start to type a response, but I see dots appear again, so I wait.

Definitely this weekend, sir.

I blow out a ragged sigh. I need a drink.

No.

What I need is Alex kneeling at the side of my chair offering me one, but since that's clearly not going to happen, a drink I make myself will have to do. I head to the bar and fix one before moving into the study. I rarely do this but, once I'm seated, I slam back the bourbon, nearly draining the glass empty. I let the alcohol settle into my system, feeling the warm burn spread through me until the edge of my anger curbs. I trail one hand over the edge of the chair, and the lack of Alex's presence is driven home acutely.

Okay. Okay, enough. This is ridiculous. Just because I want her here doesn't mean she's *required* to be. Granted, our dynamic is built around her obeying me, serving me, following my rules and direction, but I said it before: I didn't order her to start coming every night. It was an offer, a suggestion that she could do so if she wanted. That she didn't immediately take it up is no reason to get as upset as I am, nor should it be a judgment of her that she didn't read my mind.

Yeah, because remember, jackass, you were the one who told her you didn't expect her to do that.

Heaving myself out of the chair, I head back to the bar. Once I pour myself a second drink, I start heading back to the study. As I do, I remember what Deacon and I spoke about earlier today.

For the first time in a while, I'm finally feeling as if what happened between Charlotte and me is starting to fade in my relationship rear view mirror. It's not eating at me the way it had for so long after she first left. Even with Angel's comment about seeing her at Crucible, I didn't feel nearly as upset as I would if we had the same conversation a year ago. And that had everything to do with Alex.

She came into my life, and all the things I was so close to writing off returned; the pieces of a scattered puzzle coming together and falling neatly into place. Alex can't know that because I haven't explained to her all of what happened but, at this point, I'm not sure it's even necessary. She and I share a bond of trust which doesn't require every petty detail of the past be exposed and raked over the coals. All that truly matters is what we have together now.

I go to bed tonight feeling alone but a bit better than I did after our texts. I'm confident in what I told Angel. Alex will let me collar her. I'm sure of it. Like so many things about our relationship and where it's going, it's only a matter of time.

"I'M SORRY... WHAT?"

It's Friday, and I'm standing at the kitchen island while Alex kneels on her mat behind me.

"I said, have you ever thought of being collared?"

"Like... a *collar* collar"—she brings her hand up around her throat—"or did you mean something more symbolic?"

"Both, to be honest."

"Well, I mean..." Alex seems a little flustered, and I'm imagining it's for the same reasons Angel mentioned. "I mean, I think every submissive *thinks* about it at some point. I know a lot of people put great store in what it means in terms of the Dominant/submissive dynamic and how it can express that in a very visual way to others in the community. There can be actual ceremonies with friends, or it can be a very private affair just between a submissive and their Dom. Collaring can be a very intense, emotional experience."

It sounds like she's reciting a chapter from BDSM 101.

"Are you mansplaining collaring to me?" I grin down at her. "Isn't that my job?"

She drops her gaze to the floor. "Sorry, sir," she mumbles.

"It's okay, Alex. But just for the record, I know what collaring is. I've done it before."

Her head snaps up. "You have?"

"Yes. Once."

"With who?" She blurts the question, and suddenly this isn't the conversation I want to be having right now.

"Someone in the past," I say firmly. "It doesn't matter."

She stares at me intently, almost as if she's about to ask something further. Then she drops her gaze once more. "Oh."

"Anyways"—I turn back to the meal I'm fixing for us—"my question to you was more along the lines of, have *you* ever thought about being collared?"

For a moment she doesn't answer and keeps her face turned down. "Well, as I said, I think it crosses most submissives' minds at one point or another."

"Has it crossed *your* mind?"

There's another pause before she says, "It has."

The room goes silent except for the sounds of me cooking, and a tiny, jagged tip of irritation pokes through that silence. It feels as if she's being deliberately obtuse, and I don't understand why.

"Have you thought about it recently?"

She tries to hide it, but I catch the whisper of her sigh. "I find the idea of being collared intriguing, yes. Do I think I'm ready for it? No."

"Why?"

"Do you remember quizzing me the first night we were together at Black Light?"

"Yes. What in specific are you referring to?"

"You asked me about my past relationships. And after I'd told you about my admittedly limited experience, you said something to the effect of, 'Is there a possibility you don't know what high protocol really is.' At the time, I was pretty ticked off at you about that comment. You seemed like such an arrogant bastard, even if you did have more experience than me.

"However, after the time I've spent with you, I feel like there's a lot more truth to that statement than I realized then. The time we've spent together… I've loved every minute of it. I've learned a lot. I'm *still* learning. But do I think I'm at the point where I'm ready to be collared by my Dom?"

I turn my face back down to her.

She looks up as she speaks. "I'm just not sure, sir."

I turn from the counter and walk to where she's kneeling. Reaching down, I grip her chin in my hand. "Alex, if I haven't conveyed to you how stupid crazy lucky I feel to be with you, how incredible of a submissive you are, then I'm a goddamn fool and idiot. If I'm 'teaching you' anything, it's simply what *I* want from our dynamic, nothing more. As a submissive, you've already exceeded every expectation I've ever had, and more."

Alex swallows. "Thank you, sir," she says gently.

I let go of her with a parting caress. "I can tell you with one hundred percent conviction you are completely well-versed in high protocol, at least in the style I'm certain we both want. I've no doubt we'll both continue to learn things about each other as we go along. From my perspective, collaring you is simply the next step in that progression."

"Galen, that's really kind of you to say…"

"It's the truth, Alex."

"I'm sure it is. But you need to understand I might see it a little bit differently. You have the luxury of experience that I don't."

"What do you mean?"

"You were in a long-term high protocol relationship before, weren't you?"

"That… that was in the past. It has no bearing on what's going on between us now."

"Maybe for you, sir."

Ugh. Why is she bringing this up? What difference does any of that make? Our relationship is *our* relationship, and what I… *we're…* creating together is what's important, not what I had previously. Alex is everything Charlotte had been and more. She's fitting in beautifully to the high protocol dynamic we both want, and there's zero reason she should be questioning herself, and especially not comparing herself to whatever she may think I once had. I don't know why she's fighting this. She deserves to be collared. She's earned it. She may be questioning it, but I'm not.

So, what are you going to do? Force her to take it?

This shouldn't be so hard or so frustrating.

"Okay, Alex," I say calmly. "For now, just think about it. We can discuss it again another time." I turn back to the counter and continue working.

"Sir?"

Her voice is hesitant, and I fight not to turn toward it.

"Yes?"

"I'm not trying to be difficult, Galen. I swear I'm not. But… do you ever think we may be moving a little too fast here?"

What?

Okay, don't react, don't react. This collar thing's clearly thrown her, and she's just overthinking it. *Don't buy into her apprehension, just be calm and rational.* "What do you mean by that, Alex? Are *you* concerned our relationship is progressing too quickly?"

She gives another sigh behind me. "Maybe a little."

Don't. React.

"Galen, I want you to understand I truly do care for you. I meant it when I said I've loved every minute of the time we've spent together. What we've done, the dynamic we've created. It really is exactly what I was looking for."

"And yet?"

"Ugh..." she groans. "I don't mean it the way that sounds. It's just... Galen, it's only been two months. Two months, and I'm here every weekend, and I know you'd like me here more. Two months, and you're asking to collar me. Two months, and all I know about your business is the fact you get shot at, and one of your friends has hit on me, and..." The room goes quiet, and now I do turn around to look at her.

Alex stares up at me, frustration painted across her face.

"The last two months have been unbelievable, Galen. But that being said, everything's been based around *you*. Your house, your friends, your business, your super-secret special restaurant with the amazing tacos, your party, your plane." She steeples her fingers in front of her mouth. "And even though I know it sounds like it, I swear to you I'm not complaining. It's all been so incredible, and I've regretted nothing. But it doesn't change the fact that everything we've done has been on your time schedule, at the places you've chosen, and all of it revolving around your life."

"Alex, that's not—"

"Yes, it is, Galen! And I've been there for it because it's been exciting and fun and thrilling and sexy as hell. I realize you being in charge, calling the shots, making the rules, and me obeying them is all part of our dynamic, and I'm all in, I swear. But... have you not even once wondered what my life is like beyond what we have here?" She twirls a finger to indicate the house around us. "Have you no interest in who I am beyond the submissive who willingly, eagerly, pleases you?"

"You've told me what you do, Alex. Hell, I fucking saw it in action at the party! I told you how proud I was of you!"

"Yes, Galen, yes you did. And I appreciate that. But there's more to me than what you saw in that one instance."

"I understand that, Alex. And I do want to know about everything that goes on in your life. What's happening at your work, where you live, your friends... all of it. Listen, I realize I haven't been very good about talking about those things with you, but I swear, I *am* interested."

"And about my past, Galen? Is there any part of you that wants to know about that?"

"Yes, of course there is! I've... I've just been more focused on the future of our relationship and where it's going than ."

Alex leans forward as she looks up at me. "Except that's just it, Galen. We've been moving forward so quickly it doesn't seem like there's been any time or effort put into discovering who we are and where we've come from. It... it just feels like none of that is important. All that seems to matter is where we're headed. The problem is while those things may not be important to you, they are to me. And I haven't pressed, Galen. You haven't asked me about my past relationships beyond what little I told you that night at Black Light, and I've just let it go. By the same token, you haven't shared much with me about what happened in your past relationship, except to tell me to be patient and you'll get to it eventually."

God, I don't want to have this conversation right now. Tonight's supposed to be about Alex agreeing to be collared, not... this.

I move back the few steps separating us and kneel down. "Alex, I... I hear what you're saying. And I'm sorry if I've let you down. That wasn't my intention. But... as far as my past relationship is concerned, I just want to forget it. It's over, done with. All I care about is you." I reach and brush the backs of my fingers across her cheek.

She leans into it, her eyes closing briefly. "I understand, Galen. I really do. But just because something's not important to you doesn't mean it isn't to me. I'm willing to wait, but until we can get this resolved, I don't think a collar is the best symbol for us right now. It just feels... too soon."

I take a deep breath, forcing down the exasperation that wants to boil up inside me.

Angel was right. Alex isn't ready, and that makes my irritation even stronger. I'm her Dom and I could order her to do this, and a part of me wonders if she would just to satisfy me. But that's a dick move, and not want I want at all. I want her submission willingly, not coerced. That... that smacks of one of the very reasons I don't want to talk about what happened between Charlotte and me. About why she took what we had and perverted it into something I never wanted, all because she listened to...

No. No, I won't think about that bullshit right now. Instead of focusing on this momentary aggravation, I need to act like the Dom I should be. The Dom I always was for Charlotte, right up to the fucking end. The Dom Alex deserves.

"Okay," I say softly, brushing her cheek once more before I stand. "I understand. For now, let's just let it... go."

Alex looks up at me with a sincere smile. "Thank you, sir."

"Of course." I return the smile, gazing into her eyes.

There's no point in dwelling on this right now. Instead, what I need to do is exercise the one thing I've preached from the beginning of our relationship.

Patience.

There's so much I have planned for our future. Giving her the space she needs right now to overcome her anxieties is a minor inconvenience. She'll come around, in time. I'm confident of it. And when she does...

Everything will be perfect.

CHAPTER 16

ALEX

"*A*lex, it's perfection."

I smile, staring at the images on the screen. Bri's right: it *is* perfect. I'm not above preening as we watch the slide show of the resort because everything I'm seeing is going to make the principles of GSR very, very happy. And that, in turn, makes *me* very, very happy.

"I don't think we'll have any problem signing them after this," I murmur as the slides begin to repeat.

"Are you kidding me?" Bri chortles. "Hell, I'd sign just for the opening night dinner alone." She leans back from me, patting my shoulder. "You did good."

"Thank you." I watch for a few seconds more, then turn to face Bri. "Seth's confirmed all their travel arrangements?"

"Doublechecked them myself. I've got Lisa following up to make sure they have car service to and from the airport, then on standby at the resort. And limo service—none of that Uber bullshit this time."

"Oh, thank God. I do *not* want another experience like we had before." The last thing I need is an executive calling me from curbside at nine PM telling me no one was there to pick him up. It'd taken months of emails to finally smooth that over.

"And have you taken care of what you need to do?" Bri gives me a meaningful look.

"Have I taken care of..." My eyes go wide. "Oh, God, Bri, what did I forget?"

Bri groans in exasperation, tilting her head back to look at the ceiling. "Jesus, Alex! Your fiancé? Making him dinner again this week? Hmm?"

"Oh, for God's sake, Bri, you scared me." I give her the evil-eye. 'My fiancé.' That's what she's taken to calling Galen, mostly because it usually gets a rise out of me. I've kept most of what's been going on with him private, but because Bri helped me with the first dinner I made for him, she now feels she has a right to periodic updates.

"Well? Have you?"

"Yes! Thursday night. I'm going to surprise him."

"And you have everything we talked about?"

I grin. "Yep. All of it."

"Good girl."

Bri has set me up with another meal to make, this one a little more complicated than the last. It still more or less adheres to the KISS principle she used for the first one, but with the tension there's been between Galen and I, this time I want to do something extra special to help smooth things over.

There's something else I've gotten too. A second part to my special night with Galen on Thursday.

A simple leather collar.

I ordered off Amazon. It's nothing fancy, but I'm thinking of it as an olive branch, and my gut tells me he'll be pleased. It shows initiative, and it's clear the idea of collaring me is something that excited him. Not only will it send him the signal I'm not opposed to *wearing* a collar, but it'll have the added benefit of making the disappointment I won't be able to spend this coming weekend with him—because of this work event I've organized and need to attend—a little more palatable.

Galen texts me just before I leave work.

Hey, I know you said this week was going to be a really busy, but just checking to see if you might be coming over tonight?

I tap back:

Sorry, can't! But I do have something planned for Thursday. 😈

Oh really?

Yes sir.

But Thursday!? That's a lifetime.

Poor baby.

There's a long pause, and I watch the dots cycle as he types out his response.

There's easier ways of getting your ass lit up, Alex.

LOL! All that time just to write that?

You have no idea what I erased.

We chat for a little while longer, and then he lets me go with the admonishment I better not back out on him at the last minute. I assure him that won't be the case. I already told my team I'll be leaving early on Thursday, and aside from a smirk from Bri, no one even questioned it.

Wednesday is a flurry of meetings regarding the upcoming acquisition event, some planned but more than a few not. None of this comes as a surprise. The V- and C-suite types never respond to emails no matter how far in advance my team sends them, and two days before the event is scheduled to start is the *perfect* time to begin asking questions and requesting changes.

"Seth, make sure Mr. Devin's room doesn't have a south facing window in the bedroom."

"Can't fucking believe I have to—"

"I know. I can't believe I have to listen to you whine about it for the umpty-millionth time too, but here we are."

Seth gives me a sour look but jots down a note as I look around the conference table.

"We all know the drill here. I appreciate everyone having done their due diligence, but this stuff is important to them, and we've never failed to follow through in the past. I know we'll get it done again."

"We'll get it handled. You know we always do." Bri looks over at Seth, who rolls his eyes but nods his head in agreement.

The meeting breaks up, and my phone buzzes in my hand. I glance at it, and it's a text from Galen. It's already almost five, and I'm sure he thinks I'm probably wrapping up for the day, but I've got at least two more meetings I know of, and God knows how many hallway ones I'm likely to get pulled into. I'll get back to him as soon as I can, but for now I mute notifications as I head toward the Executive conference room.

It turns out to be nearly eight before I'm back in my office and able to take a moment to read the earlier texts. By now there are three, plus a missed call.

Hey, can we talk tonight? Call or text to let me know a good time.

Hey, you there?

Are you ignoring me little girl? Not a good thing to do, esp. before you show up here tomorrow. 😈

I look to see if he's left a voicemail after the missed call, but he hasn't. I roll my shoulders to try and work out some of the kinks that've built up over the course of the day, then bring up his number on my phone.

"I was wondering when you were going to call."

He sounds relaxed, and I'll admit the tone of his voice helps ease a bit of my own stress.

"It's been a day, sir."

"Sorry to hear that. You know I can come pick you up if you need some help relieving stress."

I lean back in my chair, closing my eyes and smiling. "That's a tempting offer, but I'm still not done here yet. I need to make sure everything's in place so I can leave early tomorrow."

"Ooo! Going somewhere special?"

"No, not really. Just over to this guy I know who can't cook to save his life, so I'm going to fix him dinner."

"Oh, really? Well, aren't you just the best friend ever."

"Yeah, I'm an angel, honestly. But I'm pretty sure he'll fuck me silly afterwards, so it's a win-win, I guess."

The phone goes silent.

"You do truly love playing with fire, don't you?" he growls.

I manage to keep my laughter under control. "I've no idea what you you're referring to, sir."

"Guess you'll find out tomorrow night, won't you?"

Now I do laugh. "You have no idea how much I'm looking forward to it"

Galen chuckles, and we both go quiet for a moment.

"So," he says, "not even going to ask if you're coming here tonight."

"Sir, I'm really sorry."

"Alex, stop. It's okay, I understand."

"Thank you, sir," I say softly.

"Do you have a couple of minutes to talk?"

"Of course."

"Good." There's a hint of excitement to his voice that only helps to decrease my stress level a little right now. "So, I know you'll be here tomorrow, but I'd like to talk about this weekend."

Oh, shit. In all the stuff that went on between us last weekend, and the things going on here at work this week, it dawns on me I haven't actually told Galen about the event I'll be attending.

"Sir..."

"You mentioned getting off early tomorrow, but is there any chance you could also take off early on Friday, too? I mean, you being a big-wig VP and everything, that should be possible, right?"

"Galen, I meant to tell you—"

"I've been thinking about some of the things we talked about, and I realize I've probably come across a little aggressive, especially where it concerns how our relationship is progressing..."

Oh, God, he can't be doing this right now. He can't be. I mean, I appreciate where this conversation seems to be heading, but I have to nip this in the bud right now, because there's no way he can go away from this phone call thinking whatever he's planned for this weekend is going to happen. I'll be at the Jefferson in Richmond entertaining some of the most influential talent that's come to GSR in years, not straddling the pony in Galen's playroom.

"Galen—"

"I want to correct that, so I made us reservations at this place I think you'll love. And I'll admit another reason I want to go is because it'll give me a chance to show you off, but you can forgive me for that, right?"

"Galen—"

"More importantly, though, it'll give us a chance to interact outside of the dynamic we've established here at home. Kinda a return to a little of what we had after we scened at Black Light that first night, and I thought that would be good for us, right? A callback to where we started."

"Galen!"

"Yes?"

"I can't come."

The phone goes silent.

"I'm sorry?"

"Sir, it all sounds wonderful, but I can't come over this weekend."

"What do you mean, you can't come over this weekend?"

"Just what I said. I have a company acquisition event I'm in charge of, and I have to be in Richmond all weekend managing it. It's for one of the biggest talent procurements we've arranged in years, and I have to be there to make sure it goes flawlessly."

Now the phone really goes silent.

"Galen?"

"I… don't you have staff that handles that sort of thing?"

"Umm, yes and no. They've been helping out, but this isn't something I can just turn over completely. This is a huge talent acquisition for us, and a lot of C-suite eyes are going to be on it, so I have to be there."

"Oh. Well, I guess that's okay."

You guess *that's okay?*

I'm trying not to let myself get angry, but Galen's acting like he can't understand why this is important to me. I'm not expecting him to understand all the corporate politics involved, but surely he heard me say this is a huge deal for the company. He's not a stupid man; he has to know something like this is important enough I need to be hands-on with it.

"Well, I'm glad you approve, sir. I'm sorry it'll interfere with the plans you made."

"Don't get testy with me, Alex. I went to a lot of trouble preparing for this and finding out at the last minute you can't be here is a little irritating."

"Okay, fair enough. I'll admit I did fail to let you know I'd be gone this weekend. I swear to you I meant to, but things have been so hectic this week it slipped my mind."

"Well, keeping me in the loop on your schedule is something you need to work on."

What? Okay, okay, okay, calm down, Alex, calm down. He's just upset. He's a high protocol Dom, he thinks your world revolves around him, and, yeah, he's being an asshole right now, but it's not intentional.

"Besides, honestly, Alex, you *do* realize you don't need to work, right?"

My jaw drops. "I beg your pardon?"

"I'm just saying, you don't have to work. I make more than enough money to take care of us both if you wanted to leave that corporate rat race bullshit behind you."

I go cold.

"Actually, you could come work for me. I know Mia would love that and considering how well you worked your magic on Paul Gaither the other night, it could be the perfect solution to all our problems."

I can't speak. For the moment, I can't force my mouth to let loose the torrent of words pounding their fists at the inside of my skull. I simply grip my phone tighter as the *thump thump thump* of blood hammers in my ears.

"If you weren't shackled to a nine-to-five, things like this would never be an issue," he says in a cavalier tone. "Know what I mean?"

"This is a joke, right?" I finally manage to choke out, trying desperately to keep my voice neutral.

"What's a joke?"

"Uh… everything you just said?"

"No. I mean it, Alex. Come on, think about it. No more worrying about working until oh-dark-thirty and then coming back the next morning just to start all over again. You'd set your own schedule, and we could engage in our dynamic any time we wanted."

"Are you… are you being serious right now?"

"Yes! Of course, I am! Why wouldn't I want to offer this to you? Why wouldn't I want to be able to spend more time together? I'm not saying you'd have to move in immediately or anything like that. You could still have your own place for now, but… without having that job tying you down, you could focus on the things that are important to you."

"Like pleasing you."

"Well… yes. I mean, not *just* that, but you did say one of the things you most enjoyed about our dynamic was serving, right? I'm giving you the opportunity to explore that to the fullest."

"How noble of you."

"Alex, come on. This isn't a bad thing. I mean, I was serious; I can put you to work. There are clearly things in my own business you'd be great at! And Deacon and Mia love you, so there'd be zero ramp-up time getting you acclimated. If anything, keeping Mia off you might be the biggest challenge, but I can always lock you in my office to keep her at bay." He laughs at his own joke, but he might as well be driving daggers into my skull.

The... arrogance. The total, utter bullshit, ballsy arrogance of this man.

"Well. Wow. Such an incredible offer, how could I possibly refuse?"

His laughter dies away, replaced by a sigh. "Jesus Christ, Alex, come on. I don't need that fucking sarcastic tone right now, okay? Why are you making this into such a negative thing? I told you I wouldn't press you about being collared or coming to live here. I'm giving you the space you wanted, right? All I'm doing is offering you a chance to do the very fucking thing you said you wanted the first night we met at Black Light. The ability to explore high protocol in an environment the way you have always envisioned it."

"And all I have to do is give up who I am and everything I've worked for. Where do I sign?"

Galen sighs again. "Okay, clearly you can't talk objectively about this right now. Let's just table this until tomorrow night."

"No, goddammit! We will not table this until tomorrow night because right now there's not going to be a tomorrow night!"

"Oh, come on, Alex, that's ridiculous. You're overreacting."

"What did you just say?"

I can practically hear him gulp through the phone. "I didn't mean it like that. It's just... it's been a long day, a long week, and you're tired, so this probably isn't the best time to be having this discussion."

"Don't you tell me how I'm feeling. I'm more than capable of having this conversation right now. In fact, I insist on it."

"Okay, fine, have it your way. What do you want to talk about?"

I snort. "Well, for starters, why the hell would I need to quit my job to really, truly experience high protocol any differently than we are right now? Since when is me not working a condition for that?"

"Well, I'd think this coming weekend would be a pretty damn good example of why."

"What? Just because I can't come wait on you hand and foot every time you want means I need to give up my career?"

"Pretty sure it would make things a hell of a lot easier, Alex. And I'm pretty sure you can see why."

"Yeah, except the price, Galen. And that's too damn high."

"What? Because you won't be a VP anymore? Seriously, is so much of your identity really wrapped up in that?"

"Yeah, as a matter of fact it is. I worked hard to get where I am." I don't know why I'm on the defensive here because Galen is flat-out wrong about this entire thing, and I don't have a clue why he's being so stubborn about it. "I cannot fathom how you can't understand why I'd balk at this. Here, let's flip the script: you give up *your* business, and I'll pay for everything."

"Don't be ridiculous. I have people who rely on me."

"And I don't?"

"It's not the same, and you know it."

"That's a crap answer, and *you* know it."

"Alex, why are we fighting about this? This shouldn't be something we're fighting over."

"Oh my God, Galen. You seriously can't be telling me you don't understand why I'd be upset by this!"

"Okay, sure, I get this might be a little disconcerting at first, but if you could just take a moment and look at it objectively, you'd see where I'm coming from. The problem here is you don't have the experience I do. You've never really lived in a true, fulltime high protocol relationship. All you've ever had was one single shitty experience that almost soured you entirely. And then we found each other, and now you realize how good things could really be.

"The thing is, I know what it's like to have a partner who's there beside you more than just on the weekends. You don't. You lack that experience and you're convinced without your career you'll lose your identity because up until now that's all you've ever had. You think without being a corporate drone you'll just be 'Galen's submissive,' but that's not true. I know it because I've lived it, and—"

"Galen—" If he doesn't stop mansplaining my own goddamn life to me in about two seconds, I'm going to unload on him in a way he's never experienced before.

"—and Charlotte never worked, and she was perfectly happy!"

I suck in my breath.

"Oh, she was, was she?" I respond with icy calm.

"I..."

He didn't mean to say that. He blurted it out without thinking, and it's painfully clear he wants to take it back, erase those words, scrub them into oblivion. But he can't.

I won't let him.

"Well, that's good to know. It's great your ex didn't have a life beyond being your little sex slave—"

"Don't fucking say that, Alex," he growls, trying to interrupt me, but I ignore him and press on.

"—but I do have a life, Galen. I don't just have a job; I have a *career*. I love the work I do at GSR and I'm damn good at it. I'm not about to give up everything I've worked for, the reputation I've created, just so I can kneel in your kitchen naked, no matter how much each of us may enjoy it."

"Don't fucking twist my words. You know goddamn well that's not what I meant."

"Oh, I know exactly what you meant. And I don't need to twist your words, Galen. You did a fucking fantastic job of it all on your own."

And then I hang up.

My cell starts to buzz almost immediately. I ignore it. Galen Harmon can go straight to hell. I'm done with this.

No, you're not.

I toss the phone on my desk, and it does a little dance as the vibration makes it chatter across the surface. Clenching my hands together, I take slow deep breaths to calm myself. There's a tightness in my chest, but I don't feel like crying. I can't afford to. There's one day left before I have to be on point and make sure one of the biggest events in my career goes off without a hitch.

I can't let Galen do to me what I'm sure he'd love to think is happening right now: making me fall apart. I won't let him. Even as angry as I am, I've loved every minute the two of us have spent together. I wouldn't trade a single second of what we've done for anything. But if this is the end, I'll mourn it later. Right now, I've got to get my head back in the game, and not the game he and I have been playing together.

Except it hasn't been just a game, Alex, and you know it.

No, it hasn't. It started with a game, a challenge that opened my eyes to a world I thought would never be more than a fantasy. Galen had put the lie to that. No, wait... *together* we'd put the lie to that. Together we'd been well on the way to creating the high protocol relationship we'd both been looking for. Mine for the first time, his to...

To replace what he once had.

With her.

The phone continues making a *zzzt zzt zzzz* noise, slipping away until it hits a stack of folders and comes to a stop, jittering. I don't need to look at the screen to know who it is. He fucked up, and he knows it. And if I were the submissive he wishes I would be, the replacement for a woman named Charlotte he once loved deeply, I'd probably answer it. Let him explain away what he's done with calculated words and assurances it will never happen again.

But I'm not her. I never will be. And he needs to pull his head out of his ass and come to terms with that on his own because I won't do it for him.

Ever.

CHAPTER 17

GALEN

"*J*ust..."

Don't be juvenile. Don't pretend you're not getting my messages and texts. Stop acting like we don't have anything to talk about because we fucking do, Alex.

"Please call me back when you have a moment. Thanks."

I end the call and head from the study through the living room, straight past the bar into the kitchen to the fridge. I take out another bottle of mineral water, pop the cap and slug half of it down.

And pull out my phone again to see if she's responded.

She hasn't.

Well, what the fuck did you expect, idiot? It's been, what? All of... ten, fifteen seconds, max? She hasn't responded to anything you've sent her all weekend, but now you think she'll suddenly drop what she's doing to be at your beck and call?

I take a deep breath and let it out slowly. No, I don't expect that, even if I'm acting like I do. The reality is I don't expect her to call or text me back at all, which makes my constant checking to see if she has even worse. I'd love to be one of those Doms who says 'aww, fuck it, your loss,' but that's never been my way. Not with Charlotte, and damn sure not with Alex now.

I glance back toward the living room. The bar is in there, and God knows I could use a stiff drink. Hell, it's been calling to me all weekend, but I've avoided it because if Alex does finally respond, I want to be completely clear headed, not on my third or fourth bourbon making drunken proclamations of love.

Even if it is true.

I run my hand over the top of my head, letting it come to rest at the back of my neck. I'm tense as a goddamn tripwire, but I can't think of a fucking thing to do about it. I tried working out in the gym, took a long run down the road and back, considered relentless masturbation. None of those did or would work. The one thing I know will be effective is the sound of Alex's voice, but she's still on her work thing, and even if she wasn't, her current attitude is abundantly clear.

She's mad. Furious. And she has every right to be.

All I want to do is talk. Explain myself and find out what I can do to correct the situation, but Alex isn't giving me that option. I realize she's busy, but even five minutes after she's done with work for the evening would be better than ghosting me like this.

Maybe she doesn't want to talk to you. Ever.

That's a possibility I refuse to accept.

Yeah, well you may not have a choice here, Ace.

I snatch up the bottle of water from the counter and stalk back to the study. I force myself not to look at my phone because I know I won't find anything there. I have the notification alarms on audio and the volume cranked up all the way so if there's any response from her I'll hear it. Not that it's necessary; the phone's not been out of hand's reach at any point since she hung up on me on Wednesday.

I stare down at the space next to the chair. I told Alex recently how empty the house feels when she isn't here. Now that emptiness is a physical jab because the Sword of Damocles hanging over my head is her absence could become permanent.

And whose fault is that?

I want to tell myself to shut the fuck up because I hate that I'm right. This *is* my fault, but... goddammit, I'm her Dom, and the least she can do is show me the courtesy of returning one text or call.

Oh, yeah, because she owes you, right? You're the big bad Dom, and she needs to obey you and your bullshit rules despite you having behaved like a complete fucking asshole.

I shove up out of the chair. Okay, you know what, fuck this. I stomp into the living room, heading straight for the bar. It's Sunday night, she's probably wrapped up in finishing her event, and I need a large fucking drink and I'm gonna have it.

I step to the bar and spread my hands wide along the front edge.

Go on. Pour yourself a big one. Drink yourself into a fucking stupor because that'll definitely help you forget about how you shit on the only good thing you've had in your life in years.

I clench my fingers until the knuckles crack. The bottles are right there, an arm's length away, but I don't move toward them, and I'm not going to. There's zero chance she's going to call me tonight, but I refuse to get drunk despite that. There's this infinitesimally tiny portion deep inside me that thinks—hopes— she might call, and that's all I need to stop myself.

Dit dit dit dat, doop.

Fuck.

I scramble to yank the phone from my pocket. I'm stone-cold sober and I still nearly drop it as I fumble to get it free. The chime's gone off a second time when I finally do, and for a millisecond all I see is the screen lit up with the Alex's name until it morphs into someone elses.

"Hey, Deacon, what's up?"

"Hey, brother, sorry to bother you on the weekend, but you coming by the hangar tomorrow?"

I close my eyes. "Wasn't planning on it. Why, do you need me?"

"Well, if not tomorrow, Tuesday?"

"Sure. What's up?"

"Got a call from Arthur Möller. He's got a little business he'd like us to take care of for him."

"A 'little' business?"

"Well... you know, for him, a little."

I groan. "How bad are we talking?"

"Well," Deacon draws the word out. "It'll keep us busy until Paul gets those two containers delivered."

My ears go up. "Any word on that?"

"Nope, nothing yet. But you know Paul. As soon as it's cleared, he'll let us know."

"Yeah."

I can't afford to get distracted right now because Alex is the only thing that matters. I know I can't completely ignore business, but... these two things can wait. At least until I'm able to get Alex to fucking respond.

"Okay, I'll come by on Tuesday. I have some things I need to get settled tomorrow."

"Sounds good, boss. We'll see you then." There's a brief pause, then Deacon adds "Oh, and say hi to Alex for us!"

I clench my jaw tight. "Will do," I mutter before ending the call.

I turn away from the bar. I don't need a drink. I need to clear my head somehow, so if Alex does decide to grace me with her presence, I can be ready. Glancing down the hallway, I contemplate going to work out again, or...

I hate myself for even thinking about doing... *that*. It's too late, however. I am, and it's her fault. It's a natural extension of thinking about her, and that's all I've been doing for the last forty-eight hours. Maybe if I fantasize about all the things I'd like to be doing to her in the bedroom and the playroom, it'll relieve a little of the tension that's got me twisted in knots. And even if it doesn't, at least it's better than listening to the siren's song of a bottle I'm *not* going to open.

No matter what.

∽

SUNDAY NIGHT PASSES INTO MONDAY, and I pace my house like a death row inmate waiting for word of his pardon. My hand cramps around my phone as I clench it, waiting for her to answer my at least one of my messages. I haven't sent any new ones since yesterday, but as the day stretches into afternoon, I give up all pretense and tap out a new series, each imploring her to call without trying to sound desperate.

Uh, little late for that, champ. That ship sailed about sixteen hours ago.

As the day continues to creep by, it becomes more and more clear she's not going to call back. It's the day after the event ended, so maybe she's taken the day off, or maybe she's still wrapping things up, doing a post-mortem... there's a thousand different possibilities I can conjure.

If she's not at home recovering, I could try and call her office and see if I could catch her there, except for one problem: I don't have the direct line number to her office. However, she *did* tell me the name of the company she works for, and a Google search shows they're headquartered in D.C., proper.

Since she's a vice president, I could just ask to be put through to her extension, but that's just it: she's a goddamn VP of HR, so the likelihood is she's got a secretary fielding her calls. And even if I lie and don't use my real name, I don't know anyone there I could pretend to be whose name would get me past screening. Using my real name is a non-starter because if she won't answer me on her personal cell, any call announced as 'Galen Harmon on line two' is going straight to voicemail.

Well, none of this would be an issue if you'd taken even a passing interest in what she did for a living or made the effort to connect with any of her work friends.

Idiot.

It's a little late for that now. The benefit of hindsight is worthless at the moment but, as soon as I have the chance to clear this situation up, it's going to be a goddamn priority. I may be a dumbass, but when something's as important as this, I learn quickly.

Tuesday morning dawns, and I'm determined I'm not going to spend it the same way I did yesterday. Plus, I've promised Deacon I'll be at work today at least long enough to go over the Möller stuff he mentioned.

I drag myself out of bed and through a cursory shower, then drive out to the hanger. I've barely made it inside when Mia corners me.

"'Bout time you decided to show up," she says, smoke curving away from the glowing tip of her cigar.

"I had things to take care of."

"Uh huh." Mia keeps glancing around as if she expects to find something—or someone—behind me.

"What?"

"Where's Alex?"

I force myself not to react. "I imagine she's probably at work."

"'Imagine,' huh? Or maybe you left her in bed back home?"

"No."

Her eyes narrow. "That was an awfully quick answer."

Don't do it, Galen. Don't do it...

"I don't where Alex is. I haven't spoken to her since Wednesday."

The temperature inside the hangar drops.

"What did you do?" The words are almost inaudible as Mia slowly removes the cigar from her mouth. Dropping it to the concrete, she deliberately crushes it into the dust before kicking the smoldering remnants away.

"Hey, that's FOD—"

She slams into me. Mia's small, but she has the advantage of surprise *and* she's strong as fuck. Her plane is directly behind us, and she drives my body into it, her hand pinning my chest to the aluminum body of the aircraft.

"The only foreign object damage you need to worry about is what I'm about to do to you," she says in a low, vicious tone.

"Mia—"

"What. The. Fuck. Did. You. Do?" The cadence of her words is punctuated by a series of sharp jabs she makes to my sternum.

"I didn't do anything!" I snap and immediately regret the words.

"You're a fucking liar, Galen Harmon." The hand leaves my breastbone for less than a second before it piledrives back, knocking air from my lungs. "What the fuck did you do!"

"Jesus!" I gasp, sucking in a breath. "What the fuck, Mia!"

"*Tell me!*"

"We had a fight, okay! I… I might have said a couple of stupid things which made it seem like I was pressuring her about where our relationship was heading and then I might have suggested she quit her job because I make more than enough money for the two of us to—"

"Are you out of your fucking mind!" Mia whips free of me and begins walking in a tight little circle. "Oh, my fucking God, I can't believe I've tied myself to a complete and utter fucking *MORON!*" She rounds on me, stepping in until there's no space between us.

"I did admit they were stupid."

Mia's eyes are bulging. "Stupid? Stupid? That's the best description you can think of? Because let me tell you, Galen, those are way, *way* beyond just 'stupid.'"

I bring up my hands. "I realize that and I've been trying to get in touch with her, but she's not returning my texts or calls."

"I wonder why the fuck that would be!"

"Yeah, well pretty fucking hard to set things straight when the person you need to talk to won't return your calls."

Mia's eyes burn holes through me. "Wait. Wait, is that *all* you've done?"

"Is what all I've done?"

"Call her," she growls. "Text her?"

"Umm... yeah?"

"Oh my God, oh my God, ohmigod..." Mia starts pacing in a circular pattern again.

"Listen, I've got this under control. Once she calms down and calls me back, I can set this right."

Mia spins back to me, her face incredulous. "Is that right? You think you can just lay on the ol' Galen charm and wipe away all the bullshit you dumped on her?"

"I'm not going to try and fucking 'charm' her. I seriously want to talk this through!"

"Oh, so *now* you want to talk rather than just telling her what she should do?"

"I never told her—"

"Yes, you did. By your own goddamn admission that's exactly what you did!" Mia bares her teeth at me. "You think you're some kind of cool, calculating, oh-so-fucking smart sonofabitch, but guess what, Galen? There are people in your life who see right through that arrogant bullshit. I saw you fucking *come apart at the seams* after what happened with Charlotte. I seriously thought you were gone. But you came back, and I'm pretty fucking sure a big part of that was because it was Franklin and Charlotte who screwed *you* over, not the other way around. None of what happened in that instance was your fault. But this..." Mia stabs a finger into my chest hard. "This is all you, you fucking asshole. *You* did this. You fucked things up. And *you* are going to have to be the one to make things right."

"How, Mia? How? She won't return my calls."

"Are you seriously this fucking dense?" She tilts her head back and lets a small scream crawl its way up her throat. "Go. Find. Her! Go to her office, her apartment, her favorite restaurant, wherever the fuck it is she likes to hang out. I mean, you *do* fucking know where those places are, right?"

I stare at her.

"No," she says hoarsely, shaking her head. "Oh, no, no, no, no. You *cannot* be this fucking stupid. There's no way. I refuse to believe it."

"Listen, we had other things we were focused on."

Like establishing our dynamic, learning my rules, how I liked things, what my expectations were, how she could serve and obey...

And it hits me like a blow.

"'We' language. You're using 'we' language in this discussion. Not 'I want' or 'you'll do,' but 'we' language. Now I'm impressed."

I hear her voice in my head. I picture the warm smile she'd given me, how full of pride and arrogance I'd felt managing to impress her with something so simple. Of course, I'd used 'we' language. Any good Dom would. It was always about mutual respect, mutual desires, working together toward a common goal.

Until you took the easy way out. Until you turned it into all about you. And she went along with it because she cared for you, wanted to please you. But that wasn't good enough, was it, Galen? You just had to have more.

"Fuck," I whisper.

If Mia hears me, she makes no indication of it. "God, you are such a fucking idiot. I mean, seriously, why are you even here right now?"

"Umm, because I have business to attend to?"

"Oh, so you think your precious little fucking company is as important as saving the single good thing you've had come into your life in years?" She shakes her head. "Goddamn, I can't believe I used to think you were an intelligent man."

"Hey!"

The sharpness of my tone only makes Mia's eyes flame incandescent. Before I'm able to react, she's brought her arm up, clotheslining me across the chest and pressing me back into the fuselage of the plane once more. "You listen to me, Galen fucking Harmon," she hisses. "I don't give a fuck about whatever trivial 'business' you've got going on here. What I *do* care about is you getting your shit together and straightening out the fucking mess you've made."

Mia slams her forearm into my chest, and I swear I hear ribs cracking.

"Your stupid little company can take care of itself. You need to get your ass out there and find Alex and beg that fucking woman to forgive you, no matter what it takes."

"That's what I'm trying to do!" I gasp through breath tight from lungs she won't let fill.

"Then try fucking harder!" She hits me again, and I grunt. "Fix this, Galen, or I swear to God if you don't, I'll kill you."

We've been arguing so heatedly neither of us has heard Deacon's approach.

"Hey, guys, everything okay?"

"No."

"Yes."

Our overlapping answers make him furrow his brow, and even though he's standing there watching us, Mia makes no move to pull away.

"Ooookaay." He gestures toward me. "Uh, Galen, when you're done, could you come see me? I'd like to go over the Möller job."

"I'll be there in a few," I grunt through the pressure Mia continues to exert.

"Maybe," Mia counters in a low tone.

"Yeah, you know what, I'm just gonna leave now, alright?" Deacon turns and walks away without waiting for a response.

"Fifteen minutes," Mia growls. "You got fifteen minutes to do whatever it is you need to do, and then your ass better be walking through that hanger door, Galen. And don't fuck with me, because if I find you here, I'll make sure Alex has to wear her best basic black to your funeral."

"Goddamn you are a bossy sonofabitch."

"You have no fucking idea."

I manage to work out what we need to do for the Möller account with Deacon in just under fifteen, and the man has the good sense not to question me about what went on in the hanger. I don't see Mia as I slip back out to my SUV, but I've little doubt she's around somewhere, watching.

And then I'm back out on the freeway. But I'm not heading home.

It's easy to have Siri bring up directions to GSR. Mia's right, I need to be doing more than just leaving voicemails and text messages. I need to handle this in a way that makes Alex understand I'm not just going to go away without a fight.

There may be a million reasons why she hasn't been returning my calls, but until I'm standing looking into her eyes and explaining how badly I fucked up, none of it matters. All my chatter is just background white noise. The thing is it shouldn't have taken Mia beating sense into me to admit that to myself. The reality is, though, it did, and now I'm heading into D.C. to do just what she'd said.

Fix this. Make it right.

By the time I pull into the parking garage of the building Alex works at I've come up with a hundred different things to say and ways to say it. However, as I stare out the windshield across a sea of cars, I realize I'm not going to do any of them.

The reason is simple: the damage I could do confronting her at her job is easily a thousand times worse than anything I've said to her in private to date. And God knows doing even *more* harm than I already have is the last thing I need right now.

Fuck.

Lost in trying to figure out the perfect way to set things right, I never once stopped to think I could actually make things worse. But storming into Alex's building and demanding she talk to me could potentially be the final nail in the coffin, and even though I'm sitting here less than a thousand feet from where she may be, the thought of fucking things up even worse is enough to keep me from opening the door.

I scrub my hand across my face. *Well, Galen, what the fuck now?*

Exactly. What the fuck now? What I need is someone to sound things out with, someone who understands *everything* going on between Alex and me.

Deacon and Mia are my friends, but neither of them are someone I can have a conversation with where the dynamic between Alex and I is a factor. Alex and I may have joked about Mia being a closeted Domme, but I'm not going to test that theory right now. What I really need is another Dom to help me sort through things, but I really don't have anyone left in the lifestyle I consider close enough to do that with.

Except...

Black Light's closed on Monday's and Tuesday's, but I've learned over the years on those days the staff sometimes handles special events, classes on occasion, or just generally taking care of the more mundane aspects of running a BDSM club. It's in Georgetown and a shorter drive from where I am right now than turning around and heading home. It's a longshot he'll be there, but at the moment it's a chance I'm willing to take, and the only option I have left.

"The club's closed," the woman at the counter says as I move my way through the psychic parlor that masks Black Light's entrance.

"I understand. Is there any way you could call down and ask if an employee is available? I need to speak with him."

She gives me a narrow-eyed look. "You a member?"

"Yes." I answer, nodding my head.

"I thought I'd seen you before." She purses her lips, staring hard at me for a moment. "I really shouldn't be doing this." She picks up a phone from under the counter, then holds it halfway to her ear, gazing at me quizzically. "Well?"

"Terry Robertson," I say quickly.

"Oh. Muscles."

I grin. "Yes, ma'am."

"One sec." She reaches down and taps at something, then speaks softly into the receiver, her eyes never leaving me.

"What's your name?" she asks after a brief conversation.

"Galen Harmon."

She passes it along and a moment later, she hangs up. "Wait by the door. He'll be up shortly."

I move through the curtain to what's normally the entrance to the passage under the street that leads to Black Light. The door's locked, but a few minutes later I hear a *click-clack*, and it opens to reveal Terry.

"Mr. Harmon?"

I've grown so used to seeing Terry over the years in his black pants and dungeon monitor tee shirt that it's a little odd to find him standing in front of me wearing a pair of worn khakis and an untucked white button-down.

"Hey, Terry. Sorry to bother you here, but... do you have a few minutes to talk? In private?"

He gives me a curious look. "Uh, yeah, sure, no problem. Come on." He motions me through the door, and I follow.

It's weird seeing Black Light like this. The club is normally a loud, vibrant, living space, but right now it's abnormally quiet, and eerily subdued. Without the stage and club lighting, the thumping bass coming from the sound system, the crowd of clubgoers and kinksters bringing it to life, it's a theater without an audience, an empty stage before the curtain goes up.

Terry leads me through the club to a door that takes us to a stairway. We head up three flights and through another door into a short hallway with a series of offices. Terry ducks inside an empty one, and once we're in, I find a wall with a one-way mirror that looks down over the blackened club, a large desk, and three or four chairs scattered about.

"So, what's up?" Terry asks politely, arms crossed as he leans against the desk.

I drop into a nearby chair and look up at him. "I fucked up."

His eyes narrow, and he stares at me for a long moment. "Seems like I've heard that from you before." Then his pupils widen. "Wait. Is this about Alex?"

I nod. "Yeah, it is."

"Aww, damn, man. What happened?"

I outline everything that's happened between Alex and I after our first night here, sparing nothing. Terry listens attentively, only stopping me when he needs some clarification. As I replay everything that's taken place over the past months, it seems to me much of what's happened is less my being the complete and total idiot Mia had made me out to be, and more a case of pure misunderstanding between Alex and I.

At least that's what I've convinced myself by the time I finish telling my story.

"Wow," Terry says after a moment of silence. "So, you were trying to create Charlotte 2.0."

My jaw drops. "What?"

"With Alex. All that stuff you did… you were trying to turn her into a carbon-copy of Charlotte."

"What the fuck, Terry! Everything I just told you, and *that's* your takeaway?"

"Yeah. Because it's true."

I practically come up out of the chair. "No, it's not! My relationship with Alex was *nothing* like my relationship with Charlotte."

Terry nods. "Oh, yeah, sure it wasn't. I mean, at least at first. But you were damn sure trying to make it that way."

"No, I wasn't! That's fucking crazy!"

"Is it, though? Is it really?"

"Yes!"

"Nah, bro." He points his finger at me, his voice smooth and calm. "You're fucking kidding yourself if you think it ain't the truth, because that's *exactly* what you've been doing."

Now I do get up. "If that's what you believe after everything I just told you, then clearly coming here was a fucking mistake. I don't have to take this bullshit." I've barely taken two steps when his voice cracks across the space separating us.

"Sit your ass down, goddammit. I ain't finished talking with you yet."

I turn toward him. I could take him on. I wouldn't win; in fact, I'd one hundred percent get my ass kicked, but maybe it would do me some good. Couldn't be any worse than sitting here listening to him make bullshit claims about what I've been doing to Alex.

"Go on," he says evenly. "Either take your shot or sit. I'm fine either way."

I choose to stand but I don't move any further toward the door. "What the fuck do you want from me, Terry?"

"An admission."

"An admission of what?"

"That you weren't over Charlotte. You were close, but you weren't quite there yet. Sure, you were back in the club, looking to try and find someone, but she was still there in your head, affecting everything you did. Then Alex came along at just the right time, and she was the perfect sub for you, just like I knew she would be. Problem was, instead of just letting things take their course, at some point you decided you could make her into the perfect little replacement for what you'd once had."

"That's not what hap—"

"I'm trying to remember, Galen, what was the name of the company Charlotte worked for all those years you two were together? You'll have to excuse me, name's slipping my mind right now."

"I…"

"Oh, yeah, and help me out… how long was it after the two of you met she became your full-time sub? Was it a month, or two, maybe three? I seem to recollect it was less than three, but, damn, you know me, I'm just a dumb sonofabitch, so sometimes I forget things like that."

"Terry, don't—"

"Oh, yeah, and when exactly was it Charlotte moved into your place? Like… it took at least a year, right? Couldn't possibly have been within the first two fucking months you guys hooked up together."

Terry hasn't raised his voice, but there's an intensity to it that stops me in my tracks. He's angrier than I've ever seen him before. He's standing there with arms crossed, staring at me, but if his gaze could tear me a new asshole, it would.

"Yeah, I mean, you *never* introduced Charlotte to your work friends either, did you? No… she only knew the people you ran with here at Black Light. She didn't know shit about your life beyond what you had in the club and at home, isn't that right?"

This time I don't even try and interject. I just stare at him, my jaw clenched.

"Come on, Galen, help me out here. Tell me I'm wrong. Tell me none of the things I just described happening with Charlotte ain't the *exact same goddamn things you tried to make happen with Alex.*" Now his voice does go up, and it feels like he's driven a fist straight into my gut.

"Goddammit," I whisper.

"Yeah," Terry says softly, nodding. "Goddammit, Galen."

I sit back down in the chair. "What the hell did I do?" I look up at him bleakly.

"Like you said, you fucked up. And just like the last time this happened, I told you it wouldn't be the last. And so, what you have to do now is the same thing you did before. You fix it."

"Except I didn't fix it. *You* did. You introduced me to Alex."

"And that's *all* I did. You took over from there. You gave that young woman what she wanted, what she'd been looking for."

"And then I fucked it all up."

Terry nods. "Yeah, ain't gonna lie; you did. But that don't mean it's permanent."

I blow out a ragged sigh. "God, I sure as fuck hope not."

"I told you before, Galen, you're a good man. I meant that. And I think Alex probably knows it too. But even if she doesn't fully understand *why* you did what you did, I'm betting she suspects something drove you to it. This shit doesn't happen in a vacuum, and that woman's smart. She'll get it. All you need to do is practice all the shit we preach about in the lifestyle. Communication. Honesty. Truthfulness. And not just with her but with yourself too. Don't try and pretend what happened didn't happen, and don't try to pin it on her."

I snap my head up. "I wouldn't fucking do that."

"Yeah? Need me to go over the last ten minutes of our conversation?"

I don't say anything, because... again, he's right. It's not easy to swallow, but the reality is the only path out of this mess is for me to admit what I've done. First to myself, and then to Alex.

"So what do I do now?"

For the first time in several minutes, Terry looks at me with sympathy. "Well, I'd say your friend Mia was right: you need to go find Alex and speak to her in person. Not in texts or leaving her voice mails, but face to face."

I sigh. "Well, I went to where she works before I came here, but I talked myself out of going inside because getting into a scene with her in her office would probably only make things worse."

"See?" Terry points his finger at me. "You can be a smart man when you want to be."

"Thanks," I respond with a grimace.

"So, don't do it at her work. Do it someplace where the two of you can talk in private."

"I doubt I can convince her to come to my house anytime soon."

Terry frowns at me. "Why's it gotta be at *your* house?" He points his finger at me. "That's Old Galen talking."

"Shit." I close my eyes, recognizing exactly what he's saying.

"You know where she lives?"

Mia had bitched me out because I'd told her I didn't know any of the places Alex frequented. But that wasn't entirely true: I *do* know where she lives. Alex had given me her address. The place I'd never visited, the place where she carried on her life outside of the one I'd created for her in my home.

"Yeah, I know where she lives."

"Then you know what you need to do."

I look over at Terry. A tiny ember of hope has sprung to life inside me, and I don't want to snuff it out. Everything I do now carries some risk, but the one thing I refuse to do is nothing.

That's simply out of the question.

"Yeah, I do," I say with grim determination. "I just hope it's not going be too little, too late."

CHAPTER 18

ALEX

*O*h, shit.

He's at the door. *My* door. The app on my phone shows him standing there, a bag slung over his shoulder, staring back into the camera. How did he get past security? No one is supposed to be able to get up here without being rung up, but… it's Galen. He's resourceful, and I've little doubt that's a factor in how he's managed to be standing where he is right now.

I get up and move to the door. Taking a deep breath, I undo the lock and open it a crack.

"Galen?"

"Hi. Can I come in?"

I take a deep breath, then close the door. The calls and texts from earlier in the week had tapered off, and I wasn't sure what his next move was going to be. His standing here now isn't entirely unexpected, but…

Well, are you going to do this? Let him in, or just keep the door closed and walk away forever?

I undo the safety catch and open the door. Galen waits for a second before stepping through. He turns and looks back at me as I close the door then wait in silence.

Not gonna do this for you, Galen. This is all on you.

"Umm... can we talk?" he asks politely.

"I don't know, can we?"

"I'd like to try."

I stare at him, trying to figure out what his approach is going to be. Is he going to feign ignorance about the circumstances of why what happened between us did? Is he going to try and guilt me into thinking this is all somehow my fault?

Well, he's standing there. Only one way to find out.

"I was wondering if you were going to take the hint." I say coolly.

"Yeah, umm... I needed a little push. A couple of them, actually."

I shake my head slowly. "Seriously?"

"Stupid behavior seems to be my new specialty."

"I seriously doubt that, Galen. You may be a little slow on the uptake, but you're not a stupid man."

"We'll have to agree to disagree," he responds with a polite smile. "Now, I know this is going to sound like a really weird question, but could I see your kitchen?"

I quirk an eyebrow upward. "Sure, right this way."

I step past him and walk down the short hallway before turning right and heading into the kitchen.

Galen follows, scanning the area once we're both in the room. "Can I set my gear bag over there?" He motions to the breakfast bar that divides the kitchen from my dining room.

"Gear bag." *He's got to be kidding. If he thinks for one second we're...* "Galen, before we go any further, I need to be clear: there is no way we're—"

He holds up his hand, stopping me with a placating gesture. "Alex, it's not what you think." He moves to the counter, motioning toward the top of it with his bag.

I purse my lips, then nod. "Go ahead."

He sets the tote down, then unzips it. Reaching in, he pulls out something large and black.

The cast iron pan.

As I watch in silence, Galen continues to unload the duffel. There's another smaller pan, then seasonings and spices. He's brought carefully packaged food, and though I can't be certain, it looks like everything he needs to make the exact same dinner he prepared the first night I came to his home.

A dinner I suspect he hopes will be the start of a new beginning between us.

When everything is laid out, he stands and stares at me, his hands at his sides.

"I'd like to make you dinner, Alex. And talk if you're okay with that?"

I'll give him credit: he's planned this well. The gesture itself is a good starting place, if nothing else. "Okay, Galen," I say, nodding. "Sure. You can make me dinner. And I'll listen, but I won't promise you anything more than that."

"That's all I'm asking."

He begins moving about the kitchen, spreading out his tools and utensils. His kitchen layout is different from mine, but that doesn't seem to slow him.

"Olive oil?"

"In the pantry behind that door," I say, pointing. "EVOO is on the third shelf."

"Perfect. Thank you."

As he continues, I move back to the living room and pick up the glass of wine I'd poured earlier. Once in hand, I move to the bar counter, sitting on one of the stools.

"How did your event go?" he asks politely.

It's a ballsy question to start the conversation with, considering everything that happened the other night. "It went well," I answer finally. "Except for a few minor negotiations remaining, we closed the deal. All in all, everyone was pretty pleased."

"They owe it all to you."

I frown. "Oh, they do, do they?"

"I've seen your work. I know what you're capable of. I'm positive of it."

I can't help but chuckle. "Well, that's very nice of you to say, but it wasn't just me. A lot of people put in a lot of time and effort to make it happen. I will say, though, I'm really proud of how it all came together in the end."

"As you should be."

Galen keeps the conversation light as he continues fixing dinner. My gut tells me he's doing it to avoid the 'real' conversation for now, and I can understand why. I'm sure his tactic is to soften me up a little, wear off the sharpness of my anger. It's not going to work, but he doesn't know that. Still, the food *does* smell wonderful, so I can't say I don't appreciate the effort.

"You have a beautiful home."

"That's very kind of you to say."

"I love the way you've decorated it. It has an almost post-Modernist feel, but some of the accent pieces seem more rustic than what you typically associate with the style. The dichotomy works very well."

"Ooo. Now you're trying to impress me. I'm wise to your ways though, Galen Harmon."

"You wound me," he says, placing his hand over his heart. "I was being sincere."

I laugh. "Well, even if you weren't, I appreciate the compliment."

"I meant it," he says in a serious tone. "You've done an incredible job here. I really love it."

"Thank you," I say graciously. "I'll admit, I'm rather proud of it."

We continue talking and when I gauge he's nearly finished cooking, I get up from my stool. "You're almost done, right?"

"Yeah, pretty much."

"I'll go set the table."

"Wait," he calls out.

I turn to look back at him.

"I can do it. Just tell me where the dishes are."

"Galen," I say with a sigh, "I appreciate the gesture, but I can set the table in my own home."

"I'm just saying you don't have to. I can do it, just tell me where you—"

"Galen." I shoot him a chiding look, and he snaps his mouth shut. "I'll set the table. Finish making dinner, please." Before he can argue further, I turn away and move toward the dining room.

I've almost completed the task when Galen comes out with a salad, then grabs up each of our dishes. He comes back shortly with our meals plated and sets them in place.

"I'll be back in a sec." A moment later he returns with the bottle of wine I'd opened before he arrived plus a bottle of mineral water for himself.

"Here." He motions toward my glass, and I hold it out as he pours.

"Thank you, s—"

The sibilant sound at the end is infinitesimally brief before I'm able to cut it off. I hope he missed it. I remember how powerful he said the word 'sir' is for him, and though things are going pleasantly enough right now, I'm not ready to give that to him yet.

I wait until Galen seats himself before I cut into the chicken. Taking the first bite, I can't help but smile. "This is just as good as I remember."

"I was wondering if you would."

I shoot him a look. "Of course, I remember. It wasn't *that* long ago."

"Well, considering the last five days, I thought maybe you'd purged the memory."

"Oh, come on. Don't you think that's a little dramatic?"

He stops with his next bite halfway to his mouth. "So, it was no big deal to you?"

"I didn't say that."

Galen stares at me in silence.

"Okay, no it wasn't pleasant," I say finally, pointing my fork at him. "But I was damned if I was going to be the one to go running after you. It's so damn easy as a sub to convince yourself it's your duty to make the first move, but that's not right, especially in a situation like this."

"You're right. It's not," he says firmly. "It just took me some time to come to the realization."

"And with some help from others, I think you said." I purse my lips in contemplation. "Let me guess: Deacon and Mia?"

"Close. Mia and Terry."

I lower my fork. "You went to Black Light?"

He holds up his hand in an imploring gesture. "Not during club hours. I went during the day so I could talk to Terry in private."

"Ah." It's hard to keep my voice neutral because the idea of Galen going to Black Light without me so soon after what happened...

"He had a little come-to-Jesus talk with me."

"About?"

He heaves out a sigh. "About me fucking up. About what I was doing." He pushes at the food on his plate. "I was going to wait until after dinner to get into this, but there's really no point in waiting, is there?"

I give him a tiny shake of my head.

"Okay. So, would you like to hear a story, Alex? About a woman named Charlotte?"

I freeze.

"I take it you've heard the name before," he says, his gaze piercing. "Let me guess. Mia?"

I nod.

"Figured." He sets down his fork and takes a drink before resuming.

"When I got out of the Army, I came back to Virginia and went to work for a company called GlobaLocate. They're a big outfit that does heavy machinery moves worldwide."

"You mentioned that. Not the name, but what you were doing. That was before that guy Colbie came back from Iraq and looked you up, right?"

"Exactly. But there was something else that happened during the same time. I'd always strongly identified as a Dom, but I'd never really had much opportunity to explore that part of me. When I was out of the military, though, settled into new digs, with a new job, I started doing some research. I went to a couple of munches in the D.C. area, went to Crucible, made some friends. One of them was a guy named Franklin Pierce."

There's tension in Galen's face as he says the name.

"Franklin was a Dom I met at Crucible. I can't remember exactly how we first met, but he was very much into the high protocol, Gorean lifestyle. He was some sort of lobbyist in the medical industry, but he was deeply embedded in the local scene at the time, and I'll admit I kinda ended up bird-dogging him. I was never really into the Gorean dynamic, but he was one of the few Doms I'd met who was into high protocol at all, so it made sense we fell in together. The thing about him was…he was just so charismatic. He was charming and dominant, and subs just seemed to naturally gravitate toward him. Since I was a new Dom, it made sense I spent a lot of time asking him questions, watching what he did. And boy, let me tell you, that sure as hell played into his ego. The more we hung out together, the more I genuinely believed we were friends."

"I'm sensing a 'but' here."

Galen holds up his hand. "We'll get there. Anyways, Franklin and I spent a lot of time at local munches and at Crucible, and eventually through some contact of his he got an invite to Black Light. Not long afterward, he managed to finagle one for me." He pauses for a moment, staring into my eyes.

"That's where I met Charlotte."

I do everything to keep my face emotionless.

"Franklin was the one who introduced me to her. She was new to the whole lifestyle, and she was trying out a little bit of everything to figure out what she liked. Franklin wasn't really interested in her because she had no experience, and experience was a big thing with him. He didn't like having to 'train' a sub. He expected them to know how to, in his words, 'serve a Dom properly.' Someone like Charlotte was the last thing he was looking for. But since I was a fairly new Dom, and Charlotte had expressed interest in high protocol, Franklin thought we might hit it off."

Galen smiles ruefully. "He was right. We did. In fact, I ended up falling in love with her."

He stops and looks across at me. If he thought I'd flinch at his use of the 'L' word regarding Charlotte, he's mistaken. I'd seen it in his face in all those pictures, right up until the last one. But Galen doesn't know that, so I keep my expression neutral.

"She became my life," he continues a moment later. "I was completely and utterly devoted to her. She was the perfect submissive. We learned together, discovered what we liked and disliked, created our very own high protocol dynamic, and it was *fucking incredible.*"

He stops and for a brief second smiles, lost in memory.

"Except when I had to be at work or away on business, we spent every waking moment together. Charlotte never took a job. Instead, she lived with me, working on our dynamic, building a life centered around my rules, my desires, my protocols. I can't begin to tell you how fucking amazing it was. She was flawless.

Perfection. She anticipated my needs, even when I didn't realize them myself. She and I grew together, and she supported and sustained me through the years as I built up my business along with everything else. Deacon and Mia loved her. They became our friends outside of the lifestyle because neither of them is into that, as I'm sure you figured out."

"Umm, I might disagree with you on that where it concerns Mia."

He laughs. "Okay, fair enough. If she is, she hides it well. Anyways..." Galen takes another sip of his water before continuing. "Charlotte and I were in love, and she was honestly the driving force behind how solid our dynamic became. She... she studied BDSM like it was an art form. Like she was trying to get a Master's in it. She knew all the various ways people practiced BDSM,, what seemed to work and what didn't. By this time, we'd become regulars at Black Light, and even though we weren't involved in a lot of the events they hold, people knew us. In fact, that's how I met Terry."

"He told me once you'd been a member for quite some time."

"We were. It was... even now, I can't believe how incredible it was. How lucky I was. And how much I took it for granted."

"Why do you say that?"

His mouth tightens into a thin line. "Because just like with you, I didn't see the signs."

"What do you mean by that?" I ask cautiously. "What happened?"

He takes a deep breath. "As I said, I was working on both my business and on being the Dom Charlotte deserved. At home things were great, at least as far as I was concerned. Charlotte seemed happy, and she was constantly challenging me with new ideas, new ways of serving, ways of pleasing me I'd never even fucking thought of. You remember how I taught you to make my coffee?"

"Yes?"

"I didn't come up with that. Charlotte did. There were lots of things like that, and I loved it. When we were in the club, she was fucking on point the moment we walked through the door. It was like she was in her element, on stage, the star of her own show. I realize I'm biased, but she stood out among all the other subs in the beauty of her service, the flawlessness of it. And it didn't go unnoticed by other Doms. Especially one."

"Franklin."

I didn't mean to blurt his name, but so much of what I'd only guessed at before now becomes clear. The more Galen continues, the more pieces of the puzzle start to fall into place.

And I don't like the picture they're creating.

"Yeah. Franklin." Galen's voice is bitter. "Remember when I said the reason Franklin introduced Charlotte to me was because he wasn't really interested in her? Well, that began to change. Now all of a sudden, he noticed her, and he clearly liked what he saw. He started spending more time with the two of us, and even though it was happening right in front of my eyes, I never caught on to what was taking place because Franklin was such a manipulative fucking sonofabitch."

I clench my hands together in my lap.

"He was so... subtle. So... smooth. And he did it in so many tiny little ways. You know, little comments when Charlotte was kneeling beside me about how some other sub he knew was into high protocol and they were just *soooo* fucking good at it. Or how this one sub had done this thing for him perfectly. He was fucking slick; he never made the comments directly *to* Charlotte, but he *always* made sure they were in her presence. And the closer the three of us became, the more time he spent with us inside and outside the club, which gave him all sorts of opportunities to play his little bullshit mind games.

"It was insidious. I'd be cooking dinner, and he'd be standing in the doorway to the dining room just chatting with Charlotte while she was going about her tasks, and he'd critique her on what she was doing. He was a Dom, and my friend, so I never really thought much about it. We were all friends, right? One night after dinner the three of us were sitting in the study, and I mentioned I was going to be out of town for a couple of days for work, and he said, 'I'll keep an eye on her.' Nothing more than that, and like a fucking idiot I just blew it off."

I remember the final picture from that night in the study. The lines of tension I'd seen at the corners of Galen's eyes. Something *had* been wrong. He may not have understood fully, but it's clear now he understood something was changing, and not in a good way.

"That's when it began. That's when Franklin started the slow, meticulous process of turning the woman I loved against me. See, like I said before, Charlotte was always striving to be the best sub she could be. She took everything as a challenge. Franklin manipulated that. Perverted it. It took him more than two years, but that was one thing he and I shared; we were patient. To him, taking control of Charlotte was the ultimate challenge. A game he was determined to win."

A game. A challenge. But nothing—*nothing*— like the one Galen and I had shared.

"At first, I took her comments about wanting to take our dynamic to the next level as nothing more than a continuation of what she'd been doing for years. I supported her because… why the hell wouldn't I? It started off with her saying she wanted to up her submission in the club by not just serving me, but other Doms too."

"Including Franklin, right?"

Galen shakes his head. "Oh, no, not at first. Franklin was fucking smart. It was always some other Dom we knew, or a random one. It was never sexual, just things like bringing and offering drinks or kneeling at our feet. The closest it ever came to any form of intimacy was a Dom occasionally stroking her hair. At first it was kinda intoxicating. She was my sub, and she was serving these other men at my discretion. But no matter what, at the end of the day she was still mine, and always coming home with me. I'm not gonna lie—it was ego-gratifying on a whole other level, and I'll admit I totally got into the power exchange of it.

"But it didn't stop there." Galen pauses and stares through me across the room.

"What happened, Galen?"

He blinks, coming back to the present. "You're intelligent. I'm pretty sure you have a good idea what happened next. Franklin fed her his poison in tantalizing little drops, and the more he praised her for taking it, the more she wanted. He worked slow, but within a year she wasn't just satisfied with serving drinks or performing cigar service. No, now she started talking about sex. Blowjobs. Pleasuring multiple partners, all of it couched in the bullshit high protocol language Franklin was whispering in her ear."

His voice is tight, bitterness laced with an undercurrent of rage. "We fought. I told her there was no fucking way I wanted any part of what she claimed we needed to do to take our dynamic to 'the next level.' I refused to allow her to have sex with other Doms, and all she did was argue I was holding her back from experiencing high protocol to its fullest extent. She pleaded with me to talk to Franklin, to have him explain the whole Gorean, Master / slave, freeuse dynamic. That's when it finally fucking dawned on me what he'd been doing."

Galen leans back in his chair, hands clenched vise-like at the back of his head. I say nothing, but every part of me screams to go to him, to kneel at his side and comfort him. But I don't. He needs to get through this as much as I need him to, and while I want to ease what this is doing to him, I won't, at least not yet.

"I called him out on it," he continues, his voice soft but intense. "Franklin had the fucking *gall* to tell me I was out of my league with Charlotte. That she'd grown beyond me. I kicked him out of my house and told him to never show his fucking face there ever again. Charlotte and I fought. I tried reasoning with her, but he'd done his job well, and every conversation ended in argument. I tried desperately to get things back to the way they'd been, but instead things just got worse. I stopped taking her to Black Light, and for a short time I thought that might put an end to it. But it didn't. She simply went without me. The end was the night I caught her fucking another Dom."

"Oh my God..."

"I knew she was there, even though she'd lied and said she wouldn't be. She'd ignored my calls and texts, but I searched until I finally found someone who'd seen her go into one of the private rooms. That's where I found her. With them."

"Them?"

"Yeah, Alex. *Them.* Franklin was in there with her and another man. Encouraging her. Telling her what she should do, how she should *fuck* this guy. The second I came through the door, he just turned and smiled at me. The fucker *smiled.*"

Pressure builds at the back of my eyes, but I don't let the tears fall.

"I hit him. I hit him so fucking hard, and then I hit him again, and he went down, and Charlotte was screaming, and the DMs were pulling me off him and dragging me back through the club, and..."

He stops, staring across the room with eyes that bleed both rage and pain.

"I got a one-month suspension from Black Light, but that was the least of my worries. Charlotte didn't come home that night. In fact, she didn't come home for a week. Like I did with you, I tried calling, texting, leaving her messages, but she ignored them all. When she finally did show up it was with Franklin and three other men. They were all part of some group Franklin had organized, a sort of Gorean fuckfest clique he'd formed to explore 'true high protocol.' Charlotte was going off to be his slave, and she just wanted to get some of her things before she left."

Galen stops, his gazed fixed as we sit in silence for a moment.

"I never saw her again."

I start to speak, but he holds up his hand to stop me.

"Anyways, there you go. There's the story of my wonderful, incredible, completely screwed up long-term high protocol relationship. The one I didn't want to tell you about. The one I thought I was protecting you from. And you want to know what the really, *really* fucked up thing is? It wasn't that Franklin was able to manipulate her, because the truth is somewhere deep down, I think Charlotte really *did* want all that Gorean bullshit, and I was *never* going to be able to give that to her. No, the *really* fucked up thing is this: I was trying to recreate her in you."

For a second, my throat constricts. He... he doesn't mean that. He can't mean that. Except one glance at his face tells me I'm wrong.

"Galen..." I finally manage to whisper.

"It's true. All my rules, all the instructions I gave you, all the protocols I set in place... they're the *exact same ones* I'd given Charlotte. And then I tried to collar you, get you to move in, to quit your job to be with me fulltime, all because I'm a selfish fucking asshole who never once stopped to consider whether those were things *you* wanted or not. That's what Terry made me realize. I was trying make you into her so I could pretend I hadn't fucked up, hadn't been so stupid and blind to what had happened. So, I could recreate the years I'd had with her when things were good, except this time I wouldn't let them end the way they had."

"Galen." I get up from my chair and walk silently around the table to his side. He doesn't move, but simply watches, his face a landscape of regret. Slowly, without taking my gaze from his, I kneel by his side.

"Don't, Alex," he pleads quietly. "Please don't."

"Why, sir?"

"Because."

"Because you don't deserve this? Because you're an arrogant, egotistical, selfish man who doesn't deserve someone like me? Is that what you want me to say?"

"Yeah. Pretty much."

"No, Galen. No, I'm not going to give you that because it's *not* the truth. You're a good man who has his faults but being too trusting isn't one of them. You trusted her, and she defiled that trust. Sure, Franklin manipulated the situation, but what took place with her didn't happen in a vacuum. In the end, she made her own choices. And though you may not want to believe it, ultimately there's nothing you could've done to stop what happened. You said it yourself: you were never going to be able to give her what she ultimately wanted. I will say this, though: she's a fucking fool, and I'm honestly glad she did what she did, because I've been with you, Galen Harmon, and I love the man you are."

Galen blinks.

"Yeah, I said it. And I think we both know it's something we've wanted to say to each other for a while now. You're right about one thing, though. I will *never* be Charlotte. I'll always be me, and if that's not enough, then I'd much rather we parted ways as friends than as enemies."

"That's not what I want, Alex."

"Neither do I. But you can't make me into something I'm not."

Galen reaches for me, then hesitates. I don't flinch or pull away, and eventually he continues, running his hand along the side of my face to caress me. "I didn't mean to do what I did. You have to believe me."

"I do. I've always trusted you because I'm a pretty good judge of character. It's part of what makes me good at my job. I said it before—you're a good man, Galen. You just need to put the past in the past and let it go. Especially if you truly believe there's any sort of future with me."

"I don't want Charlotte. I want you," he says softly.

"Then prove it. Show me you trust me. Fully, without reservation. Don't *hide* things from me. And don't try and protect me from things I don't need protecting from. I know you're my Dom, and some of that comes with the territory, but I also know you're a very intelligent man. You know the differences. So do what you know is the right thing to do, okay?"

He smiles. "Okay." And he bends and kisses me.

God, it feels so good. I'd be lying if I said I hadn't missed Galen this week. Now, to be here with him, having finally heard the full story of what had happened between him and Charlotte, it feels like a weight has been lifted. I mean, I'm still angry with him; what he's told me tonight doesn't make what he *did* right. But he *is* a good man. And I wasn't lying when I said I love him, because I do.

"Galen," I whisper when he pulls back.

"Yes?"

"In your home, in the study..."

He looks at me quizzically.

"I found the box."

For a moment he looks confused, and then recognition spreads across his face in a way that tells me he knows exactly what I'm talking about.

"The pictures."

"Yes." I bite my lower lip. "I'm sorry, sir. I didn't mean to pry."

"Alex, don't." He caresses my cheek again. "You've got no reason to apologize. I told you my home was yours. There was—is —nothing there I'm trying to hide from you."

"Still... I shouldn't have done it." I look down for a moment before I bring my gaze back up to his. "She was beautiful, Galen."

He nods. "She was. But you're more than she could ever hope to be."

This time his kiss is pure passion. I lose track of how long our lips connect, tasting, biting, tongues entwined. When Galen finally does pull back it's not completely, but with his forehead pressed to mine.

"We can throw out every rule I ever made, Alex. Start fresh, make new ones. Create a whole new dynamic that's strictly our own."

"But we *did*. Just because some of the rules and protocols we had were the same ones you made with her doesn't make our dynamic the same. Those things belong to us now. She doesn't own them anymore. I do."

Galen grins, and the warmth of it flushes me. "Oh. So, *you* own me now, do you?"

"You're damn right I do." And this time it's me who kisses him.

When I finally manage to pull myself away, I stand and reach down to grip his hand. "I don't think I gave you a tour of my home when you arrived. Would you like to see it?"

Galen laughs. "If it would please you."

Now I laugh. "You remembered!"

"Of course, I did. I remember every single moment I've spent with you."

"Oh, really?"

"Yes, really."

I grin, then pull him along eagerly. "This is my dining room. Over there is the kitchen, which you already know. This way"—I tug him forward—"is my living room. Sorry, no Mondrian."

Galen chuckles. "I'll buy you one."

I drag him into the hall, pointing to either side as we go. "My office—the closest thing I have to your study. A spare bedroom I'm using as a workout space, guest bath, and then..."

I drop Galen's hand as I step into my bedroom. I cross the short distance to the end of the bed, then slowly turn around. Galen's standing in the doorway, and without breaking contact with his gaze, I grab my shirt and slowly lift it over my head. I unhook my bra and toss it to the ground, then slip my pants over my hips until they're in a crumpled heap at my feet. Kicking them away, I tug my panties off to join the rest, then with slow deliberate movement I lower myself into a kneeling position before him.

I turn my face to the floor, placing my hands on my thighs in the nadu position. "My bedroom, sir."

Silence rings in my ears, then the sound of Galen crossing the short distance separating us breaks the quiet. A second later the tips of his shoes come into my vision as he comes to a stop in front of me.

"I don't deserve you," he says quietly.

"And if I offer myself to you willingly, Galen? Will you deny me that? Tell me I'm wrong? Try and convince me I'm making a mistake?"

"No."

"Good. An incredible Dom I once knew told me to 'just accept this for what it is, enjoy what we have, and see where things go.' To not overthink it. I suggest that's exactly what we do."

"Once knew?"

"Well, I'd like to think I'll have the chance to get to know him all over again."

Galen slowly lowers himself in front of me. "Look at me."

I tilt my face up.

"I'm pretty sure you only need to tell him that's what you want, and he'll make damn sure he does everything in the world to make it happen."

Don't do it, Alex. Don't do it.

"I thought that's what I was doing, but... you know, he *is* kinda dense sometimes. Maybe I better come up with a different plan."

For a moment the room goes silent once more. Then, shaking his head, Galen chuckles. "I knew I should have left some implements in my bag."

"I'm sure you'll manage to make do, sir," I say, grinning impishly.

He brings his hand up and strokes my cheek before letting it come to rest at the back of my neck. "Oh, I'm sure I will."

The delicious bite of five fingers digging into my skin sends electricity shooting up my spine as Galen pulls me up. He moves me backwards until the edge of the bed hits the backs of my knees before pushing me down onto the mattress.

"Stop me now, Alex. When I first showed up tonight, you said nothing was going to happen, and I respect that. But right now, unless you say something…" His voice trails off, and the heat in his gaze sends a shiver arcing through me.

"A girl can change her mind, can't she?"

"For you, for this?" His voice is heated with desire. "Always." The last word has barely left his mouth and his shirt is up and over his head. Tossing it aside, Galen peels himself out of the rest of his clothing as I slip further up onto the bed. When he's done, Galen follows me, pushing my legs apart as he cages me with his hands on either side.

"Gotcha."

"Oh, no, sir! What ever shall I do?" I lightly tap his chest with curled fists, my faux mewl dissolving us both into laughter.

After a moment, we stop, and Galen strokes my face with his gaze. "I meant what I said earlier, Alex. We can throw out all the old rules and start new."

"Sir. I *like* your rules. I love the dynamic we've created. I just didn't like the pressure you were putting me under."

Galen's pressing into me, and common sense tells me I shouldn't say what I'm going to next.

"That is," I go on, ignoring the voice in my head as I grind against his erection, "except for maybe *this* pressure."

Worth it.

He groans. "New rule. There'll be no more of that. Ever."

"I don't think that's going to work, sir."

"No, it won't," he says, pinning me in place with a wicked grin. "But it will make for some nice excuses to punish you."

"As if you need that."

Galen chuckles, then his fingers dig into my hip as he adjusts me into place. As the tip of his cock comes to rest between my labia, I moan, shifting to allow him access.

"Patience, little girl," he growls.

"Yes, sir," I whisper, but the sigh I give him is pure need.

Galen presses forward, and my body responds. I'm wet, which is all the encouragement he needs.

"Fuck, Alex." He grips me tightly a second before slamming into me.

"*Yesssss!*" The hiss I make as he thrusts is a mix of pleasure and pain combined. "Please sir!"

His hips come to rest against me, his length deep inside. My pussy squeezes him as he pulls back, clenching the warm flesh of his cock. Closing my eyes, I fall into the moment and let the sensation of Galen fucking me wipe away the last five days.

There's a lot we need to talk about, and while Galen may be overthinking the damage he's done to our relationship, nothing that's happened has made me contemplate what he fears the most —that I'll abandon him. After this evening, I know why that is. But dealing with all that can wait. Right now, all I want him to do is fuck me.

And he does.

Galen pounds into me hard, taking his own pleasure, and that itself is a thrill I cannot deny. I've never shied from letting him know how much I crave serving him, how arousing the act is to me, and I don't do it now.

"Do it, sir. Fill me with your cock. Take my pussy. Take what's yours."

I don't want to call what we're doing 'make-up sex,' but whatever it is, the savage way he hammers into me reminds me of our first time, and my pussy throbs with need. I'm riding him as much as he is me, and the sheer force of it pushes me toward the crest of an orgasm, an edge I'm so ready to freefall over into the release I need.

"Fuck, Alex, you feel so fucking good. I'm not going to be able to hold out much longer."

"Don't Galen. Please don't. I want to serve you. I want to feel you fill me. I want to feel your cum inside me."

The words draw a deep growl from him, and he thrusts into me harder, faster. My pussy squeezes his cock in response, a pleasure loop that grows in intensity as we feed off one another.

Galen's close. His girth swells with every thrust, the friction of my own swollen flesh pulling him toward release. I'm as close as he is, and the moment he comes inside me I'm certain I'm going to fly apart into a million billion pieces.

"Fuck. Fuck, I'm gonna..."

"*Fuck!*"

The pulse of his cock within me draws out a cry of pleasure, and the sharp bite of his fingernails into my thighs has my hips bucking up to meet his final downward thrust. As his cock jerks inside me, I fall into the blissful starburst of oblivion I've been seeking.

"Goddamn." Galen's voice is a low, breathy rumble above me, and the weight of him crushing me to the bed feels primal.

"God, I hope that felt as good for you as it did for me," I say softly.

"What the fuck do you think, little girl?"

"I'll take that as a yes, sir."

For a moment Galen continues to pin me in place, and then he bends down and kisses me. I bring my hands up from his hips, trailing up his back, one pausing between his shoulder blades while the other comes to rest at back of his head. The kiss goes on, and I'm not certain what it's doing for Galen, but for me, more than any other single moment this evening, it signals a new beginning.

Our new beginning.

Finally, he breaks the kiss and rolls to his side, pulling me up and onto his chest as he does. We lie in silence, the sweat from our lovemaking cooling.

"Galen."

"Yes?"

"This doesn't reset everything. I want you to know that."

He nods. "That's going to take time. I really, *really* fucked up."

I sigh. "Not as badly as I think you've convinced yourself, but... we def have things we need to work on."

"As long as we can do that, I swear that's all I'll ask."

"Just do me a favor, sir."

"Anything."

"I love you and I love our dynamic. Please don't take that from me. I need you to be the same man who challenged me that night at Black Light. The same man who made me set the table the first night at your home to see how I'd handle it on my own. The Dom who put me up on the pony knowing full well I'd enjoy it, even when I said I wouldn't. The man who stood behind me at his kitchen counter and showed me how to properly clean a cast iron skillet."

"Aw, shit!" The exclamation cuts me off, and Galen tilts his head back, his eyes closed.

"What?" I ask, startled.

"My skillet. It's in your kitchen, but I forgot to bring my chainmail. It's still sitting at home."

"Middle counter, top right drawer."

He turns to look at me, his eyes narrowing in confusion. "Wait. Why would you have a chainmail? I saw your pots and pans while I was cooking. You don't own any cast iron."

"No, sir, I don't. At least not right now." I give him a warm, bright smile. "But who knows? Maybe someday."

EPILOGUE

GALEN

"Galen, no!"

"Fashionably—"

"Don't say it, sir. I swear to God, don't say it."

"—late."

Alex is dressing, but when I grab her, she's only just pulled her skirt on, so it's easy enough to push it up and grab her ass, tugging it back against me. She can feel what she's done, and though she's complaining, she grinds back against me in a way that ensures I'm not letting go of her anytime soon.

"Dammit, sir, no! This… my parents are going to be there!"

"I'm sure they'll understand. If I need to, I'll explain."

"Ohmigod… you wouldn't."

"You sure you want to test that theory?"

"*Siirrr*!" Her voice is both cajoling and needy, and my dick grows even stiffer. "Fine, fine," she huffs, "I know how to take care of this…"

Alex twists from my grip and spins, dropping to her knees. She takes my cock at the base with her hand, looking up at me as she slowly draws the tip into her mouth.

"Such a good girl. Always making sure to take care of me."

Her mouth glides over my length as she takes me deeper, her eyes closing. She knows how much I enjoy this, just as I know why she's doing what she is right now. It's a matter of time management, and this is by far the quickest way to get me off. One of the things we've discussed since the first night I spent at her home is my propensity to overthink, and I'm not doing a good job of preventing that as she slips her mouth up and down the length of my shaft. She'd also warned me not to let what had happened between us change our dynamic, that she needed me to 'be the Dom I need, not the one you think I do,' and I'm trying.

"Ah, ah, ah, little girl..." I grip her hair, pulling her gently off my cock. "I see what you're doing here. And while I'm not opposed, right now I've got other ideas." I tug her up from her kneeling position and begin walking her backward toward her bed.

"Galen. Sir... please... we need to—"

I push her over the edge.

"*Oof!*" She gives a frustrated whimper as I shove the skirt up to bunch around her hips, then yank her panties down, exposing her pussy. "Dammit, sir!"

I cup her sex in my hand, letting two fingers rake their way between her labia. God, she's fucking wet, just as I suspected. I bring my fingers up, rubbing the tips with my thumb so she can see the evidence of her arousal. Her eyes widen ever so slightly as I do.

"Someone's protesting in one place while begging in another."

"Sir..."

"Yes?"

"Please."

That tone tells me exactly what she needs.

A half hour later, I have my arm wrapped around her as she curls at my side. I glance over at the clock and groan. "Shit. I knew we'd be a little late, but if we run into any traffic..."

"We'll be fine," Alex murmurs.

"Did you look at the time?"

"Yeah. But I told you the reservation was for six. It's actually for seven-thirty."

I gape at her for a second before snapping my jaw shut. "Alex."

She shifts up onto an elbow, looking down at me. "Sir, if there's one thing I've learned, I have to make accommodations for you whenever we have plans to go out. I don't know if this's some sort of hidden fetish you have, but any time we're getting ready to go somewhere..."

I pull her down into a kiss. "I love you," I whisper a moment later.

"I love you too." She pushes up and off the bed. "Now, come on. You need to shower, and I need another one."

Traffic isn't bad, and for probably the first time in my life, I'm not 'fashionably late' to a dinner engagement. I've Alex to thank for that, and she looks smug when we walk into the building ten minutes early.

I wasn't sure I had the right place when we arrived because it doesn't look like a restaurant at all. It's in the middle of Culpepper County, and it looks more like someone's farm than anything else. But Google Maps says this is the right location according to the address Paul Gaither sent me, and as we step inside, the man is waiting just beyond the door.

"Ah, you're here," he says, moving toward us. "And... early?" He stares at me for a moment, then turns to Alex. "Clearly, this is your doing."

"Hey, I can be on time when I need to be," I grumble.

"You lie," Paul says, shooting me a look before he turns back to Alex. "*Tu es magnifique, jeune fille. Non seulement cela, mais si vous pouvez le faire arriver à l'heure, vous êtes clairement une bonne. Peut-être apprendra-t-il quelques trucs avant que vous en ayez fini avec lui.*"

Alex responds in French, color rising to her cheeks.

I suppress a smile.

Patience, Galen.

Alex's parents are already here, and Paul leaves us to get them. As Alex and I glance around, it's clear this is some sort of exclusive boutique restaurant. I count maybe a dozen other people present: a mix of other customers and staff.

"Ever heard of the French Laundry?" I murmur to Alex.

"Vaguely," she replies, still looking about.

"I think we're in the East Coast version of it."

Paul returns a moment later with another couple, and I don't need more than a quick glance to see these are Alex's parents.

"Mama, Papa, I'd like you to meet my boyfriend, Galen. Galen, this is my mother and father."

I kiss Mrs. Carre's hand, then shake Alex's father's. "It's an honor to meet you both."

"What a charming man," Mrs. Carre says approvingly. "It's a pleasure to meet you, Galen."

"The pleasure is all mine, Mrs. Carre."

"Evening," Mr. Carre says politely, if a little brusquely, and it's clear he's sizing me up.

"Evening, sir," I reply in return.

"Come," Paul calls out, motioning us toward an adjacent room. "They'll be serving an *apéritif* momentarily. We can chat and get to know each other better."

I hear Mrs. Carre talking to Alex in French as we move into the room. Alex nods excitedly, and the two move off to one side in animated conversation. I gravitate to where Paul and Mr. Carre are standing, and as I approach, Paul hands me a drink.

"Some liquid courage to help bolster you, my friend."

I take the glass. "That suggests you think I need it."

"Meeting the parents for the first time? Of course, you do."

I take a sip of the drink, and I'm guessing it's Campari, or maybe Aperol. The two men take some of their own before they begin conversing in French.

"*So, this is him? I thought he'd be bigger. He needs more than just a drink; he needs to eat something, get some meat on his bones.*"

"Eh, he's American. One comes to understand these things with them."

"You said he's a good man?"

"Decent. He pays his bills. However, once your daughter has come to her senses, we can find a Quebecois suitor truly worthy of her."

I clear my throat. *"My apologies, but if I could interject here, sirs. Your daughter truly* does *deserve the best man in the world, Mr. Carre. I can only hope you'll understand that's exactly what I intend to be. Alexandria is the greatest woman I've ever met, and she's without doubt the best thing ever to come into my life. I love her. And I swear to you, I will make sure she is always protected, always cherished, and will want for nothing."*

The two men stare at me.

"I hope you'll forgive me," I continue, *"for intruding into your private conversation, but I felt I needed to make my intentions clear, so—"*

"Stop." Paul raises his hand, his voice strained. "I understand what you're trying to do here, Galen, but I beg you, please... you're butchering one of the most beautiful languages in the world. English only."

I can't help but grin. "Alex says I'm improving."

"She lies, but only because I suspect she cares for you."

"I sure as hell hope so, Paul."

Paul turns to Mr. Carre. "Well, Henri? The boy seems sincere."

"I still say he needs more meat on his bones. I shall send Alexandria some recipes to fatten you up."

I smile politely. "I look forward to it."

The two men stare at each other until finally Mr. Carre shrugs. "Eh. I've seen her with worse. I suppose we can work with it." He reaches for my hand. "You promise to take care of my little girl?"

"I guarantee it, sir."

"Good. Make sure you do so."

"I noticed Alex smiling when you came in," Paul says to me in a jovial tone. "Don't make the mistake of ever allowing me to see her otherwise." He clasps me by the shoulder and squeezes in a fashion I remember all too well from our last meeting. "I've always liked you, Galen. I'd hate for you to give me a reason not to."

"Damn, Paul. You're a hard man to convince."

"Quebecois women are the most beautiful in the world. To be in the company of one is an honor. You're a lucky man. But Quebecois men are some of the most fiercely protective you shall ever meet, and the beauty of their women means they're not protected by one, but by all. You'd do well to remember that."

"You're right," I say earnestly. "Alex is beautiful, and there's nothing in this world I won't do for her. I promise I'll never give you any reason to question that."

"Then I'll never have a need to kill you, will I?" He claps me on the back hard, and I damn near spill what's left of my drink. "Come, let's see what lies Alex has managed to fill her mother with about you." He gives me a wolfish grin, and I down what remains in my glass.

Gonna need one or two more of those before the night's over.

Dinner goes better than expected. The conversation is warm and friendly, the food incredible, and while I limit myself to two glasses of wine, the stress from earlier has melted away. It doesn't hurt my cause when Alex reaches and takes my hand into hers and no one appears to pay it any attention, which is the same reaction they give when she leans over and kisses me.

"Galen, Alex tells me you run your own business."

I look over at Mrs. Carre. "Yes, ma'am. It's a small, boutique expediting firm."

"She says it sometimes takes you away, but I assume otherwise you set your own schedule and hours?"

"Yes, that's pretty much true," I answer, nodding.

"Such a wonderful situation to be in. Not chained to a desk slaving away sixty plus hours a week working at some faceless corporation," she says casually.

Uh oh.

"Well, I suppose that's true, but there are definite advantages for working for a large company. As a small business owner, I can't tell you the number of times I've wished all the issues I face managing a company were someone else's problems." I look over at Alex. "Plus, there's that sense of pride you get from garnering the accolades of your peers which you don't necessarily have in my position. You know, like those Alex has received."

Mrs. Carre frowns. "Do be a good boy and don't dull the prick of the jab I was directing at my daughter."

"Sorry, Mrs. Carre, but I'm proud of Alex and everything she's achieved."

"Pah!" she exclaims, waving her hand. "I can see I'm going to get no help from you convincing her to quit and find something less taxing."

"No ma'am"—I glance at Alex and smile—"I'm afraid not."

"Well," she says with a sigh of resignation, "at the very least you'll have no problem taking time off to come visit when Alex decides she can drag herself away from her desk."

"Come... visit?"

"Yes. Henri and I have a lovely home near Showman Island. There's plenty of room for you both."

"Mama..."

If Mrs. Carre hears her daughter, she chooses to ignore it. "We have five acres, and the scenery is quite lovely."

Now Alex groans.

"Oh, that's a very kind offer Mrs. Carre, but I'm sure we wouldn't want to impose on you and your husband."

"I'm sorry, did I make that seem like it was a suggestion? You'll have to forgive me."

Oh. Okay.

I paste a polite smile on my face. "Well then, I'd be delighted to come with Alex for a visit."

"Good. I'll let you know when to be there."

She turns away to her husband, and I lean over to speak quietly in Alex's ear. "Are you sure your mother doesn't have a younger sister named Mia?"

"I'm starting to wonder that myself," she replies.

After dinner is finished, Paul and Mr. and Mrs. Carre move into the sitting room where the evening started, and I pull Alex aside.

"You doing okay?" I ask.

"Yes, sir," she says quietly. "Thank you for being patient with my mother."

"About what?"

"Going to their place to visit."

I squeeze her hand. "It's fine. Anywhere I'm with you is perfect."

"*You're* perfect," she says with a sigh before leaning up to kiss me on the cheek.

"I mean, sleeping in separate bedrooms for a weekend is a small price to pay if it'll make your mother happy."

Alex rolls her eyes. "I wouldn't worry about that. My mother is extraordinarily open about... sex. I think it's a French thing."

I cock an eyebrow. "Okay, good to know."

"To be honest, I'm a little worried about what you're going to say when you see her library."

"And... why would that be?"

"Let's just say her tastes in art and literature are very... cosmopolitan."

"Oookaay. And now I *really* want to go. Think she's open for next weekend?"

"Galen!" She acts shocked, but it's not fooling me. I can see she's happy.

The evening is a success, and if I needed any proof, the way Alex beams during the after-dinner cocktail and the periodic squeezes of her hand confirms it. Just before we leave, I catch a brief bit of conversation in French that passes between her and her mother.

"So, do you like him?"

"Do you like him, chéri?"

"Yes, mama. I'm in love with him."

"Then of course I like him. How could I not if he makes you happy."

'...if he makes you happy.' I watch as they hug, and a surge of satisfaction courses through me. The rest of my life is going to be dedicated to making sure that's how Alex feels, always.

"You remember what I said, Galen." Paul puts a hand on my shoulder, pulling me out of my reverie. His grip is as strong as earlier, and I wonder how many bruises I'm going to find when I get back to Alex's place. "I like doing business with you, but I like that young woman"—he tilts his head toward Alex—"even more."

"I swear, Paul." I shake my head in resignation, and he chuckles as he pats my shoulder before stepping away.

"Take care of my daughter," Mr. Carre says to me firmly. "I may not be a big man like Mssr. Gaither, but I assure you, if you hurt her, there will be no place in this world or the next you can hide."

"That will never happen, Mr. Carre."

He nods, then taps me on the chest. "And for God's sake eat something. You're thin as a corpse."

While I'm driving us back to Alex's place, I glance over and catch her wearing the same smile I'd seen earlier. The sight sends a surge of dominance pulsing through me.

Mine.

"Did you have a good evening?"

"Mmm," she hums contentedly. "It went better than I could have hoped for. You were wonderful, sir."

"I hardly did anything."

"That's not true and you know it." She leans back and closes her eyes.

Periodic light from passing lamps and the occasional building fills the interior and reflects off the necklace she's wearing. It radiates brightly, but not nearly as much as the glow coming from her. I reach across and lightly finger the gentle curve of the jewelry circling her neck.

"Alex?"

"Hmm?"

"Do you remember the conversation we had about the collar you bought?"

"The one back home?"

"Yes." I let the necklace slip from my fingers to fall back against her skin. "How do you feel about this one?"

She turns her face toward me, her brow furrowed. Reaching up, she touches the chain. "This isn't a collar, sir. It's just a necklace."

"See, that's the thing. All night tonight I've been thinking about what your father and Paul said to me about how protective Quebecois men are of their women."

"Oh, God," Alex groans, rolling her eyes

"Yeah, I know. But to be honest, I sort of get what they mean You are *mine*, Alex. Totally mine. And I look at that chain around your neck, and I don't see just a necklace. I see a collar little different than the one you bought, or the one Gilded Angel is making. It occurs to me it's not the style or the shape or how it's labeled that's relevant. It's the symbolism that's important. Between us, if it's what *we* choose to believe, that's the only thing that matters, right?"

"No one can decide what constitutes the things that make up our dynamic, Galen. We've talked about that."

"I know, I know. For some reason it was driven home tonight. Standing there with you, holding your hand, just the mere presence of you by my side... Sometimes it's not about the bold gestures: the kneeling, the being naked in our home, a specific collar around your neck. It's the little, subtle things. The making my coffee. My hand in the small of your back. Me opening and closing doors for you. Those gestures are just as powerful as any other. They define and reinforce our dynamic as much as anything else we do." I glance over and find Alex staring back at me. "I don't think I ever truly understood that with Charlotte. With her, everything was about the form, not the function. To be *seen* as being in a true Dominant/submissive high protocol relationship was what was important, not just letting it be."

"One Twue Way."

I sigh. "Pretty much. Back then, I just didn't recognize it."

"Love is blind." Alex leans back into her seat. "Admittedly, though, I believe there were other mitigating factors involved, because that guy Franklin was a complete douchebag."

"That's the fucking truth."

"Even still… she has to own her part in what happened."

We both go silent.

"Sorry, I didn't mean to spoil the night by bringing her up," I apologize.

"It's okay. Remember what we've talked about: we won't hide from what happened, but we also won't let it define our future."

"That's for us to create moving forward." I repeat a mantra born out of so many conversations she and I have had recently.

"Exactly." Alex turns her head and smiles. "Speaking of which…"

"Why did I just feel the hairs on the back of my neck stand up?"

"Oh, c'mon, sir! This is a good thing."

"And that is?"

"When are you going to take me back to Black Light?"

I pause. Aside from speaking about what took place when I went to see Terry, and the numerous stories I've recounted to her about what went on during the years Charlotte and I spent there, Alex hasn't talked about Black Light once, especially in terms of 'us.'

"Well," I say contemplatively, "we can go anytime you want, honestly. But I'm curious; why bring it up now?"

"Simple. It's where it all began. Our dynamic, our relationship: it all started with a competition there. And just like the dinner you made when you came to my home for the first time, going back to Black Light would be another fresh start."

"Ah."

"Plus, I have other motivations."

"Oh, do you now? And those would be?"

"Terry. Klara. The staff and the other members of Black Light —to all of them you were a well-recognized and respected couple. Master Harmon. Charlotte's Dom. I want to change that."

I need to be watching the road, but I can't stop myself from turning to look at her.

"Now, I'd like to have my shot. I want them to know you as *my* Dom."

Fuck.

"I'd... I'd love that, Alex," I say softly.

"Good, then it's settled. Just let me know when you're ready to go."

"I will."

Goddamn right, I will. So much of Black Light has been wrapped up in what had happened in the past with Charlotte and Franklin I hadn't given any thought to a future for Alex and I there. But now the idea runs wild in my head, and I want it more than I can put into words.

Alex's Dom.

Fuck. Yes.

"Oh, there's just one more thing, sir."

"What's that?"

"Before you set a date, please touch base with my mother first and make sure it's not going to be on a weekend she wants us to come visit. I do *not* want to have to explain to her we can't because my boyfriend is taking me to our favorite sex club."

I can't hold back my laughter.

"As openminded and sophisticated as she claims to be..." Alex looks over at me with a wicked grin.

"That's a conversation I am *not* having."

THE (sort of)END

~

THANK you for reading Galen and Alex's story! Their book may have come to an end, but there is always more fun coming to Black Light. Keep reading for an early peek at the next book coming by the very talented Samantha A. Cole. Enjoy this snippet from *Black Light: Secret* where the son of the Vice-President of the US falls for one of his super hot Secret Service agents who hasn't come out of the closet about his sexuality yet. Will they be able to keep their relationship secret?

Snippet from *Black Light: Secret* by Samantha A. Cole

His jaw ached from clenching as Hayden McKenna glared at the Secret Service agent sitting next to him in the backseat of an armored SUV with its blacked-out windows. It wasn't the first time he'd been in this situation, but each time it did happen, his anger and resentment grew. He'd never asked to be the son of the Vice President of the United States, but here he was, with unwanted protection yet again due to some vague threat against him.

As in the past, he was being escorted to his father's secure residence where the Secret Service Special Agent-in-Charge (SAIC) would explain what the current threat was and what measures would be put in place until they determined Hayden's life wasn't in danger. Which he never thought it was. The alleged suspects were just blowing off steam or hiding behind their computer screens, acting all big and bad. They were just bullies who never followed through with their threats and backed down any time someone stood up to them. In Hayden's case, the people standing up were the Secret Service agents, and if they all looked as bad-ass as the man sitting beside him, he'd concede defeat too.

Even though he lived in Washington D.C. and had a very successful art gallery there, he was so far removed from the political arena it wasn't funny. Personally, he hated politics and all the backstabbing and mudslinging that went with it.

He sighed and flopped his head against the seat back before rolling it to the side so he could address the agent. "Can you at least tell me what the threat is this time?"

He'd learned from experience it was a fifty-fifty shot for getting a decent response to that question from anyone who wasn't an SAIC—it depended on who they sent for him. While he recognized the male driver and the female agent in the front passenger seat from previous incidents, the stiff and unyielding man next to him wasn't familiar. And Hayden was certain he'd remember meeting Special Agent Rance Adams before because the man was ravishing. Michelangelo would've drooled at the prospect of sculpting his chiseled jaw, full lips, slightly-bent nose, and startling green eyes. Oh, and don't forget his Romanesque expression. Hayden could usually read a person easily, but Adams gave nothing away. Stoic. Unyielding. Gorgeous.

"Sorry, Mr. McKenna, but the SAIC will fill you in at Bubble," Adams said in a deep, rumbling voice.

Infuriating.

~

WE WILL GET Hayden and Rance's story in *Black Light: Secret* coming November, 2022.

GET A FREE BLACK LIGHT BOOK

Enjoy your trip to Black Light? There's a lot more sexy fun to be had. All of the books in the series can be read as standalone stories and can also be enjoyed in any reading order.

Get started with a FREE copy of **Black Light: Rocked** today. Your fun doesn't need to end yet!

ABOUT THE AUTHOR

USA Today bestselling author Shane Starrett loves to take his readers into the (sometimes) deeply dark but always seductive worlds of strong women and sinful romance. With a focus on BDSM themes, he explores the unique dynamics which take place between partners living 'in the lifestyle,' with an emphasis on the inherent beauty and strength of the bonds created between people who aren't afraid to tap into their kinky sides. With attention to themes such as trust, communication, understanding, and compromise (and always with a dash of humor), Shane loves to explore the ever shifting but always fascinating forces at work between people falling into or already in love.

When he isn't writing on those subjects (which isn't often), he can be found in his Texas home with his wife of thirty-three years, either working in his shop, cooking, or daydreaming about another steamy, sexy story.

To the delight of his very patient support team, Shane has new and exciting stories in the works! If you're interested in following him, you can find him online at:

Website: http://shanestarrett.com/

Amazon: https://www.amazon.com/Shane-

Goodreads: https://www.goodreads.com/user/show/100169385-

Bookbub: https://www.bookbub.com/profile/3994701705

Facebook: https://www.facebook.com/shane.starrett.9

Facebook Readers Group: https://www.facebook.com/groups/thehouseofstarrett/

Instagram: https://www.instagram.com/shanestarrett/?hl=en

Twitter: https://twitter.com/ShaneStarrett?lang=en

ALSO BY SHANE STARRETT

SUBMISSIVE LIES

JASMINE

JADED

FARIS

BLACK LIGHT: ROULETTE REMATCH

BLACK LIGHT: BRED

RAILED: 2021 DIRTY DADDIES ANTHOLOGY

CARNAL VALUE: 2021 SCOUTS ANTHOLOGY

BLACK COLLAR PRESS

Black Collar Press is a small publishing house started by authors Livia Grant and Jennifer Bene in late 2016. The purpose was simple - to create a place where the erotic, kinky, and exciting worlds they love to explore could thrive and be joined by other like-minded authors.

If this is something that interests you, please go to the Black Collar Press website and read through the FAQs. If your questions are not answered there, please contact us directly at: blackcollarpress@gmail.com

WHERE TO FIND BLACK COLLAR PRESS:

- Newsletter: http://bit.ly/2JY23Wi
- Website: http://www.blackcollarpress.com/
- Facebook: https://www.facebook.com/ blackcollarpress/
- Twitter: https://twitter.com/BlackCollarPres
- Black Light East and West may be fictitious, but you can now join our very real Facebook Group for Black Light Fans - Black Light Central

BLACK LIGHT SERIES

Did you enjoy your visit to Black Light? Have you read the other books in the series? They can all be enjoyed as standalone books read in any order.

Season One

Infamous Love, A Black Light Prequel by Livia Grant
Black Light: Rocked by Livia Grant
Black Light: Exposed by Jennifer Bene
Black Light: Valentine Roulette by Various Authors
Black Light: Suspended by Maggie Ryan
Black Light: Cuffed by Measha Stone
Black Light: Rescued by Livia Grant

Season Two
Black Light: Roulette Redux by Various Authors
Complicated Love, A Black Light Novel by Livia Grant
Black Light: Suspicion by Measha Stone
Black Light: Obsessed by Dani René

Black Light: Fearless by Maren Smith
Black Light: Possession by LK Shaw

Season Three

Black Light: Celebrity Roulette by Various Authors
Black Light: Purged by Livia Grant
Black Light: Defended by Golden Angel
Black Light: Scandalized by Livia Grant
Black Light: Charmed by Jennifer Bene

Season Four

Black Light: Roulette War by Various Authors
Black Light: Brave by Maren Smith
Black Light: Unbound by Jennifer Bene and Lesley Clark
Black Light: Branded by Kay Elle Parker

Season Five

Black Light: Roulette Rematch by Various Authors
Black Light: Bred by Shane Starrett
Black Light: Wanted by Maren Smith
Black Light: Worthy by Stella Moore
Black Light: Saved by Raisa Greywood

Season Six

Black Light: The Menagerie by Maren Smith
Infamous Trio Boxed Set by Livia Grant
Black Light: Cured by Vivian Murdoch
Black Light: Disciplined by Livia Grant
Black Light: Protocol by Shane Starrett
Black Light: Secret by Samantha A. Cole (Fall 2022)

Season Seven

Black Light: Gamble by Livia Grant (Early 2023)

Black Light: Roulette Finale by Various Authors (Coming Feb. 2023)

And many more planned!